## "Why can't Miss Ca

All the grown-ups froze. D
darling daughter just said "
herself one of Caroline's cha

Caroline's lashes fluttered as she recovered from her surprise. "I'm sorry, sweetheart. I couldn't."

Maggie's eyes clouded. "Why not?"

"Well, I'm not going to be here very long, for one thing. For another, I've never been a nanny before."

"Maybe not," Ida interjected. "But you certainly seem to have a way with the triplets."

"Ma, Miss Murray is here to visit her family, not work for ours."

"Of course we wouldn't want to impose, Caroline, but your family would be welcome to visit here as often as they want."

"Oh, I don't know." Caroline's gaze landed on his, soft as a butterfly, filled with questions.

Did he want her to help them? The answer was an irrevocable no. Did he need her help? Ida's meaningful glare said yes. When he remained silent, she prompted, "We sure could use your help. Couldn't we, David?"

He swallowed hard. "There's no denying that."

\* \* \*

### Lone Star Cowboy League: Multiple Blessings

*The Rancher's Surprise Triplets—*
Linda Ford, April 2017

*The Nanny's Temporary Triplets—*
Noelle Marchand, May 2017

*The Bride's Matchmaking Triplets—*
Regina Scott, June 2017

**Noelle Marchand** is a native Houstonian living out her childhood dream of being a writer. She graduated summa cum laude from Houston Baptist University in 2012, earning a bachelor's degree in mass communications and speech communications. She loves exploring new books and new cities. When she's not scribbling out her latest manuscript, you may find her pursuing one of her other passions—music, dance, history and classic movies.

### Books by Noelle Marchand

### Love Inspired Historical

#### *Lone Star Cowboy League: Multiple Blessings*

*The Nanny's Temporary Triplets*

#### *Bachelor List Matches*

*The Texan's Inherited Family*
*The Texan's Courtship Lessons*
*The Texan's Engagement Agreement*

*Unlawfully Wedded Bride*
*The Runaway Bride*
*A Texas-Made Match*

Visit the Author Profile page at Harlequin.com.

# NOELLE MARCHAND

## The Nanny's Temporary Triplets

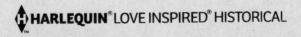

HARLEQUIN® LOVE INSPIRED® HISTORICAL

Special thanks and acknowledgment are given
to Noelle Marchand for her contribution to the
Lone Star Cowboy League: Multiple Blessings miniseries.

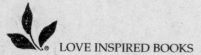

LOVE INSPIRED BOOKS

Recycling programs
for this product may
not exist in your area.

ISBN-13: 978-0-373-42522-8

The Nanny's Temporary Triplets

Special thanks to everyone involved in the creation of the Lone Star Cowboy League: Multiple Blessings series, especially Linda Ford, Regina Scott and Elizabeth Mazer!

For God is working in you, giving you the desire
and the power to do what pleases Him.
—*Philippians* 2:13

# Chapter One

*Austin, Texas*
*July 1896*

"**B**y the power vested in me by God and the state of Texas—"

*"Stop this wedding!"*

Everything around Caroline Murray seemed to blur. Yet she was more aware than she'd ever been. Time fractured until it was made up of nothing more than tiny details. Seemingly insignificant, she could still feel their indelible stamp on her soul.

Sunlight streamed through the stained-glass windows of the church, spilling a bizarre assortment of colors onto her pure-white gown. Her hands were clasped in her groom's. His grip held hers tighter and tighter. So tight now that it was almost painful, not unlike the ring he'd placed on her finger only moments ago that had somehow been forged a size too small.

None of that mattered now because through the

dreamy tinge of her veil she watched another woman march down the aisle with a baby in her arms and righteous indignation on her drawn features. Caroline turned back to her groom in confusion, waiting for him to take charge. She saw panic flash across his face before his dashing smile faded to a scowl. Yet he didn't breathe a word. It seemed she would have to be the one to deal with the stranger who'd brought their wedding to a halt.

It was silent. *Too* silent with more than two hundred people in the chapel. Even the baby, with his eerily familiar eyes, stared at her without a sound. Somehow Caroline found her voice. "Who are you? What do you want?"

Compassion filled the eyes of the woman who surveyed her. "My name is Lucette Calabrese."

"She is my sister," Nico Calabrese asserted as if his strong Italian features bore any resemblance to the delicate ones of the woman who spoke with the inflections of the French.

Lucette closed her eyes and winced. "No. I am his wife."

Caroline recoiled. "What?"

Lucette bounced the baby in her arms slightly. "This is our son."

"Caroline, don't believe her." Nico's dark, pleading eyes captured Caroline's. "She is a crazy woman who follows me from town to town. She is obsessed with my career, my music, my voice."

"Nico is right. I am crazy…for following him from city to city, standing by as he wastes the money he earns at the gambling table, then makes up for it by seducing unsuspecting women out of their fortunes." Lucette lifted her chin. "But no longer. I am going home to France. His music, career and voice do not enchant me in the least. I came here today because I could not let him ruin another life the way he has ruined mine."

Nico finally released Caroline's hands. "How can you say these things?"

Lucette ignored him. "He will take your dowry and leave you after the honeymoon. That is his plan. Save yourself and your virtue while you can."

With that, Lucette turned on her heel and walked out of the church. Nico swallowed hard. Turning back to Caroline, he asked, "Do you believe her?"

Her heart screamed no, but her head silenced it. A kaleidoscope of memories paraded through her mind. Their romance had been a fairy tale from the start. They'd met through her parents' connections in the crème de la crème of Austin's music society. He was everything they had always wanted for her and exactly what she'd wanted for herself: educated, well-traveled and, most important of all, musical. His skill at the piano wasn't particularly anything to brag about, especially in comparison to her father's, but then Lawrence Murray had been a world-renowned pianist from the age of eight.

Nico's voice, however, was the epitome of what a classical tenor should be. His control over it was astounding, his lyrical phrasing impeccable. He put new shadow, light, vibrancy into melodies she'd heard hundreds of times before and made them exciting again.

Her parents loved him. He'd become the musical son they'd never had. So much so that she'd been glad her tone-deaf brother, Matthew, had been too preoccupied with his cattle and growing family in Little Horn, Texas, to see how they doted on Nico.

He was the handsomest man she'd ever seen and the only man to look beyond the influence and glamour of her parents' lives to notice her—the girl with a voice that was pretty, but not nearly strong enough to match her mother's mezzosoprano or to even make it onto the stage. Embarrassingly enough, Caroline had little else to recommend her. Why else would her father have set aside such an obscene amount of money for her dowry, then discreetly make it public knowledge?

Nico had told her the money didn't matter to him. He loved her for who she was. In return he was destined to be her first and only love. Their romance was going to be able to meet the standard set by the tender tomes of her parents' love story. At the very least, it was meant to rival her brother's idyllic one. And it had.

Until now.

Maybe that had been the problem. All of it had been too good to be true. So much a fairy tale that it well and truly was only that—fiction.

She pulled in a deep breath, locked eyes with the man she'd just pledged her life to and suddenly felt dirty, soiled. Anger burned within her so hot and deep that it couldn't rise to the surface. She pushed it away, clinging instead to the protective numbness. "Yes, Nico. I believe your wife."

His shoulders sank, but he offered an irascible half

smile and tweaked her nose in that familiar way of his. "It was fun while it lasted. *Arrivederci*, my sweet."

She cringed away, but he was too busy rushing out the door to notice. It closed with a bang loud enough to startle some sense into her. She turned to her parents and their guests. "Wait. Shouldn't someone arrest him for something?"

A few laughs punctuated the shocked silence as a few justice-minded men bolted off in pursuit. Caroline took advantage of the general confusion that followed to slip out the side door into the harsh sunlight. She shoved her veil out of the way and hugged her arms around her waist. Wincing as the door opened behind her, she turned with a glare that softened at the sight of her brother.

Matthew didn't say anything at first. He just searched her face in concern. Finally, he ran his fingers through his blond hair and pleaded, "Carrie, let me take you away from here until all this blows over."

"Where would we go?"

"To my ranch."

A laugh escaped her. "In Little and Worn?"

His scowl lacked any real bite. "You know the town is named Little Horn."

She offered him a faint smile. "I know."

He caught her arm gently. "Come with me. Get away from the city. The country is beautiful, Caroline. The sky goes on forever. It's the kind of place that puts everything in perspective. Emma and I would love to spend time with you. You could go riding, let loose without worrying about what society thinks of you."

As though on cue, guests started exiting from the

front of the church. They walked in groups with their heads together. No doubt already gossiping about what they'd seen. Who could blame them? If she'd been a guest at such a wedding, she'd talk about it, too. The gossip in Austin was going to be unbearable for the next few weeks. Besides that, she and Nico had made memories all over town.

Someone spotted her. The society reporter from Austin's most widely read newspaper. He veered her way. Caroline tensed. Her voice came out kind of wobbly. "Matt, get me out of here."

Within minutes she was in the carriage beside her brother and sister-in-law. They went back to their parents' house, where Caroline changed into her traveling clothes. Her trunks were already packed. Having said goodbye to her parents at the church, Caroline was on a train headed toward Little Horn in less than an hour.

Relief filled her as the train lumbered into the station at Little Horn after what felt like an eternity. Soon she would be tucked away at her brother's ranch, where she might be provided some modicum of privacy.

As they stepped onto the train platform, Emma placed a hand on her rounded stomach. "I hate to say this, but the baby and my stomach are both doing flips. I think I need to eat something now before it gets any worse."

Matthew placed a comforting hand on his wife's back. "We'll stop at the café before we head home."

Caroline realized she should be ravenous. She'd been too nervous to eat before the ceremony and had had nothing since. Yet food didn't interest her, and she wasn't sure she could hold her emotions together long enough to eat an entire meal at the café. A hand reached through the fog to give hers a light squeeze. Caroline met her sister-in-law's understanding gaze. "Would you like to take a walk first and meet us there when you're ready?"

"Yes," Caroline agreed almost desperately even as Matthew protested.

Emma ignored her husband. "Go right ahead, Caroline. The church is around the corner and across the street. You might be able to find some privacy there."

"Thank you." Caroline wasted no time in finding the church, but she stopped just shy of entering. She followed the walkway between the church and what seemed to be the parsonage, hoping it might lead exactly where it did. The path opened into a small sort of…well, *park* would a generous term. It was really just a field. Though the wildflowers and grass were all but dried up, the space was blessedly empty.

A few tall live oaks provided refuge from the sun. She sank to her knees at the base of one. She opened her hand to stare at the small gold wedding band she'd carried all this way. She should have thrown it out. Yet when she'd removed the silly thing, she'd been unable to let it go.

Now it gleamed in the bright Texas sun, mocking her, berating her, teasing her with the reality of what her situation might have been had she gone through with the wedding. Not the roses, cake and laughter she'd expected, but robbery, ruination, abandonment. Closing her eyes, she clenched her hand and let the metal bite into her fingers. "How could I be so utterly stupid? So ridiculously foolish? How did I not suspect anything?"

She lowered her head to bury her fingers in her hair and fought against the tears filling her eyes. The sound of approaching footsteps made her still. She stared through blurry eyes at the man who'd stopped some distance away. He removed his hat in a gesture of respect, then went down on one knee as though purposefully making himself smaller. His broad shoulders and muscled form could be deemed intimidating. Yet there was no mistaking the gentleness or concern in his drawl. "Ma'am, I don't mean to intrude, but I couldn't pass by without asking. Are you all right? I mean, are you sick? Should I get a doctor?"

A doctor would be of no help to her. Still, it was a sweet gesture. A wobbly smile tilted her lips. "No, thank you."

There was a moment of silence. He was probably trying to figure out what to do next. Was there a polite way to ask him to leave? There had to be.

She blinked several times to clear her vision. Everything blurry came back into focus. He was handsome. So handsome that the gentle dismissal she planned to deliver died even as her lips parted to speak.

She wanted to look away, but his gaze held hers in place. More than that, it seemed to peer deep inside, where he had no business being. Then something flickered in his eyes. Recognition. Kindness. An odd feeling of kinship stretched between them as if he understood her pain and, in his own way, had felt it, too.

This time there was no question in his voice. "You are hurt."

She wanted to deny it, but her heart wouldn't listen. The ache in her chest reopened, becoming a chasm too wide to run from. Her tears would no longer be denied or controlled. They flooded her cheeks. Sobs broke free, along with more shame and self-recrimination than she'd ever felt before. She no longer cared that she had an audience. What was one more person when so many had already witnessed her humiliation?

David McKay wasn't afraid of a woman's tears. His late wife had been a crier. Anytime he'd disagreed with her or displayed the slightest displeasure over her wandering eye, she'd cried until he turned to putty in her hands. That had lasted until his mother had oh so casually mentioned she'd heard Laura instructing a friend on how to make herself cry. After that, he'd let Laura cry as often as she wanted. She'd eventually realized her tears wouldn't sway him and saved her energy for other ways to torment him.

Then his pa had been fatally gored by a longhorn. Nothing David did could stop his mother's tears. All he could do was offer a shoulder and a handkerchief to mop up her tears when she was done. She'd gone on and on to her friends about what a comfort her son had been in her grief. That was when he'd learned a secret about women strange enough to boggle any man's mind. They wanted to cry. The sooner a fellow let them do it, the sooner they'd stop on their own accord.

Of course, the difference was that the woman crying

now was a complete stranger to him…and a beautiful one at that. Yet he couldn't leave a woman crying in the dirt without trying to offer at least a little comfort. He approached her as he would an injured heifer, hoping not to frighten her. She didn't seem to care one way or the other. She just kept crying in heartbreaking sobs that shook her whole body.

He tentatively put a comforting hand on her back, between her shoulder blades. She didn't flinch away, so he left it there. Her shudder seemed to travel up his arm. She began to talk. David knelt beside her to listen to her quiet confession through her sobs. "I loved him. I really did."

His eyebrows rose, though he couldn't say he was surprised. He'd suspected she was a victim of heartbreak by the pain he'd seen in her eyes.

"I never imagined he had a wife."

Everything within him stilled. He swallowed down the instinctive aversion he had for anyone who played fast and loose with fidelity. He'd had more than enough of that from his late wife.

"How stupid can one person be? To be taken in like that? To believe every lie and ignore any sign of the truth?"

*All right.* She'd been lied to. That didn't exactly excuse it, but it did explain it. It also made her the injured party here. Her and the man's wife. He'd been in that situation one too many times not to feel compassion for her.

With a sigh, David settled in the dirt beside the woman and put his arm around her shoulders. He was kind of hoping she'd get all offended and push him away. She leaned slightly into him instead. He gave in to the moment, as crazy as it seemed, and pulled her a bit closer. Her cheek landed on his chest, allowing warm tears to spill onto his shirt. He ran his right hand up and down her arm in a calming, predictable pattern while his left hand rested on his knee in full view of her downturned face, making it clear he wasn't panning to take advantage of the situation.

Her sobs faded to intermittent shudders. The wet patch on his shirt began to cool. He dug a white handkerchief from his chest pocket and offered it to her. "You can keep this, so don't be afraid to blow your nose if you need to."

A small, watery laugh reached his ear as she took his offering. She wiped her face, then blew her nose before whispering, "Thank you, Pastor."

David's eyes widened. "I'm not a preacher. I'm a rancher."

"A rancher?" Dismay filled her voice as she pulled back to look at him with hazel eyes that were an intriguing mix of brown, amber and green.

He tried not to grimace. It figured she'd be one of those women like his wife. The kind that against all odds got even prettier when she cried. Color flushed her cheeks while reddening her nose only slightly. A rich brown tendril came loose over her right eye. It threatened to tangle in the dark lashes that her tears had turned spiky.

He lifted a hand and brushed it back. She froze. Suddenly aware of the intimacy of the moment, he removed his arm from around her and searched for something, anything, to put distance between them. "Something wrong with being a rancher?"

"Of course not. My brother is a rancher. It's only that being near the church and you being so kind and all, I assumed…" She trailed off with a shrug.

"No. I was just on my way to the parsonage and happened to see you. You say your brother is a rancher? How is it that I've never seen you around town before?"

"I haven't been around town before. Not for several years, that is. I'm visiting my brother. His name is Matthew Murray."

"I know Matthew. He's a good friend of mine." Matthew had mentioned he would be leaving town for a few days to attend his sister's wedding. The puzzle pieces shifted into place. "And you're Caroline."

Her eyes widened slightly. "Yes."

He hesitantly added, "I take it the wedding didn't go as planned."

"No." She glanced toward the church. "It did not."

That was probably for the best, though he wasn't sure she'd appreciate him saying so. He kept quiet, watching for any indication she wanted to be alone. She turned to look up at him with curiosity. "I just realized I don't know your name."

"David McKay."

Her lashes lowered toward her cheeks. "Well, David McKay, thank you for listening to my troubles and…"

"Holding you in my arms?" He probably shouldn't have teased her, but he wanted to see if he could make her smile just once before they parted ways. He wasn't disappointed.

Her laughing hazel eyes met his, acknowledging the underlying absurdity of the encounter, while her lips tilted into a smile. "That, too."

*Anytime,* he wanted to say, but that would be inappropriate. It would also be flirtatious, and David hadn't tried his hand at flirting since Laura had died five years ago. He wasn't planning to start now. Especially not with a woman whose heart had just been broken. He knew from experience how long that could take to heal.

Granted, he could use another woman's influence in Maggie's life. Preferably it would be someone who could convince his daughter to stop cutting her hair shorter and shorter anytime she got the notion and someone who could teach her that there was nothing wrong with wearing dresses or acting feminine.

Of course, there were the triplets to consider now. The ten-month-old foundlings had been abandoned at the county fair last month. Their mother had left a note explaining that she was widowed, penniless and dying. No longer able to take care of the boys, she'd asked the Lone Star Cowboy League, a group of ranchers known for their compassion and ability to get things done, to take in her boys.

As a member of the league, David had stepped up to do exactly that when the folks originally charged with their care had to give up the babies because of an illness in their house. He'd gone through a lot of trouble to hire a nanny for them and his daughter. Maggie had a tendency to run wild when he wasn't around. School being out for the summer only exacerbated that. He had a ranch to run, which meant that Ma was Maggie's main caretaker for most of the day. At seventy-seven, Ma wasn't as spry as she used to be, and keeping up with Maggie's ever-increasing energy and mischief was becoming more of a challenge.

Of course, the truth was, even in her younger days Ma never had been able to find it in her heart to discipline her only grandchild. He understood. Maggie's big blue eyes, honey-colored hair and button nose made her cute as could be. It also gave her an innocent appearance that unfortunately was too often only that—an appearance. Hence, the reason he'd been heading to the parsonage.

First, he needed to do the gentlemanly thing. That did not include leaving his new acquaintance by herself in this state. "Where is your brother?"

"He's at the café with Emma. I should probably head that way myself."

She made a motion as though to rise, so he jumped to his feet and caught her arm to help her stand. "May I escort you?"

"Oh, no. That isn't necessary." She brushed the dirt from her skirt, lifted her chin and offered one last faint smile. "Thank you again, Mr. McKay."

"You're welcome, ma'am."

He watched to make sure she was headed in the right direction before crossing the field to the parsonage. Brandon Stillwater answered the door with a welcoming grin. "Come in, David. To what do I owe the pleasure?"

"I need your advice on something." David removed his hat and stepped inside the foyer.

"Let's talk in my study. Can I get you anything? Coffee? A cookie? One of those little strudel things Mrs. Hickey is so fond of making?"

"Thank you, but I'm fine." Entering the study behind Brandon, David paced back and forth on the bright square of light falling from the window onto the floor in front of the well-hewn desk.

Concern furrowed Brandon's brow as he leaned his hip against the desk. "What's going on?"

"Maggie put a snake in the nanny's bed."

"What?" Brandon asked in alarm.

"I know." David sank into a nearby chair. "It was dead. I'm not sure if that makes it better or worse. Before I could even try to discipline her, my ma stepped in and fired the nanny for being angry at Maggie. It was a formality, really. The nanny was already halfway up the stairs on her way to pack her bags of her own accord."

"How long have you been without a nanny?"

"Two days. I've been racking my brain for a solution, asking around to see if any of the ladies in town would take the position. None of them are interested. In fact, I may have offended a few husbands and fathers by even suggesting their women might be able to use the extra income. I don't suppose you've heard of anyone in need of a job? Perhaps someone in the congregation?"

Brandon glanced away, looking deep in thought, before he slowly shook his head. "I'm afraid not. The women in our congregation are mostly married or widows with their own children. The unattached women help out on their families' ranches and farms. A lot of them are younger girls, too. Either way, you might run into the same problem of offending their menfolk. Of course, if we put the word out that you're looking for help, a few of them might be willing to do so out of pure Christian charity—and a chance to catch the eye of one of the 'wealthiest and most mysterious bachelors in Little Horn.'"

"Ugh." David winced. "Is that really what they say about me?"

Brandon grinned. "I'm afraid so."

"Well, nothing doing. I'm not letting those women into my house. The last thing I'm looking for is romance. There has to be someone else."

"What about her?"

"Her? Her who?"

*"Her."* Brandon tipped his head toward the window.

Confused, David followed his friend's meaningful look. All he saw was an empty field with a few trees. It was the same field where David had been only a few minutes ago…holding Caroline Murray in his arms while she cried on his shoulder. Heat spread across his face. He met Brandon's steady, amused gaze. "You saw that?"

"Sure did."

"Why didn't you come out to help me?"

Brandon shrugged. "You seemed to have everything well under control, so I didn't want to intrude."

"You wouldn't have been intruding."

"Are you sure about that?"

David glanced out the window and frowned. "Of course I am."

"Who is she?"

"Matthew Murray's sister, Caroline. She's just here for a visit." He shook his head. "There has to be someone I can hire."

"Maybe, but not locally. Have you checked the newspaper? That's where you found the first nanny, isn't it?"

"Yes, that's the first thing I did. I found the latest papers from Houston and Waco at the general store. None of the personal ads mentioned anything remotely close to a nanny, nurse or governess."

"Governess." Brandon held up a finger, then rounded the desk to open a drawer. "I saw something in an Austin newspaper about a governess." He pulled out a newspaper and rifled through it. "Here it is. 'Former governess of good reputation and character seeking Christian…husband.' Oh. She's a mail-order bride."

"I didn't say anything about marriage." His ma had, though, countless times. She wanted her son to be happy and for her granddaughter to have a mother. Why she thought marriage would ensure his happiness after what he'd been through was beyond him, but there was no denying Maggie would love to have a mother.

"Now hold on. Don't reject the idea without thinking about it first. You need someone to take care of the triplets until they find a permanent home, but you also need someone to help out with Maggie. This woman may have the experience you're looking for."

David gave him a doubtful look. "What else does the ad say?"

"'Please inquire at—' She doesn't give a name. Just a PO Box in…" A wistful look flickered across his face. "Boston."

"Well, that's certainly straight to the point, isn't it? Almost businesslike in a way. It doesn't mention anything about love or feelings." Hope started building in his chest. "Maybe I don't have to, either."

"What do you mean?"

"If she's willing, we could have a marriage in name only."

Brandon frowned. "David, I'm not sure that's a good idea."

That was too bad because the idea had real merit— not the least being the woman wouldn't be able to run away as soon as Maggie got into trouble. If she did, she wouldn't take his heart with him. Of course, there was a chance Maggie would get hurt if that happened. He could do his best to rule out that chance, though. In talking to this potential bride first and laying out all the parameters, they would both know from the start where they stood with each other and the marriage. There would be no passion or emotions getting in the way to confuse things. It would be a nice, straightforward marriage of convenience.

Decision made, David glanced up at Brandon. "May I borrow a pen and paper? I have a letter to write."

# Chapter Two

Caroline had lost her mind. There was no other explanation for why her thoughts kept straying to a man she'd barely met—a stranger…with the most amazing green eyes. The comfort she'd found in David McKay's embrace had been a blessing in the moment and downright disconcerting in retrospect.

"Caroline, the potatoes."

Blinking away her thoughts, she refocused on the skillet filled with potatoes in danger of being burned to a crisp. She removed it from the fire and stirred frantically. "I told you I'm a disaster in the kitchen, Emma."

"You are not."

"I am, but you're much too sweet to say so." She scooped the potatoes onto the serving dish and sent her sister-in-law a smile as Matthew breezed into the room just in time for lunch. "Matt, tell your wife I'm hopeless when it comes to cooking."

Matthew stopped in his tracks. "She has you cooking? And for Sunday dinner, too? Oh, Emma, sweetheart…no."

Emma frowned at them both. "It's just takes practice."

"No amount of practice will help my sister."

"Well, thank you for the support, Matthew. I'm not sure if I should be grateful or insulted."

Matthew patted Caroline on the back, then kissed his wife's cheek. "I still can't believe we're finally all together in my favorite place."

"I've visited here before, Matthew."

"Once. Three years ago for the wedding."

She lifted a brow. "That's still more frequently than you visit Austin."

"I have a ranch to take care of."

"And I have a job, too…" She bit her lip. She'd given up her position at the prestigious Harmony School of Music to marry Nico. "I *had* a job."

Emma's voice was soft with sympathy. "Maybe they'll let you have it back."

"I doubt it. Not after I handpicked my replacement. That's fine, though. I don't need the work."

"You needed it," Matthew interjected. "Just not for the money."

She smiled. "It did give me a sense of accomplishment, I suppose, and something to do while Mother and Father were involved in their rehearsals."

"Well, then," Emma said. "We'll all pray that a new opportunity presents itself soon."

"Yes, I think we'd better." Caroline clapped her hands. "Now, my lovely potatoes and the actually palatable food Emma cooked are getting cold. Let's eat."

Lunch was a simple and delicious affair. Caroline did her best to listen while Matthew and Emma conversed about the everyday ins and outs of ranch life. Her mind kept wandering back to Austin. Had the men who'd gone after Nico captured him? If so, what had happened to Lucette and that sweet little baby? She hoped they were on their way to France and that their family would welcome them. It wasn't her concern. She knew that. Yet she would forever be grateful that Lucette had shown up to put a stop to the wedding, as harrowing as that experience had been.

Caroline couldn't keep thinking about it, though. It would drive her crazy just as surely as her thoughts about—

"David."

Glancing up from her plate, she met her brother's gaze across the table. "What?"

He nodded toward his wife. "I was telling Emma that our neighbor David McKay rode by to ask how we were handling the drought. The creek that cuts through both of our properties has been running low. He has another spring closer to his ranch house. He wanted me to know he would be keeping his cattle closer to that so as not to tax the creek."

"Oh. I...I didn't know he was your neighbor." So much for taking comfort in the fact that she'd likely never see the man again except for across the aisle at church like she had this morning. "Does he stop by often?"

"Now and then." Matthew tilted his head to survey her. "I didn't know you knew him."

"I don't." Watchful silence descended on the table until she finally gave in to Matthew's silent probing. "I met him once."

"You did? When?"

"Yesterday. I ran into him on my walk. He was very kind."

"Was he? How so?"

"Well, I was obviously upset and he— Honestly, what does it matter?"

He grinned. "Just curious is all."

"Beware, Caroline. Your brother is on a campaign to get you to move to Little Horn by any means necessary."

He shrugged. "All I'm saying is it would be awfully convenient to have you living practically next door."

Caroline let out a disbelieving laugh. "So now you already have me married to a man I hardly know and living next door."

"Well, I think you'd know him pretty well by then."

"Matthew, give her some time to breathe. She just barely escaped marrying a—"

"No-good, low-down skunk of a man," he finished for his wife. "David is the exact opposite of that, from what I can tell. Besides, he's been a widower for five years now. He's likely to be of a mind to take another wife soon."

"The last thing I need is to start thinking about another man." Yet she already had, and Matthew wasn't helping her stop.

"All I'm saying is you could do worse."

She sighed. "That much I know."

He paused. In that moment, she was certain he saw

how much she'd been hurt, because his jaw tightened. "Mother and Father were so blinded by that Nico fellow's talent that they couldn't see his real character. If I'd been around to have my say, he never would have gotten anywhere near my little sister."

"Yes, well, you weren't around. I don't fault you for that. You have a life to live here." Caroline gestured to her auburn-haired sister-in-law, who was kind enough to illustrate the point by already having one hand on her belly. "What's more, it isn't your responsibility to keep me from making a fool of myself. It isn't our parents', either. They might not have seen him for who he really was, but neither did I. I'm the one who let myself be taken in by a…a would-be bigamist."

His brown eyes filled with worry and concern. "You didn't make a fool of yourself. He wasn't honest with you. That's on him. Not you. And you're right. It isn't entirely our parents fault, either. Though, in my opinion, they should have been paying more attention. That doesn't matter right now. What does matter is that you have to find a way to stop blaming yourself. You have to put this behind you."

"That's easier said than done, and it will be practically impossible to do if you keep bringing it up."

"Then I won't bring it up."

She leaned forward to press her advantage. "It also isn't helpful to have you pushing me toward a man I've only met once."

"Fine." This time the reluctance in his voice was almost palpable. "I'll stop, but I hope you don't rule it out."

Caroline let out a huff of exasperation. Emma jumped in with a little distraction. "Caroline, I remember that the last time you were in Little Horn, you mentioned how much you enjoyed riding. Are you still taking lessons in Austin?"

"I had to stop the lessons after I started working at the music school, but I still ride as often as I can."

Emma gave a satisfied nod. "Good. I was hoping you'd say that. About a year ago, Matthew bought me a beautiful palomino mare. Her name is Dulce, and she's as sweet as they come. You're welcome to ride her whenever you like."

"Thank you. I'd love to ride her." In fact, a ride was exactly what she needed to clear her head.

After they were finished eating, Caroline headed to the barn to saddle up. She intentionally refrained from asking Matthew about anything more than the basic layout of his land. She wanted to explore it herself as she hadn't had the chance to do when she'd arrived for his wedding three years ago. She soon found herself alone on a landscape that was a mixture of open land and tree-covered hills.

With the sun bearing down on her and Dulce from a cloudless sky, she headed for the path that led through the trees. It brought her to a creek. The sound of water rushing steadily downstream over rocks and the occasional downed tree soothed her tattered nerves.

A barking dog dashed across the path. Caroline started, and Dulce spooked a little, shying away from the puppy that was now splashing into the shallow creek. Caroline almost had the mare under control when a little boy burst from the trees yelling, "Come back!"

Dulce bolted into a gallop. Heart lurching into her throat, Caroline automatically slouched into the saddle and held on for dear life. The ground flew by beneath them. Dulce dodged through the trees and careened into open land. A fence appeared in front of them. She braced herself for the jump. Instead the mare ground to a jarring stop and lowered her head. The world turned end over end. Caroline landed on the ground with a thud.

Staring up at the sky, she couldn't move. She couldn't breathe. She was dying.

"Breathe, Caroline. Just breathe. Take a breath."

The voice was deep, soothing, commanding. She forced herself to obey it. She took in a small breath. Her lungs eased. She gasped in air.

"Calmly now. That's it. Nice and deep."

Slowly becoming aware of the strong hand holding hers, she lowered her gaze from the sky until she found David McKay's. He offered her a reassuring smile that made her breath hitch again. She concentrated on the task at hand. Did she have enough air in her to speak? If so, she'd like to ask what was wrong with her.

"You got the wind knocked out of you. On top of that, you're probably a little stunned. You'll be all right in a few minutes."

He was right. She was starting to feel better already. She tried to sit up. He pressed a hand to her shoulder to stop her. "Whoa now. Take it easy. Before you get up, tell me—does anything hurt?"

She paused to take inventory. Her voice came out a little breathlessly. "Everything hurts a little, but nothing vital seems injured. Just my pride."

"Not much you can do when a horse decides to bolt other than stick to your saddle and try to calm her down." He helped her sit up. "You did that pretty well until she decided to throw you."

"Where is she?"

Approval filled his eyes. Apparently, the way to this rancher's heart was through worrying about her horse. "My men will round her up for you."

"Thank you." She rubbed at the burning sensation on her arm.

He caught her hand and pulled it away to look at the spot. "Looks like you've got a pretty bad scrape there."

"How?"

"Probably the fence. You flew right over it on your way down. You didn't notice that?" After she shook her head, he placed a knuckle under her chin and lifted it slightly. "You've got another scratch on your chin. Come back to my ranch house. My ma will fix you up. Then I'll escort you back home."

"Oh, I'm sure that isn't necessary."

"Maybe not, but it's neighborly, and that's how we do things around here." He stood, then reached down. "Shall we?"

She hesitated only for a moment before placing her hand in his. He pulled her up. The world tilted before settling in place. She instinctively caught his free arm to steady herself, then let go. "I'm sorry."

"Dizzy?"

"A little."

He took hold of her elbow. "You didn't hit your head, did you?"

"No. My equilibrium needed to catch up. That's all."

He gave a reluctant nod. "Let's get you to the house."

She grew steadier by the minute as he guided her through the tall, yellowing grass toward the two-story house in the distance. "Thank you for coming to my rescue yet again. I promise I'm not usually this much trouble."

He smiled. "No trouble at all. Do you have any idea what made your horse spook like that?"

"A dog ran across the path with a little boy chasing him."

"A little boy?" His eyes narrowed as he scanned their surroundings. "That's mighty interesting. I don't suppose you got a good look at him?"

"Nothing more than a glimpse."

He opened the door for her. An acrid smell reached her nose. Since she was a horrible cook, it was one she knew all too well. "Something is burning."

"Uh-oh. Why don't you wait in the parlor while I take care of this?" David rushed away, presumably to the kitchen.

Left alone in the foyer, Caroline caught a glimpse of the parlor through the half-open door on her right. Her eyes widened as she stepped inside. She crossed the room to where the upright piano stood against the wall. She pressed middle C. The note filled the room until a discordant cry drowned it out. Was that a baby?

As though in confirmation, the cry seeped down

through the ceiling above her head. Hadn't Matthew said David had been a widower for five years? What on earth could he be doing in possession of a baby? She was halfway up the stairs before realizing it was bad manners to explore someone's house uninvited. Still, she couldn't ignore the baby. Not when she was so close and willing to help. She followed the cries to the nursery, then stopped short when she discovered there were *three* babies and that they weren't alone after all. An older woman with a cloud of white hair sat in a rocking chair. The baby in the nearby crib caught sight of Caroline and stopped crying in order to watch her attentively.

She gave a little gasp. "Oh my! How adorable! Are they triplets?"

The woman blinked in surprise, then offered an amused smile. "Why, yes, they are. And who might you be?"

"Caroline Murray. I promise I didn't just walk in here off the street...or range. David invited me in."

"Did he?" Surprise filled her warm brown eyes, followed by a speculative look. "Well, then, welcome to our home. I'm Ida Winthrop."

Not David's mother, then. "It's a pleasure to meet you, Mrs. Winthrop. Are you the triplets' caretaker?"

Ida laughed. "I'm everyone's caretaker. I'm David's mother."

"Oh, I—"

"It's confusing, I know. My late husband and I adopted David when he was only a little tyke. We knew that David had been separated from his two brothers.

We tried to find them. When we couldn't, we decided we'd better keep David's last name McKay in case his family came looking for him."

"Eventually they did," David chimed in as he stepped into the room and immediately lifted the baby from the crib into his arms.

Ida's face lit up with love for her son. "Yes, they did. They were both grown with families of their own and living in Little Horn. We decided to sell our old ranch and move nearer to them. And so here we are."

"Yep, here we are." David stole a quick glance at Caroline before turning back to Ida. "I took our lunch off the stove, but I think it was too late to save it."

"Oh, no! I completely forgot I had something on the stove when I came up here. Maggie could have gotten burned." Ida shook her head in dismay when David tried to reassure her. "No. It isn't fine. I can't believe I did that. It's just that I don't know if I'm going or coming these days."

It was obvious that David's mother was overtired and in need of a break. Caroline stepped forward to take the drowsy baby. "Why don't I take the triplets for a little while?"

Ida looked relieved. "Would you mind? I really do need to figure out what I'm going to do for lunch."

"I wouldn't mind at all." Caroline carefully laid the baby in the crib.

Ida sighed. "Thank you, dear. I've tried rocking them, but it doesn't seem to be doing much good."

"Are they sick?"

"No." Ida handed Caroline the baby with the little

green booties. "They aren't sleeping. Not on any kind of schedule anyway. I think that's what has them so fussy."

Caroline held the sweet weight close to her chest. "Well, I can understand that. I'd feel grumpy, too, if I was in their shoes."

"Louisa—she cared for the triplets before us—said they like to sleep touching each other, but when I put them down, one will inevitably start moving around and awaken the others. I've done everything I know how to do—rocking, pacing, singing and praying. We need to put them back on their schedule. They need their naps."

"Caroline and I will work on it, Ma. You go on and do what you need to do."

"Thank you." Ida gave them both grateful looks before hurrying out of the room.

David whispered, "Thanks for helping out, Caroline. Hey, I can't tell. Is this one sleeping?"

She met the baby's large brown eyes. "Not even close." She laughed at David's small groan. "How on earth did you end up caring for triplets?"

His brow furrowed into serious lines as he told the story, and that as a member of the Lone Star Cowboy League, he felt he should step up to care for the triplets. His answer was short, succinct, to the point and hardly revealing.

"What made you offer to take them in?"

He shrugged. "I felt responsible. After all, I encouraged the league to keep the boys together. Splitting them up into different homes would have made it easier for the community to help them. You heard my story from Ma. I was separated from my brothers for most of my life. We're reunited now, but we can't get those years back. They're gone. I didn't want these little ones to go through that."

"That's beautiful, David."

He gave her a quick smile. "Well, I don't know about that, but it was the right thing to do. Of that, I'm absolutely certain. Unfortunately, it hasn't been easy—especially now that they no longer have a nanny."

She frowned in confusion. "Oh? What happened to the nanny?"

"Pa!" A little girl yelled from downstairs. "Pa, come quick! I think I killed somebody!"

Their eyes caught and widened simultaneously. David tensed. Caroline jerked her head toward the door. "Go. I'll handle the triplets."

That was all the encouragement he needed to lower the baby into the crib and rush out the door.

# Chapter Three

There was no way Maggie could have killed someone—leastwise, not on purpose. Even so, someone might need help. Right now that person was his daughter. As soon as he descended the stairs, Maggie launched herself into his arms. He caught her close. Over her shoulder, he exchanged a worried look with his mother, who stood at the kitchen door holding a scouring pad and a burned pot. David shifted Maggie in his arms so that he could see her face. She looked downright terrified. "What happened?"

"I spooked a lady's horse. It ran off with her. She was barely hanging on. She probably fell off and died like Ma did."

He glanced at his mother. They both knew this wasn't anything like the way Maggie's mother had died. Laura's horse hadn't bolted. It had tripped because Laura had been galloping through the night in a storm—running away with another man. Of course, David couldn't tell Maggie that. He hoped she'd never find out, either. Better that she think Laura's death had simply been a tragic accident than that her mother had been willing to abandon both of them.

Tears filled Maggie's eyes. "Oh, Pa, I killed her."

"Baby, you didn't kill anyone. That lady is alive. I found her myself."

She searched his face. "You did? She is?"

"Yes, and she's fine. A little shaken and scratched, but fine. In fact, she's upstairs right now."

"Oh." Maggie's blue eyes widened. "Is she mad?"

Caroline hadn't seemed angry when she'd mentioned the boy darting across her path, but she hadn't known then that boy was actually his daughter. He'd had a vague suspicion it might be, since the incident had taken place near his property. The part about the dog had thrown him off because they didn't have a dog for Maggie to be chasing after. He'd have to talk to her about staying clear of strays. First things first, he needed to deal with the task at hand. "I'm not sure, honey. I don't think so, but—"

She began to wriggle. "Can you put me down now, Pa? I've got to apologize."

"Of course." He set her down and exchanged a look with Ma—one that was a mix of relief, concern and pride. Then he followed Maggie up the stairs. He really hoped Caroline's reaction would be appropriate to the occasion. After all, this truly had been an accident. Maggie certainly should have been more careful, but there were rarely ever any riders in those woods for her to look out for.

Maggie tugged at his wrist. She placed a finger over her lips, then whispered, "Listen."

The simple melody of "Hush, Little Baby" drifted down the hall. The soprano was bright and warm and pure. Yet its tone was so soft and soothing that he could feel the tension easing from his shoulders. Maggie moved stealthily toward the partially open nursery room door. She leaned against the doorjamb, her head cocked as she listened with a look of wonder.

He quietly stepped up behind her to peer inside. The yellow curtains infused the room with warm, muted light, outlining Caroline's willowy figure as she swayed in time to the song with a babe in her arms. She gently laid the child in the crib, lingering until the boy settled onto his stomach. She stilled. Her lashes slowly lifted until her gaze met David. She'd felt his stare. That much was obvious. He ought to look away. He had every intention of doing so when a tendril from her mussed chignon broke free to swing near her lips. His hand landed on Maggie's shoulder to ground himself in the reality of his life rather than the vision before him.

Caroline's soulful gaze mercifully lowered to Maggie. With a single sweeping glance, she seemed to take in the chopped-off caramel curls beneath Maggie's hat, her dirt-smudged cheeks and, most condemning of all, the collared shirt and worn pants Maggie had begged off her seemingly endless supply of boy cousins. Caroline's eyes lit with realization. Her mouth fell open slightly, then curved into a smile. She winked, which prompted an answering bashful smile from Maggie before the girl ducked her head.

Caroline finished her song, then tiptoed toward them. They moved out of the doorway so she could exit. She closed the door behind them softly and tipped her head to prompt them farther down the hall. Once they were out of hearing range of the triplets, she knelt in front of Maggie and gently caught hold of the girl's arm. "Are you all right?"

Maggie must have been holding her breath, because she let it out in a rush. "I'm fine. Are you? I thought I killed you."

"I'm right as rain. Even if I had been hurt, you shouldn't have blamed yourself. We scared each other. That's all."

"What about your horse?"

Caroline sent a questioning look to David over Maggie's shoulder. The palomino had seemed fine to him when he'd sent his men after it. "She looked fine to me, but I'm sure my men are making sure of that as we speak."

Caroline squeezed Maggie's arm lightly. "And what about your dog?"

"We don't have a dog," David volunteered.

Maggie bit her lip and glanced down at the floor.

He narrowed his eyes. His voice turned half questioning, half warning. "Maggie, we don't have a dog."

"The Colemans' dog had puppies. They came by this morning to see if we wanted one. I did. Grandma said I could."

David pulled in a deep breath and let out a heavy sigh.

"I named him Duke. He's really cute. I left him tied to the porch. He's probably lonely now. I should go get him." She paused to give Caroline a quick hug. "I'm sorry for scaring your horse, and I'm glad you're not dead, Miss…"

The woman recovered from her surprise to return the hug. "Caroline."

"Miss Caroline." Maggie raced down the stairs and out the front door.

Caroline stood with a smile. "There's never a dull moment around here, is there?"

"You have no idea." He ran his fingers through his hair, then remembered why he'd brought Caroline home to begin with. "Let's get those scratches cleaned up."

He led the way to the kitchen, where his mother looked up from her second attempt at lunch. "I take it Maggie didn't kill anyone?"

Caroline laughed. "No. Thankfully, everyone is fine."

"Good." Ida smiled at her. "You mentioned your name was Caroline Murray. Are you any relation to Matthew Murray?"

"I'm his sister."

"How lovely! Matthew told me that one of his sisters was getting married. You must tell me about her wedding."

"Oh." Caroline's gaze darted to David's, then back to his mother. "Matthew and I have no other siblings. I was the one getting married—only, I didn't get married, so…"

Seeing the curiosity on Ida's face, David opened the nearest cabinet. "Ma, where's that stuff you put on Maggie's cuts? Caroline hit a fence when the horse threw her and has a few scrapes that need cleaning."

"It's two cabinet doors over."

"Found it." He grabbed the supplies he needed. "Have a seat, Caroline. I'll help you out, since my ma is busy."

If her grateful smile was any indication, Caroline knew he was trying to distract his mother. The searching look Ida sent him said she knew it, too. Caroline sat on the bench at the kitchen table, so David straddled a spot beside her. As soon as he touched her arm he realized he probably shouldn't have taken this task upon himself. It wasn't the same as doctoring up Maggie. Not at all.

Seeking a distraction, he cleared his throat and pinned his watchful mother with a look. "I don't recall agreeing to let Maggie have a dog."

"I don't recall you saying she couldn't have one."

The skin around Caroline's scrape turned red, which meant the cleanser was working and likely smarting. He blew on it gently. She tensed. He glanced up at her, but she was staring at the floor near his boot. "That's probably because no one asked me."

"She has no one near her own age to play with unless one of us takes her clear across town to see her cousins. I couldn't say no."

"I know, Ma, but you could have said, 'Wait until I ask your father.'" He caught Caroline's chin and guided it away from him so that he could dab some of the cleaner on her cheek. This scrape didn't turn quite as red, and he didn't want to blow on her face, so he let it be. "How am I supposed to tell her no now that she's named the dog?"

Ida frowned. "So you really didn't want her to have one?"

"I don't want to have to take care of a dog. Especially since we're already taking care of the triplets without a nanny to help. I don't have time for that. Not with a ranch to run and a daughter to raise." He hesitated as Caroline looked at him with compassion, then swiped a bit of healing ointment on her arm.

Maggie's voice sounded from the entryway. "I'll take care of him. I promise. You won't have to do anything."

He glanced at his daughter's earnest face. It was a sweet offer, but Maggie had never had a dog before. She wouldn't know what to do. "Puppies need to be fed three to four times a day. You'd have to bathe him when he gets dirty. You'd have to train him if you want him to behave, which we do. Then there are small things like clipping his nails and cleaning his ears. You'd have to clean up after him if he has an accident and teach him to go outside."

"I'll do it. I promise." There was a determined glint in her eyes. She'd gotten that from him, so he knew she'd argue up and down that she was fully capable of tending to her pup. She probably had every intention of doing so, but when it came down to it, David knew he'd be the one to bear the most responsibility for the dog's care. Unfortunately, the dog would have to go back, but he'd save that bit of news for when they no longer had an audience.

Caroline touched his arm. "I'm sorry, but my cheek…"

One look at the redness told him it was probably

stinging up a storm. Propriety aside, he caught her chin and turned her face aside to blow cool air on it. Her tension eased a bit. He put the healing ointment on it. "Sorry about that. Almost done."

"Son, what about the lady you contacted about being the new nanny?"

David tore a strip of cotton gauze loose from the roll. He hadn't told his mother that he'd contacted a nanny. He'd simply said that he'd contacted someone about helping them out. That was all he planned to tell her until he heard back from the Boston mail-order bride. His mother wouldn't approve of it, since she wanted him to find another love match. He wanted to wait to break the truth to her until he was certain the lady was coming. "It's only been two days. There is no way she's even received my letter yet."

Maggie stepped farther into the kitchen to watch him bandage the scratch on Caroline's arm. "Why can't Miss Caroline be our nanny?"

All of the grown-ups froze. David's eyebrow lifted. Had his darling daughter just said "*our* nanny," as in she'd consider herself one of Caroline's charges?

Caroline recovered from her surprise. "I'm sorry, sweetheart. I couldn't."

Maggie's eyes clouded. "Why not?"

"Well, I'm not going to be here very long for one thing. For another, I've never been a nanny before."

"Maybe not," Ida interjected. "But you certainly seemed to have a way with the triplets. I can tell from the quiet in this house that you finally got them to nap.

Besides, we wouldn't need you for long. Only until this nanny David's trying to hire can get here."

"Ma, Miss Murray is here to visit her family, not work for ours." He tied off the bandage. "It wouldn't be right for us to impose on that."

"Of course, we wouldn't want to impose, Caroline, but your family would be welcome to visit here as often as they want."

"Oh, I don't know." Caroline touched a hand to her throat as she glanced around the kitchen. Her gaze landed on his, soft as a butterfly, filled with questions.

Did he want her to help them? The answer was an irrevocable no. Did he need her help? Ida's meaningful glare said yes. When he remained silent, Ida prompted, "We sure could use your help, Caroline. Couldn't we, David?"

He swallowed hard. "There's no denying that."

Caroline bit her lip. "Well, I'm sure my brother and sister-in-law could spare me now and then."

"We'd need you more than now and then." David offered up the potential difficulties with a little too much enthusiasm. "You'd have to stay here at the ranch. The triplets need to be fed once during the night."

"Yes," Ida interjected, "but there is a stipend that would help compensate."

Caroline bit her lip. "What about the piano?"

David frowned. "What about it?"

"Would y'all mind ever so much if I played it now and then?"

Ida grinned. "Honey, you can play it as often as you want."

"In that case..." A smile slowly tilted Caroline's mouth. "Yes! I'd be happy to help out."

Maggie let out a whoop and reached for Caroline's hands. Somehow Caroline seemed to know that was her cue to dance the girl around the kitchen in a tight little circle. Ida sank into the nearest chair with pure relief. David opened his mouth to remind everyone that he was the man of the house with the final say on all of this and he hadn't agreed to anything. Since doing so would likely accomplish nothing, he closed his mouth and let out a frustrated breath.

He ought to be happy. He had a nanny to help with the triplets—one Maggie had all but promised to mind. They could use Caroline's help. There was no denying that. There was also no denying that he'd been thinking about her almost constantly since they'd first met. He'd ridden over to Matthew's ranch earlier today hoping to catch a glimpse of her. Of course, he hadn't realized that until not seeing her had resulted in major disappointment. He'd been determined to put her out of his mind. That had lasted for about as long as it had taken her runaway horse to gallop across his land. Now he was supposed to be happy about the fact that she'd be living in his house? Not likely.

Still, there was no getting around it. Caroline was here to stay for now. He'd just have to get over his ill-fated interest in her. And it was ill-fated. More than that, it was inappropriate. She was recovering from a broken heart. He'd never quite recovered from his. There was also the little matter of him already having sent off a letter of inquiry to a mail-order bride. Not that he was thinking about Caroline in the context of marriage.

He closed his eyes, shutting off that train of thought before it could go any further. Caroline staying here wouldn't be a problem. He wouldn't let it be.

## Chapter Four

Agreeing to help David had been an easy decision for Caroline. Perhaps too easy, considering she didn't have all that much experience caring for babies. It would be worth it to have access to the piano. Her fingers were already itching to touch those smooth ivory keys. She knew from experience that as the music flowed through her it would carry her stress and anxiety with it. She desperately needed that release, and she certainly wouldn't get it at her brother's ranch. He refused to allow a single instrument into his house.

Of course, she couldn't tell him that was one of the reasons she'd agreed to move to the McKay ranch. She didn't want him to think she was being anything like their parents by putting music above family. She wasn't, but she couldn't sit around twiddling her thumbs trying not to think about what had happened in Austin, either.

David answered the door the next morning looking a little bleary-eyed but otherwise ready to start the day. He offered a welcoming smile to Caroline and extended a hand to Matthew, who had accompanied her. "Good morning. There's a fresh pot of coffee on the stove if either of you want some. Matthew, let me take that luggage from you."

He was speaking in a slightly hushed tone, so Caroline did the same. "Are the babies still asleep?"

"They were just starting to stir when I saw you driving down the road. I let them be, hoping you'd get here before they really got going."

She removed her hat and gloves. "And Maggie?"

"She was still sleeping last I checked. My ma's getting ready for the day. She'll probably be starting breakfast in a few minutes." He nodded down the hall. "Follow me to the nursery. I'll give y'all a quick tour on the way. I think y'all have both been in the parlor. The kitchen and dining room are on the left side of the house. On the right we have my study. Next door to that is my bedroom." They climbed the stairs. "My mother and Maggie are on the second floor with the nursery."

David set down the luggage to open the nursery door. One of the babies immediately grabbed on to the crib's bars and stood to greet them with a happy exclamation. Caroline dropped her hat and gloves on the bed on her way to the crib. She cooed, "Good morning."

He chortled and began bouncing up and down. Soon one of his brothers stood beside him, staring at her with big brown eyes. The last one seemed content to stay right where he sat, though he smiled shyly. They all blinked when light flooded the room. Caroline glanced at David as he tied back the curtains. "Do you know who is who?"

"The bouncing one is Jasper. Eli is the one standing beside him, staring at you all wide-eyed. The shy one is Theo."

She searched the boys' identical faces for some differences. "How do you tell them apart?"

"Mostly by their personalities. They're each pretty distinctive. If you get confused, just call one of their names. They're usually pretty good at responding to their own."

"Well, aren't you little fellas smart?" She listened intently as Eli started babbling to tell her how right she was. Once he finished, she nodded. "Yes, that's exactly what I think, too."

David walked over to the chest of clothes to show her where they kept the baby clothes, diapers and other supplies. "Everything you need should be right in here."

Matthew walked over to peer into the crib. "So these are the three cowboys causing such a fuss in town. They're pretty cute."

Caroline bumped him with her shoulder. "It won't be long before you have a little one just like this causing a fuss in your house, too."

"I can't wait." Matthew grinned. "Listen, I'd better head back to the ranch. Have fun with the kids, Caroline. I'll see you soon." Matthew turned to David. "David, would you walk me out?"

There was a questioning little lift to David's brow, but he nodded. "Of course."

Left alone with her three charges, Caroline clasped her hands behind her back and paced in front of the crib. "All right, boys, listen close. The four of us are going to make a deal. I promise to feed you, keep you clean, sing you to sleep and whatever else is necessary for your comfort. I have two conditions, though."

The shyest one finally stood up next to his brothers.

She stopped pacing to grin at him. "Well, hello, Theo! Thank you for joining the discussion."

He gave a little heart-melting grin and babbled something to his brothers.

"I do appreciate the stamp of approval, but it's a bit early. You haven't heard my conditions yet. The first one should be very simple. In return for my services, you must each continue to be adorable. Do you think y'all can do that?"

Eli yelled something unintelligible.

"I'm sorry. I know I shouldn't have questioned your talents. I just want to make sure the terms of our agreement are clear. The last and final condition is not so simple."

Jasper reached out for her.

She lifted him into her arms and hugged him close. "I'm only going to be here a short time, so you little honeybees better not make me fall in love with you. My poor heart's been through enough, and it can't take any more breaking. Is that understood?"

David cleared his throat. She spun around to find him watching her from the doorway. A blush rushed over her cheeks as she met his amused gaze.

"It was a nice speech, but I don't think they have any intention of obeying."

"You can't blame a girl for trying."

"No, I guess not." He sobered as sincerity filled his voice. "Caroline, I wanted to thank you for being so kind to Maggie after finding out she was involved in spooking your horse."

"You're welcome, but there's really no need to thank me. Maggie is easy to be kind to. Of course, that might have something to do with the fact that I was a lot like her when I was younger." She laughed at his surprised look. "I didn't go quite so far as wearing pants, but I was forever chasing after Matthew. Anything he did, I had to do or at least attempt."

"I never would have guessed that." She followed his gaze as it swept over her bottle green skirt, black shirt-waist and cream blouse. From the lace on her collar to the puff sleeves and the slender, tulip-shaped skirt that smoothed over her hips, everything about her clothing was as feminine as it was fashionable.

"What changed?" he asked with more than a hint of desperation. "I mean, what made you want to be ladylike?"

She shrugged. "I made friends with several little girls my age and wanted to be more like them."

His mouth settled into a discouraged frown. "Maggie's been around girls her age, but that hasn't changed anything."

"That's because you're more important to her than they are."

He tilted his head to stare at her. "What do you mean?"

"She could be trying to emulate you just like I was

trying to emulate Matthew." She could see him thinking about it, but she didn't have time for him to reach a conclusion. Dampness was beginning to seep through Jasper's diaper. She turned toward the changing table. "Uh-oh. Someone needs a little changing."

"They probably all do." He strode closer. "Would you like some help getting started?"

"No, I'm sure I can handle it. Why don't you head on down for breakfast? I'll bring the boys as soon as they're ready."

He hesitated. Eventually, the confidence in her smile must have convinced him she could handle this, because he nodded and left the room. That was a good thing because it took all her concentration to remember the lessons Emma had given her last night about changing diapers. She probably should have accepted David's help, but she wanted to start out being a help to the McKays, not a hindrance.

She finished changing Jasper and set him on the floor to crawl. He found her luggage intriguing. Since everything was still closed up, she let him fiddle with it to his heart's content. She opened the window that was far out of reach of the triplets to let in some fresh air before taking on the other boys. With them all clean and smelling good, she took a few moments to freshen up herself. She was just pondering how she was going to carry the triplets down the stairs to the kitchen when a tentative knock sounded too far down on the door to be anyone other than Maggie.

"Is that Maggie McKay I hear?" She opened the

door to find the little girl looking at her with a mix of sheepishness and surprise.

"How'd you know it was me?"

Caroline winked. "Just a feeling. How are you this morning?"

"Good. I'm glad you're here. Oh, I'm supposed to tell you that Grandma says breakfast is almost ready."

"Then we'd better head down—whoa, little man." Caroline caught Eli as he made a break for the stairs. Or was it Jasper? Setting them loose in the bedroom had scrambled their identities a little in her mind. It was rather like watching that street magician's game with the pea in the walnut shell. If she had to guess, she'd say this sweet pea was Eli.

Refocusing on Maggie, she realized the girl was exactly the extra set of arms she needed. "You know, Maggie, while I'm here, I could use a special helper to assist me now and then. I don't suppose you have anyone you would recommend?"

Maggie brightened. "Me, Miss Caroline. You've got to choose me. My pa said I'm supposed to help you whenever I can."

"Wonderful! I knew I could count on you. Right now, I could use an assistant to help me get the triplets safely down to breakfast. Do you think you can carry one of them while I carry the other two?"

"I can do it."

"Thank you, Maggie. Here. You take Eli." Caroline transferred the baby to Maggie, making sure she had him safely in her grasp. "Go right on down the stairs, and I'll meet you at the table."

She watched to make sure Maggie made it all right, then turned to hunt down the two others. Soon enough all three boys were sitting in their high chairs at the table, which felt like an accomplishment in and of itself. Ida greeted Caroline with a warm hug and words of welcome, then set her to work cutting the triplets' food into manageable pieces for them.

David entered through the back door with a pail of milk. He smiled at the sight of Maggie entertaining the triplets by making silly faces. David placed another chair at the table. "Caroline, the boys are pretty independent when it comes to mealtimes. At least, they try to be. Usually Ma and I split up the triplets during the meal. I watch over two while Ma takes care of one."

"I'd be happy to take one of the triplets off your hands."

"Sounds good." He nodded and placed one of the high chairs between them.

Finally, they were all seated, but not quite settled. Caroline shifted to find room under the table and accidentally bumped David's knees with her own. "Sorry!"

"It's all right. This table is getting a little too small for all of us. Ma, do you know where you stored the leaf? I can put it in before lunch."

"Yes, I'll—" Ida hesitated, her gaze flickering from David to Caroline. "I'll have to look for it."

Maggie wiggled in her seat as she impatiently eyed the gooey cinnamon rolls at the center of the table. "Is it time for grace, Pa?"

"Go ahead, Maggie."

She reached for David's and Ida's hands. Ida took Caroline's. Caroline glanced at David. He showed none of the hesitance she felt in joining hands. In fact, he was already closing his eyes by the time her hand found his. A little surge of heat went through her fingers as they slid across his palm, but he didn't seem to notice, so she determined that she wouldn't, either.

There was no ignoring that this was the hand of a rancher used to hard work and long hours in the saddle. It had a strength and a roughness to it that made for a much different experience than those few times she'd held Nico's hand. He'd had soft hands with long fingers, perfect for the piano—and for stealing from unsuspecting women, apparently. Why she persisted in comparing the two men was beyond her and beyond annoying. Especially since it only made Nico look worse, which in turn made her feel more foolish. It also had the inconvenient result of making David look even better in comparison. It needed to stop.

Thankfully, Maggie's prayer provided a timely distraction from her thoughts. "Lord, thank You for this food and for Miss Caroline coming to stay with us. Help us all have a good day. Amen."

All the grown-ups echoed, "Amen."

Caroline grinned at Maggie. "Thank you for including me in your prayer, Maggie. That was very sweet."

"You're welcome, Miss Caroline." Maggie sent her a bashful smile.

Ida gave Caroline's hand an affectionate little squeeze before releasing it. "It was well deserved. You're going to be a blessing to us. I can feel it."

"I hope so." Caroline glanced at David to see if he had anything to add. She found his thoughtful gaze trained down at the table. No. Not the table. He was looking at their joined hands. *Oh, dear.* Were they the only ones still holding hands? A quick glance around the table said they were.

Offering him a small smile to cover the awkwardness of it all, she pulled her hand free with a gentle tug. Something was troubling him. She could see that and sense it, too. His expression shuttered and he glanced back to his plate. Oddly enough, she felt cheated. After all, she'd poured her heart and her tears onto his shoulder a couple of days ago. It seemed only fair that he would be just as vulnerable with her.

Of course, they were technically little more than strangers, and the best place for sharing confidences probably wasn't at the breakfast table. But still. The principle of it bothered her. And it annoyed her to be bothered by it.

"Caroline, dear, the boys like to try to feed themselves, though they don't quite have the knack of it yet."

Caroline blinked away her reverie and focused on copying Ida's technique in making sure the baby, whom she was relatively certain must be Theo, was well fed. It took far more energy and creativity than she'd imagined to keep him interested in the food. Maggie filled the lagging conversation. "Are you riding with the ranch hands today, Pa?"

"Yes, I need to check on the herd."

"May I go with you?"

David paused to look at Maggie, then at Caroline before returning to Maggie. "I thought you were excited about helping Miss Caroline today."

"I am, but I also like helping you. I can do both."

David chuckled. "You stay here with your grandma and Miss Caroline today. I'll take you riding another time."

Caroline lifted a brow at David slightly, wishing she could say, "See? I was right. You're the most important person to her." Instead Caroline smiled at Maggie. "We'll have fun today, Maggie. I promise."

Ida took a break from feeding the baby to nudge the bowl of biscuits toward David. "David, will you be back in time for lunch?"

"Probably not, but I'll be here for dinner." He finished his plate and set it in the sink before grabbing a biscuit on the way out. "Y'all have a good day now."

"Bye, Pa." Maggie returned her father's parting wave and watched until the door closed after him. Her eyes filled with tears. Her lower lip trembled.

Caroline tensed in alarm. She was about to try to comfort the girl when Ida caught her eye. The woman shook her head in warning. Pressing her lips together to keep them silent, Caroline did her best to listen as Ida went over the triplets' daily schedule with her. Even so, Caroline couldn't help glancing at Maggie now and then. The girl's eyes eventually cleared of tears. Finally, Maggie reengaged in the conversation as though nothing had happened.

Did that happen every morning? It must if Ida was

so used to it. Caroline's heart went out to the girl. At Maggie's age, she used to do the exact same thing when her parents left for the theater. She'd known she wouldn't be able to see them again until the next morning, and the small amount of attention they'd paid to her at breakfast was never enough to fill her aching heart. Matthew had always done his best to distract her until she was able to forget about her parents and enjoy the rest of the day. It had bothered her less and less as she grew older. Eventually she'd learned to accept the fact that her parents cared more about their work than they did about their children.

Could the same thing be happening here? If so, Caroline was a living, breathing example of why that was a disaster waiting to happen. She'd fallen for the first man to show her any attention and ignored every sign of his dishonorable intentions. Caroline couldn't let the same thing happen to sweet little Maggie. Something had to be done. And she was just the woman to do it.

David tugged his hat lower to block out the mid-afternoon sun. Even its scorching heat couldn't quite rival the intensity of Matthew's warning glare from earlier this morning. The man's exact words had been "Watch yourself around my sister. She's been hurt, and that won't happen again on my watch. At least, not without some serious repercussions for the man who does the hurting. Understand?"

David understood, all right. He'd done his best to assure Matthew that Caroline would be safe from any romantic entanglements at the McKay ranch. For some reason, Matthew hadn't seemed entirely convinced. The man really had no need for concern. The only thing David intended to do with Caroline was to stay out of her way. That should be easy enough, since as long as she was doing her job, he'd have plenty of time to do his.

That in and of itself was a blessing. After spending the last few days helping his mother with Maggie and the triplets, he had a lot to catch up on. Beyond the normal day-to-day running of the ranch, David was also battling the drought that continued to wreak havoc on the ranches surrounding Little Horn. He'd grown up on a ranch in west Texas, where rain and water was far less abundant than in the comparatively lush Hill County, so he felt he had an advantage in that fight that many of the nearby ranchers didn't.

He was used to conserving water and stretching resources. Unfortunately, that didn't make it any easier to watch the once-green pastureland fade to yellow, then dry up in patches of brown. Nor did it stop him from being concerned about his cattle—especially since the land had to support the extra two hundred head he'd brought with him from out west last year.

Bringing along his best breeding stock had seemed like a good idea at the time. He'd planned to focus on rebuilding the herd and extending his adoptive father's legacy right here in Little Horn. Now it would take his best efforts to keep the stock healthy and fed through the winter. While the fresh spring near the house looked to be holding up, his hay crop was going to be much smaller than he'd hoped.

David sent a questioning glance to his nearest ranch hand. Ephraim Campbell had been a part of the McKay operation in west Texas and had followed the outfit to Little Horn, along with David's foreman, Joaquin Reyes. They'd joined together with Isaiah Upkins, an older cowboy who'd worked for the previous owner of the Windy Diamond. As appreciative as David was for Isaiah's knowledge of the land, David had worked with the other two men long enough that they could all but read his thoughts when they worked together. Proving that, Ephraim simply said, "Twenty-four."

David nodded. Twenty-four calves still nursing so far. They'd likely find a few more before the day was through. That meant he'd have no choice but to buy additional feed. Other ranchers in the area were going to find themselves in the same position, which meant feed prices were bound to go up. The sooner he got his order in, the better.

The only thing left to determine was how much he'd need to spend. He considered his options for a moment. "I'm thinking about weaning early."

Ephraim wiped his golden-brown brow on his shirt-sleeve before placing his hat back over his dark curls. "Cutting feed cost?"

"Yep."

Ephraim nodded his agreement. David glanced across the thirty or so cattle they had corralled in search of his foreman. "Hey, Joaquin, what do you think about weaning early this year?"

Joaquin tipped back his hat to eye the calves in the bunch. "They look good. I think they can handle it. Want us to separate them out?"

"Yes, as soon as we get a final tally."

Far in the distance, Isaiah headed their way, returning from a scouting mission with a couple of strays. Catching sight of a limping calf, David rode out to meet him. "Have you checked the injury?"

"Not yet. This red-spotted steer has a mind of his own." As if to prove Isaiah's point, the steer bolted left.

"I'll doctor the calf. Have fun with the steer." He grinned as Isaiah grimaced and redirected the steer.

Joaquin cantered over as David doctored the calf's leg. "What's the matter with him?"

"Looks like he got caught up on some barbed wire." David untied the calf and watched him lope back toward his mother. "If so, his mother might be scratched up, too, even though she isn't limping. Once we're done counting calves, let's bring them into the corral by the barn. Examine the mother. Keep an eye on the calf."

"Sure thing, *jefe*." Joaquin tipped his hat back. "Do you want us to check the fence? It might be damaged."

David remounted his horse. "I'll ride over now and take a look, since I wanted to check on the crop anyway. Meanwhile, y'all keep looking for nursing cattle."

"We'll take care of it."

With a nod of thanks, David rode the hay field fence until he found the spot where the cattle had tried to break through. Oddly enough, a large branch blocked the opening. It had to have been put there after the cows had broken in. Had one of his men coaxed the cow and calf from the field and placed the branch here as a temporary fix?

It seemed a strange thing to do when fixing the breech was a relatively simple task with the right tools. Stranger still was the fact that none of them had mentioned it. No. His men hadn't done this. They'd started rounding up those heads of cattle two days ago. That meant whoever had helped them out by blocking the fence was long gone.

Shrugging off the matter for now, David set about mending the break. He was nearly finished when he spotted Jamie Coleman riding toward him. They'd missed each other yesterday when David had returned the puppy to the Coleman ranch. Tug, Jamie's father, had promised to send his son out to apologize for giving Maggie the dog without David's permission. David had insisted it wasn't necessary.

Apparently, Tug hadn't agreed, because the nineteen-year-old in question greeted David with a wave of his hat. "Howdy, Mr. McKay! I came to apologize. My pa is right. I should have checked with you before I gave Maggie that puppy."

"It was only a misunderstanding. Don't worry about it."

Jamie nodded, though worry entered his hazel eyes. "I hope Maggie wasn't too upset by it all."

Oh, she'd been plenty upset. The fact that Caroline was coming to live with them had been the only thing to save the evening. "She'll be fine. I softened the news by telling her we'd get a dog someday when everything calms down. Right now adding an untrained puppy to the mix is just too much."

"I understand." Jamie hesitated. "What if I kept the dog for a little while and trained him for you? That way you and Maggie both get what you want and I'll feel a whole lot better about the whole thing."

David stopped wrestling with the barbed wire fence to consider the offer. "That would be a huge help. I'd be happy to pay you for the training."

Jamie grinned. "Great! No need to pay me. Would it be all right if I bring him around now and then so Maggie could have a hand in training him?"

"She'd love that. Thank you, Jamie." David held out his hand and they shook on it. "You've just made my daughter's day."

"Happy to help. I'd better get back to work. I'll be by with the dog in a couple of days."

"See you then." David let out a sigh of relief. With the dog training out of the way, he'd still have to deal with its day-to-day care, but that shouldn't be too much of a problem now that Caroline was caring for the triplets. Maggie would help out, too. He'd hold her to the promise.

He'd tell her the news when he tucked her in tonight. For now, he had a fence to finish repairing. With that done, he rode the fence to check for other breaks in it. That took David well to the north side of his spread, so he took the road back around toward the house.

He hadn't gone far before he spotted two children riding a mule ahead of him on the road. Neither of them seemed to notice David's approach as they talked to each other. David called out, "Hello there!"

The children startled. The girl kicked her heels into the mule's side and sank low to its back as though she expected him to gallop away. Instead the mule brayed in stubborn protest and continued its plodding progress. David easily caught up with them. Up close, the children looked so much alike that they had to be siblings. The girl seemed to be around Maggie's age with brown hair and serious brown eyes. The boy matched her in coloring but looked to be several years younger. Noting their wide eyes, David spoke in a friendly, gentle tone. "Evening, folks. My name is David McKay. I don't believe we've met."

The two exchanged a look rife with meaning before the boy answered for them. "My name is Gil. This is my sister, Jo."

"Do you two have a last name?"

"Satler."

*Oh. The Satler siblings.* He'd never met the pair, but he'd heard enough about them to make sympathy stir in his chest. Their widowed mother had died recently, leaving them orphans. The last David had heard they'd been taken in by some friends of their family who lived in town. However, that didn't explain what they were doing way out here by themselves.

"It's nice to meet you both. What brings you to these parts?"

"We're out for a ride, sir."

"I see." That sounded innocent enough, but they had the same look on their faces that he saw on Maggie's whenever she had something to hide. "Do your guardians know you're out here by yourselves?"

Gil shrugged. "Don't reckon they much care, sir."

"Hmm." David hoped that wasn't true, but he couldn't help taking a closer look at the pair for signs of neglect. They were both a mite thin. Otherwise, they appeared to be well taken care of. Sometimes appearances only went surface deep, though.

Jo poked her brother in the ribs, loosening his tongue a bit more. "I mean, they let us do what we like so long as we stay out of trouble and make it back in time for supper."

Jo nudged the mule's side again. This time the mule picked up speed. Gil waved. "We've got to go now, Mr. McKay. Don't want to miss supper. Bye!"

David watched them take the turnoff toward town and shook his head. It was a shame that the Satlers didn't feel cared about at home. David had every intention of following up with their guardians to see if there was anything he could do to help support the siblings. Even so, he wished there was something more he could do for them. Something like what exactly? Take them into his home? He'd expanded the former Windy Diamond homestead into the ranch house it was today. Even after adding a second floor with three bedrooms, the McKay house was full up to the rafters. Actually, that wasn't entirely true. He could ask Maggie to share her room or he could clear out the study, which operated as his business office. But he was already struggling to care for the children under his protection now.

The sad fact was he simply couldn't take in every

orphan in the county—no matter how much he might want to. No matter how much they needed a home and not just a transient one, either, but a permanent place where they could grow up or stay until they found new families.

"Wait a minute," David whispered to the quiet woods. "That's it. That's the answer."

A children's home would provide the town's orphans a permanent place to stay where they knew they would be safe and cared for. It was the perfect solution. Not just for the children, either, but for him. He wouldn't need a nanny. He wouldn't need a wife. Not if the children had a permanent place to stay. Selfishness aside, the children needed this, too. The triplets needed stability. The other children in the community, children like the Satlers, should have a place to go where they knew they would be cared about. This was the perfect solution. He simply needed to develop it more.

He said a quick hello to his family when he entered the house, then all but locked himself in his study to do just that. Once he ran out of ideas, he switched his focus to pinning down the feed order. Before he knew it, his mother was calling him for supper. He took one look at the table and asked, "Ma, did you find the table leaf?"

She shook her head. "I'm still looking. Sit down, son. Supper is getting cold."

He hesitated only a second, then took his seat. Maggie extended her hand to him. Caroline's fingers slid across his palm to rest in his grasp. He stole a quick glance at her only to find her watching him expectantly—just like everyone else.

Grace. He was supposed to be saying grace. Clearing his throat, he kept his prayer brief and released Caroline's hand even faster once it was over. No romantic entangles. Not even the merest possibility of one. That was what he'd said. That was what he'd meant. End of story.

# Chapter Five

Caroline sang one last lullaby as she watched to make sure Jasper's droopy eyelids stayed shut. With her three little charges snuggling together in their crib, she silently padded toward the door. She pulled it open as quietly as possibly only to hear a grunt as Maggie tumbled into the room and landed at her feet. Caroline's eyes widened. Putting a finger to her lips, Caroline helped the girl stand. A quick glance at the crib showed her the babies hadn't been disturbed. She ushered Maggie out of the room and closed the door behind them. She spoke softly as they walked down the stairs. "Are you all right, Maggie?"

"I'm fine," Maggie mumbled.

"How'd you end up on the floor?"

"I was listening to you sing. The door opened. I fell in." Maggie paused at the base of the stairs to cross her arms and pout. "How come you never sing to me?"

Caroline's eyebrows lifted. "Do you want me to sing to you?"

Maggie shrugged. "I don't know. I just like hearing you is all."

"Well, that's very sweet, Maggie. I'd be happy to sing for you anytime you like."

"Now?"

"Oh. Well…" She glanced back at the nursery. Too much noise would awaken them. She had a feeling Maggie wouldn't particularly appreciate Caroline using that as a reason to refuse.

"Can we? We still have a few minutes before Pa has to tuck me in."

"Pa" had been locked away in his study since shortly after dinner. Honestly, in the three days that Caroline had been living with the McKays, she'd hardly seen the man. That meant Maggie hadn't, either. The more time Caroline spent with the girl, the more she noticed how much Maggie wanted to spend time with her father…and how often those requests were denied. Determination filled Caroline. "Let's make an adventure of it, Maggie. We can go a little away from the house and serenade the moon. Maybe your pa would like to join us."

Delight filled Maggie's eyes. "I'll ask him."

"Good. Meet me at the front door." Caroline dropped off her writing box in the parlor, where Ida was sewing in a comfortable armchair near the fireplace.

Ida lifted a brow. "Serenade the moon?"

Caroline laughed. "What else could I do? We can't sing here. We'd awaken the boys. I didn't have the heart to tell her no."

"I don't suppose it would hurt to indulge her once in a while."

Caroline tilted her head as she caught sight of the garment Ida was working on. "Is that a skirt? For Maggie?"

"A grandma can hope, can't she? Besides, I have every confidence in your positive influence on her. She'll be begging me for this in no time."

"Oh, I don't know about that."

Ida winked. "I do. That reminds me. I wanted to thank you for folding all that laundry for me this afternoon. I have no idea how you found the time."

"Laundry? I didn't—"

"Pa can't come," Maggie said, poking her head into the parlor. "He has to work. He says not to walk too far. Just to the rise. He can see that from his study. How come you aren't at the door? That's where we were supposed to meet. Aren't you coming?"

"Coming." Caroline caught the girl's hand. They rushed out the front door, hopped down the porch steps and raced each other up the rise next to the house. A heavy wind rushed across the open field, barreling past them in its haste to reach the woods. Maggie let it knock her off balance until she laughingly collapsed in a heap on the grass. Caroline laughed with her, then closed her eyes and stretched out her arms to allow the last of the fervent rush to blow past her.

She pulled in a deep breath. There was something so special about that moment. Something so sweet and simplistic. A child's laughter. The rich scent of earth and grass. The darkness and the stars shining in spite of it. Emotion welled in her throat and came out in a song. "Oh, Lord, my God, when I in awesome wonder, consider all the worlds Thy hands hath made. I see the stars. I hear the rolling thunder. Thy power throughout the universe displayed."

One of Caroline's hands rested over her heart and she shook her head. "Then sing my soul, my Savior God to Thee—"

"How great Thou art," Maggie's voice joined in with a voice that was clear, soulful and sweet. "How great Thou art."

Caroline turned to smile at Maggie, who came to stand beside her, but the girl's eyes were closed in innocent reverence. They sang the rest of the chorus together, and that set the pattern for the entire song. Caroline sang the last two verses, with Maggie joining in for the chorus until the triumphant finish that faded into silence.

Maggie gave a happy little gasp. "It's Pa!"

David walked up the rise toward them with... Was that a guitar strapped across his shoulders? It certainly seemed to be. He gave Maggie a one-armed hug as she rushed over to greet him. "I thought y'all might be able to use some accompaniment."

So they'd finally managed to pull the man away from his work long enough for him to spend a few minutes with his daughter. Caroline flashed a smile that didn't feel altogether sincere. "Always. I had no idea you played an instrument."

"Oh, he's really good, Miss Caroline. Just wait until you hear him."

Caroline wasn't aware of the challenging look she

was sending David until he peered back with an inscrutable look of his own. "Don't talk me up too much, Maggie. I've never played in front of a real music teacher before."

What was wrong with her? She'd always hated when her parents' musical society friends turned their noses up at beginner musicians. Everyone had to start somewhere. Very few were born virtuosos, and even the most talented of those had to practice just like everyone else. She was letting David's neglect of Maggie influence her treatment of him. That wasn't altogether fair.

David may not have been around all that much during the short time she'd been staying with his family, but when he was present, he was always kind and respectful. His fostering of the triplets showed that he was compassionate. She'd witnessed that firsthand when he'd comforted her in the churchyard. Besides, he was here with Maggie now. She should encourage that and avoid making him feel the least bit unwelcome.

"No need to be nervous, David. We're simply out here to have some fun."

Maggie giggled as she sat in the grass, tugging her father down along with her. "Yep. We're serenading the moon."

He grinned. "I see. Well, to me, it sounded like y'all were serenading the one who created the moon. How about we continue with that instead?"

Caroline sank to the grass across from him to complete their little circle as he strummed the opening chords of "Amazing Grace." Her eyebrows rose. *All right, then.* He wasn't a beginner. The ease and confidence with which he played made that abundantly clear. It also made him even more attractive.

Biting her lip, she steeled herself against this. Against him. After all, it was a proven fact that she had a weakness for men who made music. It hadn't been just Nico, either. She'd had her fair share of crushes on her father's piano pupils and her mother's opera associates. Nico had simply been the first one to reciprocate. She'd been enamored at his attentions. She was wiser now. Far too wise to let a man slip past her defenses simply because he knew how to play an instrument.

She'd simply smile and watch the tall, handsome rancher strum a guitar against the backdrop of a starry sky. After the song was over, she'd go back inside the house and leave the father-daughter duo to finish their night with a lovely duet. Everything would be fine.

Then he just had to open his mouth and start singing.

She was riveted—utterly and completely. His voice was untrained, yet that gave it a natural quality that seemed altogether fitting for the kind of man David was. Someone genuine and real. Nothing like the folks she'd known in Austin. It would be like comparing a falsetto to…well, to a voice like his—one that was purely masculine with a hint of rawness. There was an underlying smoothness to its tone that made it seem comforting. It was also a little adorable that he didn't entirely lose his drawl. And his range!

She closed her eyes. *Calm down, you silly ninny. You've heard some of the finest voices in the—*

Someone poked her. Caroline opened her eyes to

find Maggie leaning closer. The girl whispered, "Do you know this one?"

"Hmm? Oh. Of course."

Maggie gave her an expectant look.

Caroline cleared her throat. *Right.* She should sing. That would help. She'd be too focused on her own voice to notice his. She waited for the chorus, automatically calculated the correct harmony and joined her voice with his. It blended seamlessly. Actually, it was more than seamless. It was exquisite. That wasn't just Caroline's opinion, either. She threw a startled glance toward Maggie, who mouthed, "Whoa."

David's eyes widened. Somehow he managed to move a bit closer. To hear her better? She wasn't sure. She didn't question it. She found herself leaning forward, as well. It really was incredible how her silvery, refined tone brought out new depth and dynamism in his. Conversely, his masculine voice brought out an unexpected richness in hers. Added to that, the spiritual nature of the song, the beautiful lyrics, the act of worship made her feel vulnerable in a way she'd never experienced before while singing.

The sound of the guitar faded into the breeze. Their two voices were the only sound arching through the still night. There was no pulling away or holding back now. His expression told her as much. He wanted to see what their voices could really do together, only the two of them. So she tilted her head, listening to every timbre and nuance of his voice. She gave her own the freedom to merge, tease and play with his to the slower tempo he set. By the time their last notes wafted toward the sky, they were both grinning at each other…and perhaps staring at each other a little.

One silly, ridiculous thought entered her mind. *It is entirely possible that I may have just fallen in love with David McKay.*

She held back a giggle. Even she couldn't possibly be that silly. No. They'd shared a song. Nothing more. Nothing less.

Maggie's voice intruded on the silence. "Are y'all going to kiss now?"

"Maggie!" they both chided, in harmony once more.

Maggie's eyes widened. "What? The way y'all were looking at each other is the same way Aunt Lula May and Uncle—"

"Hush, child, please." David groaned out the plea even as he washed a hand over his face.

At least, that was what Caroline thought he did. She couldn't quite see through the fingers she was using to cover her own face. She slid them to her cheeks. "We weren't going to kiss. We were only singing. Sometimes that happens when people sing. They—"

"Kiss?" Maggie asked.

"No. They connect. It's perfectly natural." She wasn't certain who she was trying to convince most, Maggie or herself. She stole a look at David, who seemed content to look anywhere but at her.

Finally, he met her gaze with a quick searching look of his own before refocusing on Maggie. "Time for bed."

"Aw, Pa."

"No arguments. Let's go, young lady." He stood,

pulling Maggie to her feet. "And don't tell your grandmother about this."

"Why not?"

Caroline managed to stand before David could offer his assistance. She let David convince his daughter that what happened wasn't worthy of being mentioned as they headed back to the house.

Since her room was the baby's room, she wouldn't want to risk awakening them with a light, which meant she'd have to go directly to sleep in the dark room. Feeling too keyed up for that, she dodged into the empty parlor, where she'd left her writing box. She should write a letter to her parents. They'd seemed genuinely concerned for her after the wedding. She'd let them know she was doing better and would be staying in Little Horn for the foreseeable future.

She was just blotting the letter when David stepped inside the parlor. He stopped in surprise when he saw her. "I thought you'd retired already."

"No, I was finishing up a letter to my parents."

"I see." He nodded, then hesitated. "Listen, about what happened out there... Please, excuse Maggie for speaking out of turn."

She waved away his concern. "Oh, don't worry about that. Children say all sorts of silly things. I've learned not to take it seriously."

"Yes, and what you said was right. What happened was a normal thing."

"I didn't say it was normal." The words were out before she could stop them. *Wonderful.* Now he looked puzzled, and she had to explain. "I said it was natural."

"Natural," he repeated before looking at her more closely. "That isn't the same thing."

She lowered her gaze to the letter. "No. Not quite."

He was quiet for a long moment. "Good night, Caroline."

"Good night, David." And that was it. The distance between them was restored. Everything went back to the way it had been before, which was exactly as it should be. If that was disappointing…well, there was no reason to admit that to anyone. Least of all herself.

# Chapter Six

David had decided that his best chance of getting a children's home in Little Horn was by going through the Lone Star Cowboy League. The county fair the league had hosted last month left them with funds earmarked for the needy in the community. Orphans certainly met that requirement. All he had to do was convince the other members that this should be their main cause.

He was doing his best to fine-tune his idea about the children's home to prepare for the Lone Star Cowboy League meeting that would take place in a few days. In preparation, he'd paid a visit to the Satler siblings' temporary residence. The children had been right about their guardians not caring what they did. He'd surmised that wasn't because the caretakers were bad people. It had more to do with the fact that they'd gotten in way over their heads by adding two more children to their already expansive brood.

He'd recognized that exhausted look in their eyes

because he'd seen it in his and his mother's own when they'd first started taking care of the triplets. Unlike him, they didn't have the means to hire outside help. Besides, he seemed to have procured the only person in town willing to act as a nanny—even if he was avoiding her at all costs.

Today had made that pretty easy, seeing as it was Sunday, her day off. He had to admit he'd breathed a sigh of relief when Matthew had arrived to pick her up, even if Maggie had pouted something awful in the several hours since then. That was a shame really because for the first time in days he felt free to move around his own home. While Maggie retreated to her room to read, David took the opportunity to play with the triplets in the parlor. He gave Jasper a light toss in the air, caught him easily, then blew on his tummy, still slightly rounded with baby fat. Jasper screeched and giggled in delight. Eli grabbed on to David's knee to pull himself into a standing position. Theo crawled closer, then banged his hand on the floor and yelled out something in the language only the triplets understood.

David exchanged Jasper for Eli and kept making the rounds until his arms got tired. Finally, David collapsed on the floor with them and let them crawl over him at will. Jasper seemed to mistake him for a fine piece of cabinetry and the building block for a hammer. Eli had been rather fascinated with ears of late, so David let the boy pull and twist his as long as he kept it gentle. Theo was content to snuggle up on David's chest. Now, if Maggie would only join them, David would be content.

"Mags!" he bellowed, knowing full well the girl's

bedroom was above the parlor. "Maggie! Magpie! Sweet-heart, come down here."

"David Bartholomew, how many times have I asked you not to yell like that?" Ida yelled from the kitchen.

David grinned. "Too many times for me to remember. The funny thing is you're always yelling when you do it."

Ida poked her head in from the kitchen, where she was making lunch, and lifted an eyebrow. "Are you sassing me, David Bartholomew?"

"Yes, but I'll stop as soon as you let my middle name rest in peace."

"There's nothing wrong with Bartholomew."

"Makes me feel like a day-old kitten."

"It does not."

"Mew. Mew. Mew." He meowed in a high-pitched voice that absolutely delighted the triplets.

Ida shook her head, then disappeared back into the kitchen. "You're awfully unencumbered today. I don't suppose that has anything to do with a certain nanny we know."

He flopped his arms out on the rug while whispering under his breath, "Freedom."

"There's no reason you can't have freedom while she's here. If you weren't so afraid of feeling what I know you feel—"

"How on earth did you hear me?"

"I told you. Mothers have special hearing when it comes to the children."

He harrumphed. "Then how come you never hear when I remind you about finding that table leaf?"

"What's that? A stable wreath? Why would you want one of those? It isn't even Christmastime."

"Funny." He stared up at the ceiling, a sudden suspicion growing. "Maggie? Come down here right now please!"

Silence filled the house. Ida stepped into the parlor. "Oh, David, you don't think she climbed out her window to run through the woods again. Not after she almost got someone seriously injured."

"And after I expressly told her not to? I sure hope not." He gently freed himself from the triplets' grasp and went up the stairs two at a time. He opened Maggie's door, hoping against hope she was lounging inside with a book and a sullen expression that would explain her reluctance to answer. The room was empty. Her window was wide-open. It didn't take much imagination to envision her stretching herself across the gap between the windowsill and the oak tree outside. He checked the other hiding places in her room and the rest of the second floor. Coming up empty, he shook his head and headed back downstairs. His mother exited the study. Resignation filled her eyes as they met his. "She isn't in the house."

David grabbed his hat from the hat rack. "I'm going to look for her. Ring the dinner bell if she comes back."

Within minutes he was searching the woods on horseback and checking all her known hideouts along the path toward the Murray ranch. Matthew was just leaving the house when David rode up. "Matthew, is Maggie here?"

"No. I haven't seen her. You might want to look down

by the creek. Caroline and Emma were headed there. I was on my way to join them. Why don't you ride ahead and check?"

The section of the creek Matthew described was on Murray property, which meant Maggie would have had to have gone farther than she ever had before. Emma waved at him as he got closer. "Maggie was here. She's fine. Caroline is taking her back to your place on the northern path."

Relief filled him. No wonder he hadn't seen her. They'd been on the other side of the creek. Likely they'd crossed each other in passing. With a quick thanks, he rushed back home. He strode into the parlor, where Caroline played the piano. His gaze landed on his daughter, who sat next to her on the piano bench. He desperately searched for any sign that she might be hurt. "Are you all right?"

"Yes."

Relief filled him even as his jaw tightened. "Good. Come with me, please."

Maggie swallowed, "But, Pa—"

*"Now."*

Maggie hopped up from the piano bench and followed him into the study. Hands clasped behind her back, she stared down at her muddy boots as she stood in front of the desk. David turned the desk chair toward Maggie and sat in it, letting the silence build for a moment. "What do you have to say for yourself, young lady?"

She heaved in a deep sigh. "I'm sorry, Pa."

He nodded his acceptance. "Do you remember why

I told you not to disappear without telling anyone and why you shouldn't wander through the woods on your own?"

"Because it's dangerous."

"So why did you do it?"

She opened her mouth, then set her lips in a line that soon began to wobble. Tears were surely on their way. Or so he thought. Right before his eyes, his remorseful daughter turned reticent. Defiance glinted in her eyes. Her jaw clenched in pure stubbornness. She stared straight at him and said absolutely nothing. He gave her one more chance. "Why did you leave, Maggie?"

She glared or at least got as close to that as she dared.

Her actions proved there was a definite reason behind her actions. If they could address that, then he could nip the behavior in the bud, which meant there would be no need to punish her in the future. It would keep her from getting hurt or injured out in the woods with no one knowing where she was. He was determined to get to the bottom of this once and for all. "Go to your room. You can come out as soon as you are ready to tell me."

She whirled on her heel and marched out the door. He followed behind her to make sure she was headed for her room. She flew up the stairs. Her door closed with enough force to rattle the hinges. Before he could stop himself, he yelled up the stairs. "We do not slam doors in this house."

Realizing he'd all but issued a challenge and knowing how he might have reacted in his rebellious youth, he waited to see if she'd slam it again. Much to his relief, silence filled the house. Caroline stepped into the hall. He'd forgotten she'd been in the parlor with his mother and Maggie when he'd walked in. Embarrassment filled him at the realization that she'd been privy to their little drama. She seemed to suffer from the same malady for she offered an apologetic smile that looked more like a wince. "I'm heading back to my brother's place now."

"David," Ida called from the parlor doorway. "You should walk her back."

"Oh, there's no need. I know the way." She paused at the bottom step and glanced back up the stairs. "On second thought, would you walk with me a bit of the way?"

"Of course." David ignored the speculative look Ida was giving them and sent her a warning look of his own. *Honestly.* This was hardly the time for matchmaking. Caroline's request likely had nothing to do with romance. His suspicions were confirmed as soon as they'd put a little distance between themselves and the house.

Caroline slid her hands into the pockets of her skirt as they walked down the rise toward the creek. "Maggie and I talked on the way over here."

"You did?" David stopped, then gently caught Caroline's arm to make her do the same. "Did she tell you why she left the house?"

Caroline nodded and stepped a bit closer. The intensity in her eyes told him she was just as concerned about this situation as he was. "She said that she left because she didn't think anyone would notice she was missing."

"What? Of course we noticed. Why would she think we wouldn't?"

"She said that you and Ida were both playing with the triplets."

"What does that have to do with anything?"

A soft, knowing smile drifted across Caroline's lips even as she gently said, "David...she's jealous."

"Jealous? Of the triplets?" He shook his head in a denial. Yet it made sense. In fact, it would explain a lot. The distance she kept from the babies, how much she avoided helping with their care, the snake in the previous nanny's bed, her once asking if someone else could take the boys. To be fair, he had been giving them a lot of attention since they'd arrived. Perhaps more than Maggie. It was hard not to when the babies screamed and wailed for help. Then again, hadn't Maggie been doing the same in her own way?

"I think she's been feeling overlooked. She misses having her father's undivided attention. I realize that isn't entirely practical with the triplets living at your house. They need care and devotion, too. Perhaps you..."

Barely mindful that Caroline was still talking, he glanced up at Maggie's window. Was his daughter really up there thinking he didn't love her anymore? He staunched Caroline's words with a hand on her arm. "I'm sorry. I have to go."

"But—"

He gave her arm a small squeeze, hoping she'd understand the apology and appreciation in the gesture, then turned on his heel and hurried toward the house. Whatever else Caroline had to say could be dealt with later. Right now his little girl needed him.

## Chapter Seven

David wasted no time in knocking on Maggie's door. Not a peep sounded from within. Worried that she may have managed to run off again, he opened the door. Maggie lay on the bed, pretending to sleep fully clothed on top of the covers. Tear tracks showed on her cheeks. He knelt beside the bed and gently rubbed his thumb across them. Her pale lashes fluttered, then lifted to reveal her blue eyes. She froze. Emotion flickered across her face as she seemed to be trying to decide whether or not she was still angry or sad. He didn't give her the chance to think too hard on it. He kissed her forehead, then looked her in the eyes. "I love you, baby. You know that, don't you?"

She shrugged and looked away as her eyes filled with tears. He scooped her into his arms and placed her in his lap as he sat on the floor. That was all it took to convince her to cuddle with him. "It's true. I love you so much. I guess I don't tell you enough."

He pressed a kiss on her hair. "You need to know

something, Maggie, and I want you to remember it, all right?"

She nodded.

"People may come and go in our lives, but you and me—we're forever. You will always be my precious Maggie. I'll always be your daddy. Nothing and no one is going to change that. Do you understand?"

"Yes."

"Good. Now, here's the thing about a love like ours. It's big. So big that it can't help but include the other people in our lives. People like Grandma, for instance."

"And Miss Caroline."

David held back a frustrated sigh and worked to keep the droll tone from his voice. "And Miss Caroline."

Her next question came softly. "And the triplets?"

"Yes, Maggie. Them, too."

She pulled back slightly to look up at him. "They're going to be staying awhile, aren't they?"

He nodded. "They are. Do you know why?"

"They're orphans."

"Right." He eased her head back onto his chest and settled his chin on it. "I've got a story for you, sweetheart."

Suspicion filled her voice. "A real story or a made-up one?"

"This is a real story. Many years ago there were three brothers who were the very best of friends. Granted, the smallest one wasn't much bigger than a mite, but they enjoyed playing together all the same. They were all real happy until one day both of their parents went up to heaven to be with the Lord."

"Like Mama did when her horse threw her."

He sighed. "Yes. Now, these little boys had cousins and uncles and aunts just like you do, but the three boys were going to be a lot of work to take care of, so it was decided that they would be separated. The oldest, he ended up with a real nice family who taught him how to be a good man with a family of his own. The youngest boy lived with a widowed relative. She didn't treat him all that well, so he struck out on his own and had a rough time of it. Despite all that, he turned out to be a good man and made a family of his own, too. The middle boy was taken in by a maiden aunt who gave him to a loving couple. He grew up and had a sweet little daughter named Maggie."

She pulled back again to grin at him. "I knew the middle one was you."

"You're a very smart girl."

"The other boys are Uncle Josiah and Uncle Edmund."

He rubbed a circle on her back. "That's right. Those boys reunited, as you know, but they're still kind of sad about all that time they missed having together when they were growing up. That's why I am so set on keeping the triplets together, Maggie."

"Oh." She narrowed her eyes in consideration.

He should have made sure she understood why they'd taken in the triplets long ago. The babies had set the household in upheaval, and in the hectic busyness of it all, it hadn't occurred to him that he needed to explain why taking them in was so important to him. "They don't have any relatives like I did. They're all alone. They need someone to look out for them and make sure they have the chance to grow up together, knowing each other. I don't know how long they're staying, but I do know God's got a reason for putting us in those babies' lives—especially you."

"Me?"

"Sure. God gave them you so they'd have someone special to look up to and to look out for them. You can teach them the things a big sister would. You can play with them and let them know they aren't alone in ways grown-ups can't. You're real important to them, Maggie. They may not be able to say that just yet, but they would if they could."

She was quiet for a while. Finally, she asked, "I've never been a big sister before."

"Well, here's your chance."

"I suppose..." She rubbed her chin. "It could be fun."

He held back a grin. "It sure could."

"But they're going to go away, and they aren't my real brothers." She paused, and he let her deliberate. "Seems to me this could be good practice, though, for when I do have real brothers. I am going to have real brothers, aren't I? And a sister?"

"Uh...well... Maggie, you can't have real brothers and sisters unless I get married again so they have a mother."

"Shouldn't I have a mother?"

Heartache competed with laughter. His mouth opened and closed without a sound. She seized on his silence. "When will you get me a mother?"

"Oh, Maggie, I never said—"

She brightened. "I like Miss Caroline. Can she be my mother?"

He frowned. "Maggie."

"Grandma says you—"

"Maggie!"

She blinked at him.

He patted her back weakly. "You just focus on being a good sister. Leave the rest up to God."

She didn't seem all that satisfied with that answer. Truth be told, he wasn't, either. Not if leaving it up to God meant he'd fall in love again. After all, that was the only way David would ever have more children. He wasn't ready for that. He wasn't even ready for the possibility of that. Then what in the world had he been thinking sending out a letter to a mail-order bride?

He'd been thinking he needed help—desperately. At the time remarriage had seemed like the only option. Now that Caroline was taking care of the triplets and Maggie, he had some breathing room, some thinking room. He was beginning to suspect there might be a better way out there. A less drastic one that didn't involve him tethering himself to a stranger for the rest of his life.

The children's home could be that option. He almost had his proposal ready. There was nothing he could do until the meeting but hope and pray that it got approved. In the meantime, he wouldn't borrow trouble by worrying about it or the nanny he was still determined to keep his distance from even though she had proved herself helpful.

* * *

Caroline had hoped that her unfinished conversation with David two days ago would prompt him to spend more time with Maggie. That didn't seem to be the case. However, whatever he'd rushed off to say to Maggie had spurred a major change in the girl's attitude toward the triplets. While Maggie had done her best to make herself useful to Caroline, she hadn't displayed much warmth toward the triplets until now. Her favorite new activity seemed to be finding ways to make them laugh.

The girl was a little firecracker, no mistake about that. There was rarely a dull moment around Ida, either. When she wasn't doing chores, the woman always seemed up for anything that smacked of mischief. If Caroline didn't know better, she'd think some of that mischief was directed toward trying to matchmake.

That didn't make a bit of sense, though. Caroline had made it clear she would be going back to Austin eventually even if she hadn't shared any of the particulars about the botched wedding that had brought her to Little Horn. As far as she could tell, David didn't seem to think anything was amiss. Of course, he'd either been shut up in his study or out working the cattle, so perhaps he hadn't had time to notice. In fact, he—

Caroline gasped as frigid water splashed onto her blouse, pulling her from her reverie. Some of the water must have landed on the triplets, too. They screamed in delight, then rolled with laughter on the picnic blanket beside her. Maggie gasped from where she waded in the knee-high water of the creek. "Oh, Miss Caroline, I'm sorry! I didn't know it would splash that far."

Caroline laughed even as she shook the water off her arm. "It's fine, Maggie. The boys seemed to enjoy it. Truth be told, so did I. Think you can do it again?"

Maggie grinned and tried her best. The next few minutes were full of baby giggles and screams. Even Caroline let out a few when Maggie got particularly enthusiastic. Still, the cold creek water was a blessed relief from the heat that continued to blaze even in the shade of the oak and willow canopy that stretched along the banks. She couldn't help gazing longingly at the creek, wishing she could join Maggie and wade for a while. She couldn't figure out how to manage with the triplets, so she contented herself with being splashed.

Maggie was beginning to tire out when Caroline's sister-in-law stepped through the trees with another young lady Caroline hadn't met before. Emma waved at them. "Fancy meeting you folks here. We were just on our way to visit y'all."

Maggie waved back but didn't move from the creek. "Hello, Miss Emma and Miss Annie."

The ladies returned her greeting as Caroline hurried over to give Emma a hug. "What a wonderful surprise!"

"I wanted to see how you were settling in, and Annie was just dying to see the triplets, so we decided to walk on over. I don't suppose you've met Annie Hill?"

Caroline shook her head, surveying the cheerful-looking blonde in a homespun blue dress who looked to be around eighteen. "I'm glad to have the pleasure. I'm Caroline Murray."

Annie grinned as she fanned herself with the magazine she carried. "Oh, I know who you are. Emma told me all about you."

"Good things, I hope."

"As if there is anything else to tell," Emma chided, then nodded to Annie. "I'm so glad y'all are finally able to meet. I've known Annie as long as Matthew and I have lived out here. She and her family are our northern neighbors."

Annie's blue eyes sparkled with laughter. "Honestly, Emma, the way you say it always makes us sound like we're Yankees or something. My family has lived in this area for generations. My ma does own the spread just north of Matthew's, though."

"Which makes you our northern neighbors." Emma winked, then grabbed up Jasper, who'd decided now was a good time to go exploring. He stared up at Emma and reached out to touch her face with his damp fingers.

"A spread?" Caroline lifted Eli onto her hip as she glanced over at Maggie. She tried to hide her grin when she saw the girl was now sitting in the creek with her toes wiggling toward the sky. "Does that mean your mother is a ranch owner?"

Theo was reaching for Annie. Expectation and a hint of impatience furrowed his brow, which surprised Caroline to no end, since he was the shyest. He seemed quite content in Annie's arms. Annie smiled down at him. "She sure does. She's got plenty of helping hands with me and my siblings."

Emma nodded. "There are four of them."

For some reason, Caroline's gaze instinctively went to Emma's belly.

Emma immediately covered it with her hand. "Don't look at me like that, Caroline. I'm only having one."

Annie shrugged. "Oh, you never really know for sure until the day comes. It seems like this town is full of multiples. We've got the Stillwater twins, Bo and Brandon. Then these triplets showed up out of nowhere. Well, I guess that's only two sets."

"That's more than enough," Emma said rather enthusiastically.

Maggie yelled from the creek. "Excuse me, Miss Caroline? May I swim a little?"

Caroline couldn't hold back her laughter another second. The girl was drenched from head to foot. It wasn't as though she could get any wetter than she already was. "Go right ahead. Just stay close to the bank and where I can see you."

Maggie let out a whoop. Emma stared at the creek with what seemed like the same longing Caroline had felt a few minutes ago. The three women exchanged a glance. Seconds later, they were all kicking off their boots, tying up their skirts and wading into the water with the babies in tow.

They did a little splashing, then settled down enough to lower the triplets into the shallows. Jasper hit the water with his hands, making himself and Theo laugh. Eli seemed content to watch his toes move beneath the clear surface of the water, stirring up little clouds of dirt. The water came up to his chubby thighs, but he didn't seem to mind. In fact, he barely seemed to need Caroline's grasp for balance, though she held on plenty tight enough to keep him safe. Theo's legs went limp as noodles until Annie moved him to even shallower water where he could sit down and wave his arms in the water. He cooed in delight as though that had been his aim all along.

Caroline shook her head at the baby and his current caretaker. "I'm amazed at how well y'all get along. Theo tends to be the shyest of the three, but he seems so comfortable with you."

"Actually, Theo and I know each other pretty well. Before David took the triplets in, Louisa Clark and her father, Dr. Clark, cared for them at their house in town. Louisa is the midwife, and I work as her assistant whenever she needs me. Those few weeks with these cute little fellows gave me a soft spot where they're concerned."

"I'm experiencing that firsthand, too." The sun shifted through the trees, calling Caroline's attention to the patch of sky overhead. The sun wasn't wasting any time and neither should they if they wanted to be home in time for the visitor David had scheduled as a surprise for his daughter. "Maggie, find a patch of sunlight and try to dry out a little. We'll be heading home soon."

"Yes, ma'am." Maggie dunked herself under the water one last time before swimming for the banks.

Emma's curious gaze landed on Caroline. "Home?"

"Maggie's home. Not mine. My home is still in Austin."

Emma shrugged as though it made no difference to her. "Home is wherever you decide it should be."

"And whomever you decide it should be with?" Annie asked with a hint of something more than idle curiosity.

"Maybe. Ida told me something the other day that stuck with me. I don't even remember how it came up, but she said something about how in our lives we have two families. One of them we're born into. The other we create for ourselves."

Emma smiled. "That's beautiful."

Annie looked more than a little perplexed. "What did she mean, Caroline? How do you create one for yourself? Does she mean the children you have?"

"Yes, and the choice of whom you marry, whom you let close to you, whom your friends are."

Emma nodded. "That can shape your life just as much if not more than the family you grow up with. I think that's particularly true for women. I know the Bible says for the man to 'leave and cleave.' These days, or at least in these parts, it's more often the man who stays right where he is and the woman who leaves everything she knows to cleave to something unknown."

"That's why it's so important to choose a good man—a man of character," Caroline added as if she had any experience doing that. Then again, why shouldn't she? At the very least, what she'd been through ought to qualify her to give advice on what not to do. She'd learned her lesson. No more rushing into things. Maybe even no more falling in love if she could help it.

"My mother told me something I'll never forget," Emma began with a wistful smile. "She said, 'Emma, don't even think about marrying a man unless you'd be proud to have a son exactly like him.' Now that I am going to have a son or daughter, I feel as though I understand the importance of that at an even deeper level."

Caroline frowned. "Yes, but what if that man seems to be everything a woman dreams of, then he turns out to be something else entirely?"

Emma reached over to touch Caroline's arm and offered a reassuring smile. "Then we thank the Good Lord that He revealed it to us before it's too late."

Annie looked back and forth between Emma and Caroline as though trying to read between the lines. Apparently unable to find the answer, she frowned. "How does God reveal it to us?"

Caroline lowered her gaze to the clear creek water. "Sometimes it becomes too obvious to ignore."

"Otherwise," Emma added, "a woman has to make a careful study of a man's character, reputation and values. Get to know him real well. See how he reacts in different situations and around different people. Don't ignore that little niggling sensation in your gut that tells you something isn't right no matter how tempting it is—or he is."

Caroline felt her cheeks warming at the idea of letting a man's looks sway her better judgment. Had that contributed to what happened with Nico? If so, it wouldn't happen again. Not that there was anyone in her life at the moment who could make that happen.

After all, David certainly didn't count, even though he was handsome and…

She shook her head, realizing her mind was headed down a dangerous path. A quick glance at Annie proved the girl looked just as uncomfortable as she felt about the current line of conversation. Caroline wasn't surprised when after a small, thoughtful nod, Annie drifted over to talk with Maggie. Of course, that left Caroline with nowhere to hide from Emma's concerned look and quiet voice. "How are you handling things, Caroline?"

"Better. So much better. The children have been a perfect distraction." She watched Maggie and Annie, with Theo on her hip, walk over to the picnic blanket before meeting Emma's gaze once more. "You don't have to worry about me, Emma. I'm putting it behind me. You can tell Matthew that, too."

Emma grinned. "Good. I'll tell him. Whether that will be enough to stop his worrying, we'll have to see."

Caroline barely had time to shake her head in exasperation when a deep, unfamiliar voice called out from the woods "Hello the camp!"

Eyes widening, Caroline kept hold of Eli while using the other hand to unknot her full skirt enough for the fabric to plunge into the creek. A tall young man stepped onto the creek bed a good distance away. He waved a hand, while the puppy tucked against his chest yipped in greeting. Maggie gasped and ran toward the pair with a happy cry of "Duke!"

That meant the young man was probably Jamie Coleman. David had told Caroline and Ida that the nineteen-year-old would be stopping by soon to train the dog for Maggie. She watched as he surrendered the puppy to Maggie's care. Emma muttered something that sounded like "Uh-oh."

Caroline sent her a questioning glance, then lifted Eli onto her hip before reaching out to shake Jamie's hand. "Hello, you must be Jamie."

"Yes, ma'am. Sorry to sneak up on y'all like that. I went by the house first. Miss Ida told me I should come by and let y'all know I was here."

"You were perfectly right to do so. We were planning on heading back to the house soon anyway. We just stopped to cool off a little first. Emma and Annie, you'll come back to the house with us, won't you? I'm sure we'll be able to visit a little more."

Concern furrowed Emma's brow as she looked to her companion. "What do you think, Annie? I don't want to cause any trouble between your families."

Now it was Caroline's turn to try to read between the lines. Why would her invitation cause trouble and between whose families? None of this made any sense. Annie didn't seem to be of a mind to explain. In fact, an awkward silence enveloped the group. Emma finally cleared her throat. "Annie, do you need to go home now?"

"I—um. Well…" Annie stole a glance at Jamie, who was staring at his shoes. "No. No. It's fine. I'll just stay a few minutes."

Jamie ducked his head, but Caroline was almost certain she caught a glimpse of him smiling. Emma frowned. Caroline glanced back and forth between everyone for some sort of context for the interaction and came up empty. Maggie rushed over with the puppy still in her arms. "Are we going back to the house to train Duke now?"

"Yes," Caroline said. "As soon as we clean up our picnic."

With everyone helping, they were on their way back to the house in no time at all. A still-soggy Maggie led the way, wrapped in the picnic blanket they'd used to dry off the triplets' legs. Jamie carried the basket, and Annie walked beside him carrying Theo.

Caroline waited until they were out of hearing range before edging closer to Emma. "I know I'm being nosy, but I can't help asking. What was that all about?"

Emma gave a soft laugh. "I'll indulge your nosiness because I don't want you to accidentally get caught up in the middle of the feud."

"There's a feud?"

"Unfortunately." Emma released a tired sigh and shifted Jasper on her hip. "Jamie is a Coleman. Annie is a Hill. Their families have been feuding for...oh, I don't know how long it's been now. Too long. That's for sure."

"Why are they feuding?"

Emma shrugged. "Something about a diamond ring, I think. Each family thinks it's rightfully theirs. It escalated from there. Jamie and Annie's brother Peter got into a fistfight about it at the county fair last month."

"Whoa. They're pretty serious about this, then." She eyed Jamie in the distance. "That's so strange to me. Jamie doesn't seem like the type to get into a fight. David speaks well of him, too."

"That's because Jamie is a good man. So is Peter. The same goes for both of their families, but when you put the two factions together..." She shook her head. "It's like a powder keg and kerosene. All it takes is one little flame, and suddenly everything is exploding. I hate seeing them like that. The Colemans live on a spread north of David, so all four of us are neighbors in a way. We should be helping each other out, not fighting. Especially the Colemans and the Hills. I've tried talking to Dorothy about it, but does anyone listen to me about these things? No, of course not."

Caroline frowned. "Dorothy?"

"Annie's mother. She's a widow. Matthew has tried talking to Jamie's father, Tug. That didn't help, either. Tug is a widower, or I would have spoken to his wife, too." Emma paused in the yard while the others went into the house. "I've learned the best thing to do is leave it to God. We also try to keep the families as separate as possible. It's odd, but they all seem drawn to each other. I guess some people like having a good fight."

Caroline glanced toward the barn, where David had disappeared to first thing this morning before heading out with his men. "Speaking of confrontations, I was hoping you might be able to give me some advice."

Emma's gray eyes refocused on her. "About what?"

"Well, I'm a little concerned about Maggie. She doesn't get very much attention from her father. He always seems to be in a hurry to leave the house or locked up in his study. She finally cajoled him into singing with us the other night, but that's the first time

I've seen them spend more than a few minutes together. I thought after—"

Emma held up a hand. "Wait. You sang together? You, David and Maggie?"

"Well, technically, I sang a duet with each of them. By the way, did you know he plays the guitar? Not to mention that his voice was incredible, and why are you looking at me like that?"

"Like what?"

"Like you're concerned but excited and I don't know what else."

"No reason. It's only that…" Emma bit her lip, then shrugged. "It's so soon after Nico."

"What does Nico have to do with—" Suddenly realizing where this was going, Caroline felt heat rise on her cheeks. "Listen, just because I happen to have a weakness for men who make music doesn't mean I'll fall in love with every man I sing with."

Even if she had felt for a moment during the song that—

"I know. I know. I just want you to be careful. That's all."

"I will be. Don't you worry about that." She eagerly brushed aside the subject with a wave of her hand. "What I was trying to say is I've been considering speaking up about Maggie to David. I've never been a nanny before, so I'm not entirely sure that it's my place to do so, but Ida doesn't seem to think anything is amiss."

Emma tilted her head. "Do you think he'd listen to you?"

"He listened about the triplets." At Emma's questioning look, Caroline smiled. "I know you don't know what that means, but the short answer is yes. I think there is a good chance he'd listen."

"I don't think it's wrong for you to bring up your concerns to him. He did hire you to see to the well-being of the children." Emma shrugged. "Trust your own judgment, Caroline. I'm sure you'll do the right thing."

Caroline nearly laughed out loud at that but somehow managed to hold it in so as not to offend Emma. Trust her own judgment? That seemed like a great idea. It wasn't as if Caroline hadn't almost ruined her whole life by doing that very thing. No. It was far better to trust logic. Logic said that if she didn't speak up, no one else would. Eventually Maggie would be the one to suffer for it. It was decided, then. She'd try to talk to David. She just had to catch him first.

# Chapter Eight

Walking into the Lone Star Cowboy League meeting, David was confident that his plans for the children's home would be approved. That didn't stop his palms from sweating as it got closer to his turn to speak. He mumbled a soft prayer under his breath, earning himself a curious look from his brother Edmund, who sat beside him. Edmund's wife, Lula May, stood at the front of the church. She'd served as chairwoman of the LSCL almost from the very first meeting. The strawberry blonde's large blue eyes met David's. "That's it for old business. I've been told David has some new business he'd like to discuss. David, the floor is yours."

"Thank you, Lula May." David stepped out from the pew to join her at the front. He wanted to be able to see everyone and include them in his plans. Of course, that meant he had a roomful of ranchers staring back at him. Worse yet, the effects of Lula May's famous chocolate macaroons would soon be almost entirely worn off. That meant the natives would be getting restless soon.

Before David could say a word, Bo Stillwater, the preacher's twin brother, called out, "How are the triplets?"

A murmur of interest swept through the room, causing David's chest to swell a little. Jasper, Eli and Theo were blessed to have so many people concerned with their welfare. Surely those same people would take an interest in any plan that would make life better for the triplets and other orphans like them. With renewed confidence, David smiled. "They're doing real well. They've gotten so they can almost sleep through the whole night. They're even learning how to take a few steps here and there with some help."

"Heard you had some trouble with a nanny," a woman near the back said.

David tilted his head for a better look at the woman; everyone else turned to look, as well. None other than Constance Hickey, town gossip and well-known troublemaker, stood in the back of the church. David glanced at Lula May in time to see his sister-in-law bristle and narrow her eyes. David cleared his throat. "Mrs. Hickey, this is a private meeting for ranchers only."

Mrs. Hickey huffed and muttered something unintelligible about "secret meetings" before sauntering out rather slowly. Once the door closed behind her, David addressed the issue she'd raised. "The original nanny did leave, but Matthew Murray's sister, Caroline, was kind enough to step in. Today I want to talk about a more permanent solution for the triplets' care."

"You here to say you don't want 'em anymore?" Casper Magnuson asked from his seat near the aisle.

Second to Mrs. Hickey, Casper might just be the most…contentious person to deal with in Little Horn. David refused to let the man get him off track. He pulled in a deep breath. "No, sir. Taking on triplets can be a challenge. I'm sure Bo can attest to that, since he helped out when Miss Clark cared for them. However, it's also a privilege. One I don't take lightly. The problem we face is bigger than the triplets."

CJ Thorn smiled from his seat in the front row as curiosity filled his eyes. "For a man who usually gets straight to the point, you sure are beating around the bush today, David."

A few others called out in agreement. Someone mentioned a roast waiting for him at home. Apparently, they were also completely out of macaroons. David held up a hand to silence the lot of them. "All right. Listen. I'll tell it to you straight. The triplets aren't the only orphans in this town. We've also got the Satlers. If I could take all of them in, I would. I can't. None of us can. At least not on a long-term basis. That's why I think we need to create a place for them where they can stay until they find a permanent family. Otherwise, they're going to be tossed from pillar to post."

Bo frowned. "What kind of place are you talking about? An orphanage?"

"No," he said quickly. "Children shouldn't be raised in a clinical setting. They should feel as though they have a home—a real home—for as long as they need it. That means having a loving married couple to serve

as houseparents. The orphans would attend school with the rest of the town's children. As they grow older, vocational training could be made available."

Everyone seemed to be listening intently, but David couldn't tell if he was winning them over or not. "The facility itself should be a real house. None of that dormitory-style living that orphanages are known for. Only two or three children to each bedroom. We'd have a nursery for the babies. Of course, there would need to be a dining room and kitchen. The house would need to have a large yard for the children to play. A garden, some chickens and other livestock to give the children some responsibility and provide food for—"

Casper shot to his feet. "That's the biggest load of nonsense I've heard in a long time!"

Stunned at the man's vehemence, David could only blink mutely.

"Where do you think we're going to find a house like that in this town? Or were you planning on building it? Doesn't matter. We ain't got the money."

David swallowed. "The county fair we had—"

"Made us flush, but for how long? That money needs to be saved to get us all through the drought. If you think I'll agree to using the funds to buy a big fancy house for five little kids that already got someplace to stay, you must be crazy. No, their situation ain't ideal, but whose is in this town? We're all a couple weeks away from being in desperate straits, losing ranches and animals." Magnuson shook his head. "This is no time to talk about expanding."

David pulled in a calming breath. "Listen, I under-

stand that, but the drought won't last forever. Once it's over, the children will still need a home. We need to think beyond our own needs and consider the needs of others."

Magnuson crossed his arms. "Let's consider it now, why don't we? Short-term. You'd have us build a house or buy a house. Furnish it. Hire a staff. All of that and more even though folks are struggling right now as it is. Long-term. We'd be supporting five children all the way to adulthood. And if you think it would be only those five, you're kidding yourself. Soon as word gets out about this, every parent who's in trouble or negligent is going to start abandoning their babies on our doorstep. That means more staff, more food, more housing. Fact of the matter is, despite the whole lot of Good Samaritans we've got in this room, the LSCL isn't a charitable organization. It's here to support the ranchers' interest. I don't see how any of this is in the interest of ranchers."

David had no response as Magnuson's words hung in the air. As much as he hated to admit it, the man was right. The Windy Diamond was doing all right considering, but many of the ranchers in this room were struggling. Every indication showed the drought would get worse before it got better. All his grand plans were for naught.

Lula May came to stand beside David in a silent show of support. "Does anyone else have an opinion they'd like to share?"

For a moment David hoped that someone might speak up to champion his idea. That hope withered in the silence that followed. Bo finally met his gaze and nodded in appreciation. "It was a nice thought, David. A real nice thought."

The other ranchers agreed, each in their quiet way. Magnuson shook his head but finally sat down again. David kept his chin up. "Thank y'all for hearing me out."

David took his seat. Lula May soon called an end to the meeting. The other men filed out as Edmund clasped David on the shoulder. "I'm sorry your idea got shot down, David. It was a good one. If circumstances were different, I'm sure you would have gotten more people behind you."

Lula May reached over to give him a hug. "I'm sorry, David. I could tell how much that meant to you."

He hugged her back, then stepped away to shrug. "It's fine. Sunday supper at Josiah's place next week, right?"

"Yep." Edmund nodded. "We'll be there."

Someone else needed Lula May's attention, so David took the opportunity to slip outside. Only after he stepped into the summer sun did he finally acknowledge the disappointment seeping through his chest. Lula May had been right. The children's home idea had meant a lot to him. It would have meant even more to the orphans in their community.

"Seems to me you've found yourself in a bit of a predicament."

David blinked as Matthew's voice jolted through his reverie. He suddenly became aware of the fact that the man was walking beside him, toward where their horses waited. "How's that?"

"If you're looking for a more permanent solution to the triplets' care, it must mean you don't have another one." Matthew untied their horses from the hitching post. "You haven't been able to find a nanny to replace Caroline when she leaves, have you?"

David stopped beneath a rather barren tree to survey the man. Recognizing that the question stemmed from more than just idle curiosity, David nodded as he accepted his reins from the man. "Actually, I'm still waiting to hear back from the woman who I... Let's just say I'm open to other suggestions. I don't suppose you have any?"

"Before I answer that, I have a question for you." Matthew mounted his horse, then waited for David to do the same before searching his face. "Is my sister happy with you?"

Alarm made him stiffen in the saddle. "*With* me?"

"At your ranch."

"Oh." David thought about the glimpses he'd caught of her in the past week she'd been living at his place. "Sure. She seems happy to me."

Matthew nodded. "Seems that way to me, too. I've been concerned about how she'd recover from that near miss at the wedding. She tells me she's fine, but you know how it is with women. *Fine* can mean about a hundred different things."

David chuckled as they headed out on the road that led east. "I know what you mean. It seems to be true in this case, though. Of course, I'm not privy to her most inward feelings, so I can't say for sure."

Matthew lifted an eyebrow. "Aren't you, though?

She told me that she ran into you when she first got to town and that you were a help to her. I appreciate that."

Feeling heat crawling up from his jaw, David rubbed the nape of his neck. "It was the least I could do, but that was a onetime thing. I've kept my distance since then…as per your instruction the morning you dropped her off at my place."

"I didn't mean you had to keep your distance. Just that I wanted you to be careful. She's been through a lot lately."

"I believe your exact words were 'Watch yourself around my sister. She's been hurt, and it won't happen again on my watch. At least not without some serious repercussions for the man who does the hurting.'"

Matthew chuckled. "Well, now, the man does pay attention."

David rolled his eyes. "Let's just say you made an impression."

"Not too deep of one, I hope." Matthew lifted a hand to wave off David's confused look. "What I'm trying to say is I don't want to see her hurt, but I don't want her to be isolated, either. She needs friends around her right now. Seems to me she chose you as one of those as soon as she got off the train."

If that was the case, then he hadn't done a good job at being a friend to her at all. Truth be told, he hadn't had many women friends in his life. He'd been too busy pursuing them. That had been back when he was young, foolish and more interested in a woman's face and figure than her character. He was different now. He didn't have to do things that way anymore.

Did that mean he could be friends with a woman without expecting anything more? Honestly, he wasn't sure. After all, Caroline wasn't just any woman. She was special. She was caring. She was downright beautiful. Still, she could also be a friend. If he let her. If he kept his wits about him.

Realizing Matthew was waiting for a response, David couldn't be anything but honest. "I haven't seen much of her. I've been pretty busy with the ranch. I had a lot to catch up on now that we have someone to watch the children."

"Well, I'm sure being around them has helped her a lot, as well."

He smiled. "Yes, she's likely too busy chasing after them to focus on what happened in Austin."

"Things are still happening in Austin, actually. She doesn't like me bringing it up, so I plan to let things develop a little more before I tell her this. The man she was going to marry was caught by the authorities. He'll likely be going to prison before it's all said and done."

Surprised, David turned to look at Matthew. "He was a criminal?"

Matthew nodded. "A con man to be exact. Nico pulled the same con in several states. His victims have been coming forward."

"Victims?" David found himself bristling at the idea of someone trying to turn Caroline into a victim.

"It seems he preyed on women like Caroline— sweet, trusting, beautiful, wealthy, unprotected and lonely."

"That's awful." He couldn't imagine Caroline being

lonely. There was something about her that seemed to draw those around her. Look how quickly Maggie, the triplets, his mother and, by all appearances, the town had taken to her.

Matthew grimaced. "It gets worse. He'd court them, take advantage of them, then disappear in the middle of the night with their money, never to be seen or heard from again."

David shook his head in disbelief at the man's action and how close Caroline had been to suffering the fate he'd had in store for her. "No wonder you're protective of her."

"Someone has to be. Actually, someone *should* have been. I wish I'd been there to do it. And that's what we're all doing right now. Blaming ourselves for what happened—Caroline included. She thinks she should have seen it coming."

"Well, I hope in time she'll be able to let it go."

Matthew nodded. "I think it would be a whole lot easier for her to do that here than in Austin."

Truth be told, Caroline seemed to fit right in to life in Little Horn. Granted, he hadn't been around her all that much, but from what he'd seen she looked to be adjusting well. "Do you really think she'd be willing to stay here in Little Horn?"

"With the right incentive? I think so."

David tilted his head to survey the man riding beside him. "And what's the right incentive?"

Matthew grinned. "Well, she seems plenty happy at your place, doesn't she?"

Matthew was right. The triplets. Maggie. The opportunity to sing and play the piano. All of that seemed to make her plenty happy. David would be happy, too, because with a live-in nanny, he wouldn't have to marry anyone. Of course, he'd have to figure out how to be in the same house with her without avoiding her, but surely that would be less of a problem than having a wife. David squared his shoulders. "I'll do all I can to convince her to stay."

"Good." Matthew held out his hand across the empty space between their horses, and they shook on it. "Very good."

Caroline had waited all evening for a private audience with David. One look at his face when he returned from the ranchers' meeting told Caroline that the children's home idea Ida had mentioned hadn't worked out. That one look was pretty much all she'd gotten because she'd needed to get the triplets bathed and into bed. By Maggie and Ida's request, she played a few nocturnes until it was time for Maggie to go to sleep.

David stayed in the parlor rather than retreating to his study, but a private conversation was impossible. Finally, Maggie was put to bed, and Ida retired to her room. Caroline heard David shut Maggie's door, but she hesitated to open her own. Maybe this wasn't the best time. After all, he seemed to have had a disappointing evening. He might not be in the mood to listen.

She squared her shoulders. If she didn't take this opportunity to talk to David, she wouldn't have another one for…well, who knew when she'd find another chance to corner the evasive man?

Caroline crept down the stairs to find the first floor dark and quiet. As disappointing as that was, she could hardly knock on his bedroom door and demand an audience. Even she didn't have that much gall. Releasing a sigh, she turned to go back upstairs only to notice the front door was cracked open slightly. Perhaps that meant he was sitting on the front porch. She stepped outside—the porch swing was empty. Her gaze scanned the shadows of the barnyard, and that was when she heard it. The faint sound of a guitar drifted through the air from the direction of the barn.

It must be David. Beneath that was an equally faint but persistent rhythm. Someone else on the ranch was a percussionist? She bit her lip and stared across the darkened expanse to the barn. Her caution gave way to curiosity. She lifted her skirt to rush across the grass toward the sound. She stopped to lean against the side of the barn. Someone began to sing in Spanish. The man was a tenor with a smoky quality to his voice. Well, then. That was definitely not David.

A banjo joined in...or was it a mandolin? Feeling as though she'd been transported to some exotic location, she sank to the grass to listen. Someone else began to sing—still not David. This voice was full, rich, soulful, deeper. My, but this was beautiful. Where was David, though? Something within her desperately wanted to hear his voice. When the piece was over, yet another voice spoke. This one was older. "You boys need to write down the music you create."

She barely smothered a gasp. They'd created that?

The others, including David, suggested different reasons why it wasn't necessary. It was all Caroline could do to keep herself from jumping around the corner to volunteer for the job. That music deserved to be preserved in some fashion. It seemed too good to be true that so much talent resided on one ranch. Then again, she'd heard tales of cowboys who sang and played to calm their cattle, so perhaps this wasn't unusual at all.

David spoke. "Listen, we'd better call it a night, men. Morning comes early."

Realizing she was about to get caught, Caroline struggled to get to her feet. She almost toppled over as her boots tangled in her skirt, and she heard an unmistakable rip. Thankfully, that was covered by the men's protests. The Spanish-singing tenor chided, "You won't get away that easy. We want to hear the piece you've been practicing."

"That's the problem. I haven't been practicing."

"You always say that," the rich voice chimed in. "And it's always perfect."

The older voice made it unanimous. "Yeah, let's hear it."

David grumbled a bit, picked a few strings in practice, then played something Spanish, classical, romantic and downright lethal to her good sense. As the last notes faded, she hotfooted her way toward the house. She was barely halfway there when a whisper shot across the yard. "Hey, slyboots! Where are you going?"

She froze. Her heart gave an extra hard thump, but she ignored it. Turning to face David, she clasped her hands behind her back and offered her most innocent expression. "Oh. Hello, David."

He offered a nod as he continued toward her with a knowing half smile flashing in the dark. "Caroline."

Was that all he had to say? It was an old trick she'd used as a music teacher to get her students to admit to fudging their practice hours. Stay quiet and let the person in trouble implicate themselves with their own words. She wasn't about to fall for it. "I guess I'd better turn in. Good night."

She ignored his chuckle and turned toward the house, hoping he'd let her go. Instead he locked step with her. "How'd you like the music?"

Her gaze shot to his face. She could see his face pretty clearly now that they were nearing the lantern on the porch. Her mother hated not knowing she had an audience, especially during practice. David didn't seem to mind. Letting her nervousness ease, Caroline tried to ignore the embarrassment at getting caught sneaking around the barnyard. It wasn't that hard when she focused on the memory of what she'd just heard. "It was beautiful. How did y'all learn to play like that?"

"Joaquin, my foreman, learned the guitar from his father, who also happened to be my father's foreman many years ago. Joaquin taught me after...after my wife died. It helped me deal with the grief, I reckon. Ephraim arrived at my ranch knowing how to play the banjo. I'm blessed that he chose to be a part of my outfit. A cowboy with that fine of a voice is highly sought after. Isaiah Upkins was employed by the previous owner of this ranch. I don't think he realized he had any musical talent until Ephraim caught on to how his toe was tapping in a rhythm, not only a beat. Joaquin had an old drum. That was that."

Caroline laughed in delight. "That's incredible. I love hearing how people discover their musical gifts."

"Naw." He tilted his head. "I suspect you just outright love music and almost anything having to do with it."

"Am I really that obvious?"

"Afraid so." He grinned, then leaned on the stair railing. "What about you? How did you discover your musical gifts?"

She tried not to stare at him with too much suspicion. Why was he being so friendly? Then again, he'd been friendly enough when they'd sung together. Perhaps that was the secret, then—music. "Growing up as I did with a piano prodigy for a father and a renowned soprano for a mother, I was surrounded by music. They gave me the lessons. I took to it."

"Just like that?"

"Just like that." She offered a smile and a shrug. "See? My love story with music isn't quite as grand as one might imagine."

"The beginning might seem ordinary to you. What you have now, though…" He shook his head. "It's something else."

She reached out to trace the newel post. "You mean an obsession?"

Matthew had accused their parents of it often enough that she was afraid it might be true of her, too. David searched her eyes as though examining the validity of that fear. Finally, he shook his head. "Not obsession. Passion. I saw it when we sang together. I heard it when you sang with Maggie. You become almost... transcendent."

"I think that can be true for everyone when we find the thing we were meant to do. Especially when it connects us with God. For that song, in that moment, the melody and my voice lift me higher than the things of this world. My cares and troubles melt away. It's just me. The creator. Worship. Praise."

"Power."

"Passion." She stared into his eyes, feeling something unlock between them. Mutual understanding? Her heart responded with a warning. *Don't. Don't fall in love.*

His question was a welcome distraction. "So music is what you're meant to do?"

"On a basic level. I believe so. It's what motivates me." She somehow knew that he was asking himself the same question. The answer came to her, though it really shouldn't have been hers to give. "Compassion."

Their eyes met once more. "What?"

"That's what motivates you at the most basic level. It's rather obvious from the outside looking in."

"Is it?"

She nodded. "The triplets are evidence of it. I met Louisa Clark this past Sunday at church. She told me how you championed them when they were first found abandoned at the county fair. On top of that, you didn't hesitate to take them into your home the moment they could no longer stay with her. There's also the matter of the children's home."

His jaw flexed slightly as he glanced away. "Heard about that, did you?"

"Ida told me. It was a good idea."

"And an impractical one."

She shrugged. "I didn't hear of anyone else proposing another solution."

"Yes, well, mine wasn't completely altruistic."

"What do you mean?"

"I'd like to keep the triplets long-term. I might even be able to see myself taking in the Satlers, but I can't do any of that without some sort of permanent assistance. The most practical solution is for me to find a wife."

Her eyes widened. She searched his face. The discouragement there told her the truth. "You don't want that?"

"No." He rubbed the back of his neck and glanced into the darkness. "After my first marriage, I…"

He must still be grieving. She placed a hand on his arm so that he wouldn't need to find the words. "I understand, David. Trust God. Maybe He has another way."

As soon as the words left her mouth she felt convicted. She was a fine one to talk about trusting God. The woman who hadn't stopped long enough to consult God on the man she'd planned to marry. She'd wanted so badly to be loved, valued and deemed worthy of attention that she'd allowed herself to be taken in by Nico.

She didn't want that to happen to Maggie. With David talking about taking in even more orphans, it seemed even more imperative to speak to him about her concerns. As much as Caroline hated to strain this unexpected new accord with David, she'd sought him out for a chance to talk about Maggie. This looked to be it.

# Chapter Nine

David was amazed at how easy it was to talk to Caroline. Too easy, actually. He hadn't planned on telling anyone about the possibility of him remarrying yet. Why he'd chosen Caroline to confide in was a mystery to him, and a discomforting one at that. "Listen, I haven't told anyone I'm actually considering remarrying, so I'd like for that to stay between us."

She nodded. "I won't say a word. As for the idea of taking in the Satlers, well, I do worry that maybe…"

She bit her lip, and it was plain that she had something to say. She was holding back on him. He wasn't sure why. For some reason, he didn't want her to have to do that. Maybe it was because she seemed to understand him in ways and with a depth that she shouldn't be able to on such a short acquaintance. Or maybe it was because her large hazel eyes looked troubled. He stepped a bit closer, feeling her hand slide from his arm. "Go on."

She swallowed hard. "I don't want you to forget about Maggie."

"Forget Maggie?" The concept made no sense to him.

Caroline seemed to flush in the golden lantern light. "I'm not saying that you would. It's only that I've been that daughter. The one who feels forgotten by her parents. I know that I wasn't. I mean, obviously, they remember who I am, but I was never a focus for them. I don't want that to happen to Maggie."

He frowned. "And you think there's a danger of that happening?"

"You're gone quite a bit, which I realize is necessary due to your responsibilities at the ranch. However, once you're home, you tend to close yourself off in your study as soon as dinner is over. At least that's what you've done nearly every night since I got here. Maggie misses you…"

Her voice faded into the background as he realized she was right. He had locked himself in his study nearly every night. Technically, he'd been working on the accounts and making decisions about winter feed. He'd had to because he'd been riding with the hands during the day and trying to catch up on the work he'd missed since the triplets had arrived. He could have handled it differently, though. He could have found a way to spend more time with Maggie. He knew that because it was exactly the way he'd always handled it until this week.

There was one simple reason for that. Maggie stuck to Caroline's side like a burr to a saddle blanket. Being around Maggie would mean being around Caroline just like avoiding Caroline had the unhappy consequence of meaning he also avoided Maggie. He had good reasons for avoiding Caroline. Reasons that he'd already wrestled with once today while talking to her brother.

Caroline was genuine and sweet with an inherent vulnerability that made a man want to protect her—particularly after what he'd learned she'd been through. Her hazel eyes drew a man deeper and deeper until he didn't care which way was up. He'd like to say that he hadn't noticed them, but he had. That and pretty much everything else about her.

That was the reason he tried to avoid her. He'd simply refused to acknowledge his attraction to her. He surely shouldn't be doing it now. After all, he wasn't interested in getting married. He'd told her that only a minute ago because he'd meant it a minute ago. He still meant it now. Didn't he? Strange how he suddenly wasn't sure.

What was he supposed to do about that? Stare at Caroline Murray, apparently. Try to focus more on the words Caroline said than the soft caress of moonlight against her cheek and willing his fingers not to trace the same path.

He swallowed hard. Clenching his fists, he forced himself to refocus. Finally, her words began to make sense. He couldn't help but smile just a little as she ever so gently told him what a horrible father he was being. She meant well. That was obvious from the concern in her eyes. She was also incredibly afraid of offending him. The slight waver in her voice told him that much. Maybe he ought to be offended. Still, it was hard to be angry at someone advocating so strongly on behalf of his daughter, so he listened intently, offering a slight nod now and again until she finally deigned to ask him a question. "Did you know she holds back tears when you leave the house in the morning?"

"Yes. She's always done that, ever since she was little. I think it might have something to do with her mother's death." He rubbed his hand over his jaw, feeling the prickle that told him he'd need a shave come morning. "Actually, what you've seen is a big improvement over how it used to be."

"Oh." Even in the darkness, he could see the blush rising in her cheeks along with a healthy dose of self-doubt.

He found himself reassuring her with another nod. "You were right about me not being around much this past week, though."

"Then you'll try to be more present?"

He hesitated. Could he afford to be? He doubted it, but saying no to Caroline meant saying no to Maggie, too. The scary part was he didn't really want to say that to either one of them. Caroline's hand came to rest on his arm again. "David, please. Set aside a little time for her even if it's only once a week. I promise you won't regret it."

Of course he wouldn't regret it, and no one needed to beg him to spend time with his daughter. In fact, he already set aside time for her. He took Maggie riding every Sunday afternoon. Caroline didn't know that because she'd spent her day off with Matthew and Emma.

How could he tell her that without revealing the true reason he'd been absent lately?

He couldn't. So he looked deep into her eyes and said the only thing that seemed anywhere close to being right. "I love my daughter. I believe she knows that. I usually try to spend as much time with her and my mother as I can. This past week was out of the ordinary. Please don't think that's the norm. You'll be seeing a lot more of me this week. And I'll be seeing a lot more of Maggie."

"Promise?"

He nodded. "I promise, Caroline."

She squeezed his arm and gave him a smile of approval that filled him with a warm glow he knew better than to analyze too closely. It stuck with him all the way to the next morning when she greeted him with a smile as he entered the kitchen for breakfast. He tried to ignore it…ignore her.

Then he realized it would be downright rude to do that after what they'd shared last night. Besides, he didn't want to. Unfortunately, with his guard lowered, what came out was…well, a wink.

It was just a small one. A friendly one, but it reminded him too much of that cocky, flirtatious younger version of himself that hadn't questioned his ability to win the heart of the belle of the county. The older, more mature and love-worn man he was now should know better than to go around winking at nannies.

He glanced around the kitchen to see who'd noticed his lapse. His ma was still at the stove with her back turned to the table. Maggie was distracted by the triplets. That still left Caroline, who surely couldn't help but notice, since it had been directed at her. It was far too late to pretend he had something in his eye. He stole a cautious look at her.

She leaned forward slightly to capture his gaze. Her eyes danced with something friendly and teasing. Her lips tilted in some mixture of amusement and surprise. "Did you just—"

"Maggie," he called a bit too loudly, already reaching for Caroline's hand. "Why don't you say grace?"

Ida gave a slightly indignant snort as she placed a bowl of biscuits on the table. "Maybe because I haven't even had a chance to sit down yet. Land sakes, son. Are you that hungry?"

He wasn't. He simply hadn't wanted Caroline to mention his winking in front of his ma and Maggie— two people who would surely get the wrong idea. His eagle-eyed mother was already narrowing hers rather speculatively at the way he was still holding Caroline's hand. He released it and ignored the curious look he was getting from all three females. He cleared his throat. "Sorry. I'm thinking it would be good to get an early start today. I need to head into town."

"Well, I suppose there's no harm in saying grace. You can start eating while I finish the bacon. Go ahead, Maggie."

Once Maggie finished, David steered the conversation back to safer subjects. "Ma, do you need me to pick up anything from the general store for you while I'm in town?"

"We could use a few things." Ida placed strips of

bacon on his plate. After doing the same for Maggie and Caroline, she took the seat across from him. "I'll make a list for you."

He turned to Caroline to ask her the same, but she nodded toward Maggie instead. Apparently, she still thought he needed prodding to spend time with his daughter. He wasn't entirely sure what he could do to disabuse her of that notion other than go along with her efforts to help him. "Maggie, would you like to ride into town with me?"

Maggie's brow furrowed. "Would I have to wear a dress?"

He gave her a firm look. "You know the rules. Skirts are required when you go to town."

"Hmm." She poked at the last piece of her scrambled eggs. "I don't know if it's worth it, Pa."

David barely held back a laugh. Caroline looked appalled and more than a little confused at Maggie's hesitancy. "Maggie, I'm sure wearing a skirt is a small price to pay for a chance to go riding with your father."

Curiosity filled Maggie's eyes. "Do you want to go with him, then?"

The last thing David needed on this particular errand was Caroline watching over his shoulder. "She needs to take care of the triplets. Come on, Magpie. I'll let you pick out a few pieces of candy while we're at the general store."

"Oh, all right, I guess." She wrinkled her nose. "May I be excused to change clothes?"

"Go ahead." David barely managed to hold back a

laugh as she tromped up the stairs with a decided lack of enthusiasm.

A quick glance at Caroline revealed her cheeks had turned a dusky pink. "I'm sure she'll enjoy it, David."

"Well, she'll like the candy. That's for sure. What about you, Caroline? Is there anything I can get for you while I'm in town?"

"Oh, I don't know. I don't think so. I packed more than enough of everything for my—" She bit her lip, and he knew she was thinking about the fact that she should have been on her honeymoon. She continued, "For my trip. I do have a letter that is ready to be mailed if you don't mind taking it along."

"I wouldn't mind at all." In fact, visiting the post office was his main reason for going into town. He should be hearing back from the mail-order bride soon. He doubted any woman would agree to travel all the way to Texas from Boston to enter into what was little more than the equivalent of a business arrangement. If that was the case, he'd be free to... He stole a quick glance at Caroline. Well, free to consider other solutions should he find the courage.

Caroline had a problem, and that problem was David McKay. He'd done exactly what he'd promised he would over the past three days by being more accessible to and engaged with Maggie. He'd also been going into town to check the mail every day. If Caroline didn't know better, she'd think he had a sweetheart he couldn't wait to hear from. Ida had finally mentioned that he was looking for a response from a nanny who might be interested in staying on more permanently. Caroline hadn't felt any less threatened by that.

Not that she was threatened by the idea of him having a sweetheart. Really, it was none of her business. Well, the replacement nanny was, but—

This was the problem. He kept distracting her. What had she been thinking about? Maggie. The girl was blooming under her father's attention. It was lovely to see. Of course, Caroline hadn't minded having David around more, either.

And she was still thinking about him *again*.

Despite the current evidence to the contrary, she hadn't allowed their deepening friendship to go to her head. Most important, she wasn't allowing it to go to her heart. Just because they'd played one board game together with Maggie and Ida like a real family didn't mean she had any illusions that they'd become one. Just because he seemed to understand her love for music and had gone so far as to encourage her to share that with Maggie through lessons didn't mean that...

She nearly groaned. Who was she fooling? Now that David was actually present, it was hard not to notice that he was incredible. She was doing her best to ignore it. Mostly because she'd be silly to allow herself to get caught up in the idea of another man so soon after Nico.

Doing so would be even more proof that her emotions weren't trustworthy, and she'd already had plenty of that. Still, she couldn't help being grateful that he'd encouraged her to give Maggie singing lessons. Maggie slid onto the piano bench beside Caroline. "Do I get to sing now?"

The girl had been admirably patient all morning as Caroline took care of her duties with the triplets. The boys now played happily at Ida's feet as she worked on some mending. Caroline didn't miss the excited look on Ida's face. Nor did she forget that this was Ida's piano to begin with. The woman was clearly eager to hear her granddaughter sing. Caroline didn't waste another moment. "You sure do. Let's start with some exercise to warm up the muscles we use to sing. Ready?"

Maggie glanced back at Ida, who gave her an encouraging nod. "I think so."

"Wonderful! Stand up nice and tall beside the piano. Very good. Now relax your belly muscles. Remember you're going to breathe way down there for me." And it was so good to feel as though life was getting back to normal. With the hustle and bustle surrounding the wedding and resigning from the music school, she'd missed this. The familiarity of sharing her love of music with an eager young mind was so comforting. She felt her mood lifting. "I'll go first to show you how it's done. Then we can do it together, all right?"

She started out with a simple humming exercise. Maggie caught on quickly, her pitch perfect. Caroline moved on to vowel sounds. Maggie's vocal range and ability were impressive for one so young and untrained. Her voice was surprisingly rich. Beyond that, her enthusiasm and concentration on the simple exercises were adorable. Caroline finished the warm-ups, sending the girl an approving nod. "Good job, Maggie. You have a beautiful voice."

"She certainly does," Ida seconded.

A grin flashed across Maggie's face even as she ducked her head. "Thank you. Are we going to sing a real song now?"

"I think that's a great idea. Why don't we—" A knock interrupted her. Ready to save Ida a trip to the front door, Caroline hopped up. "I'll get it."

She opened the door to find Annie Hill standing on the porch. The girl was so busy scanning the woods in the distance that it took her a second to realize Caroline had answered. Annie removed her bonnet and offered a nervous smile. "Hello, Caroline. Sorry to bother y'all, but I left my magazine here the other day. I thought now was as good a time as any to get it back."

"No trouble at all. Come in. I haven't seen your magazine, though. Let's ask Maggie and Ida if they have."

After Annie asked them about it, Maggie retrieved it from her room. Presenting it to Annie, Maggie said, "I meant to bring it to you at church, but I forgot. Oh, I couldn't find that cyclone thing you were telling me about. All I saw were pages and pages about dresses."

"You mean the bicycle. The article about it was near the back." Annie perched on the settee to flip through the magazine. She turned it around so they could all see it. "Here it is, Maggie."

Ida leaned forward for a better look, then shook her head. "Can you imagine balancing on such a contraption?"

Maggie traced the wheels with her finger. "Maybe it's like riding a horse."

"Now, there's a thought." Caroline lifted a brow.

"Can you imagine cowboys trying to round up cattle on that?"

They all laughed, but Annie shook her head. "Oh, no. These could never replace horses."

"Maybe not on a ranch, but they're becoming popular in the city."

Ida's eyes widened. "Don't tell me you've had a chance to ride one of those."

"Not yet. I've seen a few people riding them in Austin, though. You should see the ladies in their cycling suits. It's quite a sight."

"Actually, there's a sketching of a cycling suit in here, too." Annie turned a few pages, then held up the magazine again.

Ida lifted a brow. "Are those pants?"

"Technically, they're bloomers," Caroline offered. Seeing Maggie's fierce frown, she couldn't help asking, "What do you think, Maggie? Would you wear bloomers?"

"I think they look silly."

Ida sent Caroline a wide-eyed glance. "You do?"

"Sure I do. Grown-up ladies should look like ladies." She hooked her thumbs in the pockets of her denim trousers. "'Course, when you're a kid, they just aren't practical—especially for climbing trees and running in the woods."

Ida's shoulders relaxed in what seemed to be relief. Before she could comment, another knock sounded on the front door. Ida grinned. "Aren't we popular today."

"I'll get it," Caroline offered, since she had yet to sit down.

Jamie Coleman greeted her when she opened the door. A puppy sat next to him on the porch. She hadn't really had a chance to see the dog up close. She'd seen only a flash of him from her horse when he'd run across the pasture. The last time he'd visited, Jamie and Maggie had kept him outside while Caroline had been busy cleaning up the triplets after their playtime in the creek. Now she couldn't help noticing that Duke wasn't just cute; he was actually kind of beautiful. Fashioned with elegant lines and droopy triangular ears, his coat had a white base with a mixture of gray spots and black spots. His paws were awfully big for such a small fellow. His wagging tail set the entire back half of his body wiggling. Caroline grinned. "Well, hello there. May I pet him, Jamie?"

She glanced up when Jamie didn't respond. He didn't appear to have heard her. He was too busy scanning the woods in the distance. Caroline followed his gaze but saw nothing of interest. "Is something out there?"

"What?" His face turned slightly pink. "Oh. No, ma'am. I was just...um, is David around?"

"I'm afraid not. He went into town to check the mail. He should be back soon." She glanced down at the puppy, who was looking back and forth between them as though he understood the conversation. "Are you here for another training session?"

"Sure am. Maybe David will be back by the time I'm through." Jamie peered past her. "Hello, Maggie."

"I knew it would be you and Duke." Maggie grinned. Caroline stepped out of the way so that Maggie could greet the dog, who was now beside himself with joy. "Grandma says to bring him inside. She wants to see how he behaves around the triplets."

Jamie wasted no time accepting the invitation. His only pause came when he saw Annie in the parlor. Caroline tensed as she remembered their two families were feuding. She watched them both for any sign of aggression or hostility while half expecting Annie to make her excuses and hurry from the house. The visitors' gazes connected, then held. Jamie smiled. Annie didn't have to. Her heart was in her eyes.

Caroline's mouth fell open, and she couldn't quite seem to get it closed. Apparently, they'd both found what or should she say *whom* they'd been looking for in the woods right here in the McKays' parlor. Well, this was an unexpected twist on the story Emma had told her about their feuding neighbors. Who else knew that Jamie and Annie had feelings for each other? She clamped her lips together as she stole a glance at Ida and Maggie. Either they hadn't seen what Caroline had or they already knew because they didn't act like anything out of the ordinary had happened. They were both focused on the triplets and the puppy.

Reminded of her duty, Caroline knelt beside the triplets to keep watch as Duke caught sight of the babies. The dog tilted his head as he studied them. Theo seemed more interested in trying to take the magazine from Annie despite her attempts to point out the new visitor on the floor. Eli stared at the dog intently. Jasper slapped his hands on the floor playfully at the puppy. Duke's tail started wagging again. He sank to his belly and slowly crawled toward the boys until he was close enough to nudge Jasper with his nose. No longer worried about the puppy, Caroline sank to her knees beside Jasper and took his hand in hers to show him how to pet the dog. "Gently, gently."

Eli crawled over to carefully investigate Duke's ears with his little fingers. Theo crawled over to talk to Eli in that language only the triplets could understand. Frustrated with being ignored by the boy, Duke barked at him. Theo started. He stared at the dog, then a laugh slipped out. Duke barked again. Theo laughed some more. Jasper giggled. Eli chortled. Maggie sank to the floor beside the boys. She put Theo in her lap, and he reached out for the dog, sliding onto his stomach toward Duke as he continued giggling. Maggie grinned. "They laugh at everything—don't they?"

"Sure seems like it," David said as he entered the room, his arms full of brown paper packages. He winked at Maggie, then nodded to everyone else. "Hello, Annie, Jamie. Caroline, someone left this bag of old toys in the wagon for the triplets. Would you mind sorting through them? See what they might like to play with."

"Of course." She took a small flour bag full of toys from him.

"Ma, the things you asked me to order from the general store a few days ago finally arrived. I'll put them in the kitchen for you."

Ida stood and took a few of the packages. "Let me help you with that. I was about to head for the kitchen to get some refreshments for our guests anyway."

While Maggie and the triplets played with Duke, Caroline sorted through the bag of what turned out to be several wooden blocks. She couldn't help stealing glances at Jamie and Annie. They exchanged small talk, but the conversation between them was more than casual despite the common words they used. It went deeper than mere politeness all the way to caring, concern, focus. Especially on Jamie's part, since he was the main one asking the questions.

A longing filled Caroline's chest at the sight of it. Wasn't that what she'd wanted so badly? Wasn't that why she'd been so eager to embrace Nico's presence in her life? Because of that need to matter to someone. To be another person's central focus if only for a moment. It was a dangerous thing. She wouldn't let herself make that same mistake again. No matter how much she might long to experience what Jamie and Annie seemed to have.

# Chapter Ten

Caroline refocused her attention on the triplets as Ida bustled into the room with a tray full of refreshments. Meanwhile, David paused in the doorway to call Caroline's name. She met him there with an inquiring look. He gave the package he held a little wave. "This is for you. The postmaster heard you were staying at my ranch, so he entrusted me to give it to you."

She took the thick envelope from him and eyed the return address. "It's from my parents."

"That's good, isn't it?"

She wasn't entirely sure. They'd been too stunned by the events of the wedding to have much of a response in the immediate aftermath. Then Matthew had whisked her away to Little Horn. Now that her parents had been given a chance to process all that had happened, she had no idea what their reaction might be. The large envelope surely had to contain more than sympathy. Trepidation closed her throat. She swallowed hard and gave a light shrug. "I don't know."

He caught her gaze, searching it in concern. His hand settled on her forearm, and he gave it a gentle squeeze. "Why don't I put this in my study for now? You can open it later when you have more privacy."

Reminded that they weren't the only ones in the room, she glanced over her shoulder. Ida, Jamie and Annie appeared to be in a deep conversation of their own, while Duke continued to entertain Maggie and the triplets. Relief filled her at the realization that no one else had noticed their exchange. She gave David a grateful smile. "Thank you."

"Of course." He gave her a small nod, then left to stow the envelope.

Jamie joined them when he returned. "David, I came by to let you know Duke is housebroken now. We just have to remember to let him outside often. A good rule of thumb is that he'll be able to hold himself one hour for every month of age. Other than that, he's caught on quickly with his training. As long as Maggie keeps making him practice, he should be fine to stay here if you're willing to let him."

David nodded. "I reckon I've held off on this long enough."

Caroline grinned. "Maggie will be ecstatic."

"Let's see." He gave her a conspiratorial smile before calling out, "Magpie, what do you think about letting Duke stay here from now on?"

Maggie gasped. After staying frozen for a full second, she jumped to her feet. "You aren't pulling my leg—are you, Pa?"

"No, I'm serious. Do you want him to stay?"

She nodded.

"Then he stays."

Maggie didn't say a word at first. She just rushed over to hug her father. He lifted her into his arms and hugged her even closer. Finally, she whispered, "Thank you! I'll take good care of him. I promise."

"I know you will, and you're welcome, sweetheart. Thank you for being patient." He set Maggie down as she began to wiggle a little.

She immediately went over to place a kiss on Duke's head. "Can I take him outside to play?"

"Stay close to the house."

"Yes, sir."

"And what do you say to Jamie for helping train the pup?"

"Thank you, Jamie!" Maggie gave him a quick hug, then clapped her hands. "Duke! C'mon, Duke. Let's go outside."

Jamie gave the dog a parting pat as Duke rushed out the door after Maggie. "I'd better head on back to my pa's ranch. I'll come by to check on Duke later this week."

David shook Jamie's hand. It didn't escape Caroline's notice that Annie readied herself to leave, too. Caroline bit her lip as the young couple walked out together. Ida lifted Annie's magazine off the settee. "Oh, dear. She left it again."

"I'll take it to her," Caroline volunteered. "They couldn't have gotten that far."

Knowing they were likely headed north, Caroline rounded the corner of the house and caught sight of them. She called Annie's name. The girl whirled around. Caroline held up the magazine. Annie slapped a hand to her forehead and rushed over. "I can't believe I forgot it again. Thank you for bringing it to me."

"You're welcome." Caroline hesitated. However, when Annie began to turn away, the words rushed out anyway. "So you and Jamie, huh?"

Annie's blue eyes went wide as red suffused her cheeks. "You know. How do you know?"

Caroline smiled. "The way you look at him. The way he talks to you. Honestly, it's one of the sweetest things I've seen in a long time. But I'm worried about y'all. Your families—"

"They have their suspicions, but they don't know for sure." Annie placed a hand on Caroline's shoulder. "I'd like to keep it that way. Please say you won't tell them."

"I won't."

"Thank you." Annie released Caroline and let out a relieved breath. It seemed Annie was somehow able to sense that Jamie was heading their way even though her back was turned. She lifted her hand in a little wave that made him stop. "It's actually a relief to be able to admit this to someone."

"That you've been seeing each other?"

"That we're in love."

Caroline blinked. "Oh my."

"Jamie wants to marry me. Only, he says we can't tell our parents yet. It would only make the feud worse."

"So you're sneaking around instead?" She shook her head. "Oh, Annie, are you sure that's a good idea?"

Annie shrugged helplessly. "I don't know what else

to do. We've talked about him speaking to my mother on my behalf, but what's the point? All she would do is refuse to let him court me or ban me from seeing him altogether."

"Are you eighteen, Annie?" When the girl nodded, Caroline offered a shrug. "Then it's your decision to make. You'll need to decide whether you'll abide by your mother's wishes or marry Jamie anyway."

Annie stilled as hope and trepidation filled her eyes. "You think...I could marry him even if my ma doesn't want me to?"

"Ultimately, it's your choice. If y'all are serious about being together, then you'd best tell your folks before they find out on their own." She paused, then frowned at the yellow grass beside their boots. "Listen to me giving advice. I'm hardly an expert when it comes to love or relationships. I just want you to be careful, Annie. You've been so nice to me. I don't want to see you get hurt."

"Jamie would never hurt me."

"I thought the same thing once about—" She cut herself off with a wave of her hand. "I don't mean to be so maudlin. Never mind about me. Have—"

Annie caught her arm gently. "Who hurt you?"

She sighed. Was this what moving on was supposed to look like? Lugging around the embarrassment Nico had caused? Bringing his name into every situation? Unwilling to give him that honor, to let one more person know who he was, she kept it simple. "Let's just say I made the wrong decision. I trusted the wrong man. I almost ended up in a horrible situation because of it."

Annie was quiet for a moment, then smiled. *"Almost."*

"What?"

"You *almost* ended up in a horrible situation. Don't let that stop you from trusting again and making the right decision this time."

Caroline eyed the girl. "What are you saying?"

Annie lifted one eyebrow in a direct challenge. "You and David. There's something between you two, isn't there?"

"Oh, I wouldn't say that."

"Tut-tut. I've seen it with my own eyes. It's awfully sweet. Seems to me that you should do something about it." With a final teasing grin, Annie backed away. "Now, I've got to go. Jamie's waiting."

She skipped off to join Jamie, and the two of them set off down the path toward their families' ranches. Caroline found herself staring after them with her hands on her hips. *Honestly? Me and David? Something between us? That is... Well, that is just...*

She caught her lip between her teeth, then turned to face the ranch house. It simply couldn't happen. That was all there was to it. It was far too soon after all that trouble she'd had with Nico. She couldn't possibly have feelings for another man already. Especially not a man she'd known for only a little more than a week. Her heart couldn't be that changeable or...fickle. The word she was looking for was *fickle*. Or *foolish*. That would work, too.

"No. No way. This can't happen. It won't."

She set off toward the house, ignoring that niggling sense that, with or without her permission, it already was.

* * *

David couldn't go through with it. He'd known it the moment he'd read Elizabeth Dumont's reply to his letter in town this afternoon. She was willing to come to Little Horn as his mail-order bride. She had no qualms about entering into a union that was little more than a business arrangement. She was sure she'd get along with Maggie. She wasn't at all intimidated by the idea of triplets. She was ready for adventure in the Wild West. All he had to do to finalize their agreement was send the train ticket. David was the one with ice blocks for feet. It wasn't only the reality of getting married again that had him running scared, either. For some reason, the whole idea just felt wrong.

He'd find another way. Somehow. He had the time. As long as Caroline stayed at the ranch, there wouldn't be an urgent need for him to take action. Nor was there any need to tell his mother that he'd been considering marriage. It would only encourage her attempt at matchmaking between him and Caroline. Oh, she'd been subtle about it, but there was no mistaking her efforts for anything other than what they were. Never finding the leaf for the table had been only the start.

One of her more obvious tactics was giving him as much time alone with Caroline as possible in the evenings. Ida used to stay up late with him in the parlor to talk about their day. Now she went to her room as soon as Maggie was in bed. That left him with only two options. Hole up in his room for the remainder of the evening or spend time in the parlor with Caroline. So far he'd always gone to his room.

Tonight he was finally giving in. The parlor was empty, but the porch swing wasn't. Maybe it was just a trick of the lantern that made it seem as though Caroline lit up at the sight of him. It was hard to tell, since she sobered the moment she saw the envelope he carried. She slid over to one side of the swing to make room for him, then took the missive as he settled beside her.

She offered a weak smile. "I suppose there's no use putting this off any longer, is there?"

He immediately began to stand up again. "I can give you some privacy if you like."

"No." She placed a hand on his arm to keep him from leaving. "You're fine. I'm probably making too much of this."

Once he relaxed again, she pried open the envelope. She pulled a small letter from the larger missive. He found himself leaning closer even as he stared out toward the woods to make it clear he wasn't trying to read the letter but only offer support. Finally, curiosity got the better of him and he studied her face. The lines across her brow eased a little before smoothing out entirely. Her lips curved slightly. Her hazel eyes sought his before returning to the page. "They're actually being really understanding about it."

"It?"

"What happened at the wedding."

He nodded, but the fact that she'd questioned whether they would understand made it hard to fight back a frown. Caroline blinked. Her eyes widened. Setting the letter on her lap, she tore open the rest of the package to reveal a book with a pirate on the cover. When her silence lengthened, he broke the tension as best he could. "Did they send you a treasure map?"

She laughed. "No, silly. It's a vocal score."

"You seemed puzzled."

"I am." She went back to the letter. "They secured a role for me in an operetta. One of their friends is producing it. He's heard me sing a few times and believes I'm perfect for the part. Supposedly, he'd wanted to ask me all along but held back, since I was getting married."

He stared at the book, seeing it for what it was— concrete proof she'd be leaving soon. *Unless...* "That isn't a good thing?"

"I don't know. I'm not sure what to think. Mostly I'm surprised Mother and Father would arrange it for me. They always said my voice wasn't suited to opera. Then again, this is an *operetta*, so it isn't quite the same."

"It isn't? What's the difference?"

"For one thing, some would say an operetta isn't as vocally challenging." She gave a light grimace, then shrugged and flipped through the book. "They gave me a good part, though. I'm supposed to play Mabel in *The Pirates of Penzance*."

He tried to smile. "Well, it seems that congratulations are in order."

A smile touched her lips, but she didn't glance up. "Thank you."

"So I guess that means you're leaving? Going back to Austin?"

She stilled. Her dark lashes swept upward to reveal her hazel eyes, which searched his for a breath or two before she said quietly, "I didn't say that. I'm not even sure I'm going to take the part."

She glanced back to the page and traced a finger over the sheet music. "Of course, the hard truth is I don't have very many options. I gave up my music-teaching position before the wedding. I even went so far as to handpick my replacement. I can't go back to that. It's far too late to find another position with a different school for the upcoming school year. I suppose I could try to teach independently."

She sighed. "All I know is if I don't do something, I'll be rattling around my parents' house all by my lonesome with no purpose."

"You can always stay on here." The offer was out before he even made the decision to make it. That was what he'd been angling toward ever since his talk with Matthew, though, wasn't it? She didn't immediately reject the idea, so he continued. "I know this arrangement was only supposed to be temporary, but I never found another nanny. If you still want to give music lessons, you're welcome to do that on our piano. We'd all love for you to stay."

She smiled up at him. "That's so kind of you to say. I do appreciate the offer. I'll need to think about it. Being here has lifted a burden from my mind. That's for certain. As for the operetta, rehearsals don't start until the second week in September, so if I did leave, it wouldn't be until around then."

*If* she left. He liked the sound of that. He liked it even better when she closed the book, curled one leg beneath her and shifted to face him. "So you haven't been able to find a nanny?"

Tongue-tied was not a familiar sensation to David. Usually when he didn't talk, it was because he didn't care to. This time it was because he didn't trust his words not to implicate him. What could he say? He hadn't exactly tried to find a nanny. Not beyond the first few days after the previous nanny left. Instead he'd settled on the idea of a mail-order bride. One who, as it turned out, was willing to agree to everything he wanted. Only, he didn't want that anymore, and he was afraid that had everything to do with the woman sitting next to him.

That scared him silly. He wasn't sure what he should do about it. Or what he wanted to do about it.

Caroline tilted her head. "David?"

"No nanny." The words came out gruffly, but she didn't seem to notice.

"No children's home, either." She glanced thoughtfully out toward the barn, then back to him. "You have no plans to keep the triplets long-term?"

"I can't without a nanny willing to stay long-term… or a wife."

"And you don't want to get married again."

He glanced down at her bare left hand. "Not for convenience's sake."

She smiled. "Well, then. I think there's only one solution."

He sat up straighter. "What's that?"

"We need to find the triplets a permanent home."

"Oh." He leaned back into the swing and stared out

at the night. That wasn't what he'd thought she was going to say.

"Unless… Do you think their mother will come back to claim them? Or some of her relatives?"

He shook his head. "I think their mother might already be dead, God rest her soul. We tried to find a permanent arrangement for the triplets when they were first discovered at the town fair. No one in town was able to take all three of them in. I doubt that's changed in the last month."

She gave him a conspiratorial look. "No one in *this* town was able to take them in. That doesn't mean someone in another town wouldn't."

"You know, you might have something there. There are a couple of towns within a few hours' ride of here. I could ask around and see if anyone is willing to adopt the triplets."

"What about the Lone Star Cowboy League? Will you tell them your plan?"

"No. I've learned my lesson. I don't want to go to them until I have a willing and viable option for the triplets' adoption. No use giving anyone the chance to shoot it down. Even if the Lone Star Cowboy League would think it's unrealistic, I'd like to try."

She gave him a nod of approval. "Good for you."

He grinned, unable to staunch the well of affection within him. She poked his arm much like Maggie might, then lifted an inquiring brow. He shrugged. He couldn't remember the last time he'd opened up to a woman like this. Or a time when he'd felt this comfortable with one.

Her vulnerability seemed to unlock his. Her lack of pretension was nothing short of refreshing. Never before had he been so tempted to take another chance at finding romance. He ought to be running the other way, like he had when she'd first arrived. Instead he pulled in a deep breath and settled in. "Care to swing awhile?"

She nodded and lifted her boot off the porch floor. He gave them a little push. The momentum took over, and off they went as effortlessly as their conversation flowed and as naturally as the bond between them grew. His past warned him that wasn't a good idea. In the end, she'd leave him. Perhaps it wouldn't be for another man, but another opportunity would seduce her away just as surely.

He should listen. He knew that. But he was so tired of resisting that undeniable pull toward her. Maybe... just for a while, he wouldn't. Maybe Matthew was right. If all she needed was a reason to stay, he could give her plenty. Ignoring the uneasiness that told him that might not be the wisest choice, he planned on doing exactly that.

## Chapter Eleven

How Caroline ended up seated alongside David McKay in a buggy headed to some little town called Oakalla was still something of a mystery to her. It had all started two days ago when David had mentioned the idea of trying to find a home for the triplets to his mother. Ida had gasped and proclaimed the idea heaven-sent. The notion of David going about the task alone hadn't sat nearly as well with her. A woman's opinion on the prospective adoptive family was indispensable. None of that had seemed suspicious, but then Ida declared that a woman her age could hardly be expected to go traipsing about the countryside, so the duty must fall to Caroline.

Caroline had protested, citing her responsibility to the triplets. Ida had insisted. David had shrugged and rented a buggy. And so here she was, clinging to the right side of the buggy as it made every attempt to throw her against David's side. Was the seat tilted? How else could it be possible that she kept sliding toward him no matter how much distance she tried to maintain between them? Was he the one moving? Surely not. The fabric of her traveling skirt was too slippery; that was all.

"Best get comfortable," David said over the rhythmic clop of the horse's hooves. "We've got a long drive ahead of us."

"How much longer, do you think?"

"An hour and half to two hours depending on the conditions of the road."

Her fingers tightened on the buggy's padded arm. "And how long has it been so far?"

"About five minutes."

"Oh." He was right. She should get comfortable. Seated as she was, she'd likely tumble from the buggy at the first sizable bump. Besides, this wouldn't be much different from sitting next to David at mealtime. Except that meals were relatively short and there were always five other people at the table. It didn't help that Ida had packed them a picnic lunch. It made the business of finding a home for the triplets seem more like... well, like they were courting, which they weren't, even though she had been spending an awful lot of time with him on that porch swing in the evenings.

"Caroline."

She snapped back to attention. "Yes?"

He caught her gaze as amusement filled his. "Relax. It's a beautiful day. Let's enjoy it."

"Right." She offered a wan smile and gave it a valiant effort. Releasing her death grip on the buggy's armrest, she braced her boots on the floor to see if that would keep her from sliding. It did. Companionable silence settled over them as little by little she relaxed.

She pulled in a deep breath, smelled the sharp scent of grass, rich leather and the spicy woods. Streaks of wildflowers painted the tall grasses alongside the pale dirt road. The branches of oak, willow and cypress trees intertwined, almost but not quite forming an arch overhead. A ribbon of cloudy blue skies danced between their branches. She gasped as a blue jay darted across their path into the woods, where its mate chirped a welcome. "Did you see that?"

"Sure did. Pretty little things, aren't they?"

"Yes, and you're right. It's beautiful out here. I'm glad Ida insisted I come. Other than horseback riding around Austin's parks, I'd never spent much time out in nature until I came here."

"You've been to Little Horn before, though—haven't you?"

"My parents and I came for Matthew and Emma's wedding three years ago. We didn't stay long. Just two days. Then we went right back to Austin." She finally chanced a glance at him. "Matthew told me that you and your family moved here last year. Where from?"

"Near San Angelo."

The brevity of his answer, so different from their conversations on the porch, made her look a little closer. He stared straight ahead with the brim of his slouch hat casting a shadow over his eyes. In anticipation of the day's heat, he'd left his suit coat tied to the top of the picnic basket in the back. A white shirt, black suspenders and charcoal-gray pants gave him the appearance of a man in total control. Only the tension in his muscular arms and tight grip on the reins gave away the truth.

He was as nervous as she was, if not more so.

What was he nervous about? Finding a home for the triplets…or being with her? The buggy hit a small bump, sending her shoulder careening lightly into his arm. A flash of heat shot between them before she straightened. A muscle in his jaw tightened. His brow lowered slightly. Yet his attention never strayed from the road. *Interesting.*

She allowed her gaze to trace his features, wondering if he could feel her watching. "Did you like it there?"

"Where?"

"San Angelo."

"Sure, I—" He stole a quick glance at her with guarded green eyes. He took a deep breath. A hint of rawness tinged his baritone. "No. There were too many memories. Good and bad. All mixed together. Everywhere I looked I saw reminders of the people I'd lost. My father. Laura."

"Laura?"

"Laura was my wife. She died when Maggie was three. She was leaving me—leaving *with* a traveling salesman—when she got thrown from her horse."

"Oh my."

He seemed to shrug away the scandal of it. "It wasn't entirely unexpected. She was always leaving. A couple of times she left for several days. This time was different. She'd left a note that said she wasn't coming back.

I went after her, hoping I could catch her and convince her to stay for Maggie's sake. By the time I caught up with them, she'd already died in another man's arms. I wanted to be heartbroken. Instead I was just numb and sad and angry. At myself, not just her."

Caroline shook her head. "She made her own choices."

"Yes, and so did I. The truth is I never should have married her." He straightened and shot her an alarmed look. "That isn't to say— I love Maggie. I wouldn't give her up for the world, but Laura wasn't a good choice for me."

She could understand that. She'd experienced it on a smaller scale. "Why did you choose her?"

"Stubbornness? My parents didn't approve of her, and I wanted to prove them wrong."

"That doesn't sound like you."

"It isn't. Anymore. Back then I was cocky, sure of myself, thought I knew everything. Obviously, I didn't. Every man in town was after Laura. She wouldn't give them the time of day. At least not for long. I thought that made her a challenge worth winning."

"So you won."

A rueful smile tilted his lips. "I did at that. We were happy for a while. Then I guess the shine wore off. She got bored with me, with everything. She felt as though she'd settled. She could have had more, done more. She felt pinned down on the ranch. She was lonely."

"Lonely?"

He nodded. "We had one of the larger spreads in the area, which meant plenty of space between us and our nearest neighbor. She never got along well with my parents. I worked long hours. She thought a baby would cure the loneliness. Having one only made her feel more closed in. She needed company, freedom and excitement. Leastwise, that's what she said the first time she found company elsewhere. After that, she stopped trying to excuse it or hide it."

Sympathy filled her voice. "Oh, David."

"Betrayal, hurt, frustration, resignation… I went through the gamut, then settled on not feeling anything at all. It's taken me a long time to shake that woodenness."

"You don't seem wooden to me."

"I still have a tendency to withdraw. In fact…" He hesitated, glancing at her as though there was something he wanted to tell her, then shaking his head. "All I can say is that time helps. I've had five years of time. The distance I've had this last year since we moved helped even more."

"No more tripping over memories." She bit her lip. Perhaps Matthew had been right to insist she leave Austin following the wedding.

"Exactly." He shrugged. "I've still got a few scars. There's no denying that, but I think I might finally be able to move forward."

It took a moment for his words to settle before she grasped his meaning. She turned toward him and searched his profile. "You mean with someone else?"

"Maybe. When the time is right."

"Huh." The thoughtful little sound escaped before she could stop it. That was a good thing, wasn't it? A healthy thing? Suddenly she didn't want to talk about

David's former wife or potential future one anymore. She leaned in a little. "Tell me about your father."

His mouth tilted into a fond smile. "My father was wonderful. He was one of those men who seem larger than life. He was the most genuine, down-to-earth person I've ever known. He started out with practically nothing yet created a successful cattle empire. It nearly broke my heart to sell off the ranch. The cattle are from the same lineage, so I feel as though I'm still continuing that ranching legacy in my own way."

"You're his legacy, David. He raised a good man."

"You think so?"

"Absolutely." She couldn't hold back a smile of her own when he glanced at her as though for confirmation. "I'm sure he'd be very proud of the man you've become."

He refocused on the road. "Thank you. That means… so much."

She reached over to give his arm a comforting squeeze much as she would Maggie or Ida or Emma or anyone else. Only, he wasn't anyone else, which meant touching him wasn't like touching anyone else. It was more like passing her hand over a flame. Close enough to feel the heat. Quick enough not to get burned.

"Caroline…" He hesitated, then continued slowly. "Do you feel it, too?"

Her stomach tightened. Her gaze latched on to his. Her voice came out a bit breathless. "What?"

"This." He transferred the reins to one hand. Lifting the hand she'd placed on his arm, he kissed her palm. Her lungs froze in her chest only to race back to life as his lips strayed a few inches to her wrist. She tugged her hand free, cradling it with the other one. Her gaze sought his even as he turned away.

Bright red crawled up his neck. "Caroline, I'm so sorry. I shouldn't have presumed. That was way out of line. It won't happen again."

Her mind reeled as it tried to catch up with what had just happened. His apology finally filtered through. That was when she realized he was positively mortified. What was more, he was bracing himself for a first-class dressing-down. She could see it in his face as he stared at the road so hard she feared the earth would split in two.

She could leave things as they were and let him think he'd overstepped, but that seemed unfair. Especially since… "I feel it, too, David."

His gaze shot up to search hers. "You do?"

"Yes." She stared down at the space between them, hardly aware of him stopping the buggy. Now that she'd started, the words refused to remain unsaid. "In fact, I've never felt anything quite like it, but that—"

Her voice came out quietly, gently. "David, this isn't real. It can't be. We've known each other for less than two weeks. Before that I was ready to marry another man. I couldn't possibly consider—"

"You could."

"Of course I could, but it wouldn't be wise." She smoothed her skirt, refusing to meet his gaze. "Besides, it's a simple matter of chemistry."

Amusement filled his voice. "Chemistry."

He didn't believe a word she was saying. So what

was he doing? Testing her to see how far she'd plunged into denial? The answer was as far as it took to prove she wasn't a silly girl who fell in love with any man who paid her the slightest attention.

David slapped the reins to get the horse going again. She couldn't take her gaze from his profile. She wanted more than anything to know what he was thinking and feeling. He seemed to have no intention of telling her. Feeling a little put out by that, she clutched the dash. "Aren't you going to take me back to the ranch?"

"Why would I?" He glanced her way with a look of challenge. "The triplets still need a home, don't they?"

"Yes, but it's hardly wise for us to—"

"I promise I'll behave myself. Of course, I wouldn't mind if you sat a little closer—just so you don't fall out of the buggy, mind you. I'm very concerned about your safety." His teasing broke some of the tension between them. She fought a smile as he caught her gaze, then tipped his head to beckon her closer. She cautiously slid across the leather seat. He offered his elbow. "Better hold on tight. It's liable to get rough in a couple hundred yards."

"The road looks perfectly smooth to me."

He shook his head. "No, it's filled with all sorts of unexpected bumps, hills and turns."

She lifted a skeptical brow but cautiously threaded her arm through his.

He gave a satisfied nod. "Now we can both relax."

"Hardly," she mumbled, forgetting for a second that he was plenty close enough to hear her. Giving in to her more foolish side, she surrendered with a sigh and leaned her cheek against his shoulder. "What am I going to do with you?"

"You'll figure something out."

That was exactly what she was afraid of.


Caroline was right. Shifting their relationship into more romantic territory probably wasn't a wise thing to do. But then, that had always been his problem, hadn't it? He'd never moseyed into a relationship with caution. No, he rushed in impetuously, brimming with emotion, not even bothering to think through all the consequences. He didn't want to think about them now, either. He just wanted Caroline to sidle over to his side of the buggy like she had on the way to Oakalla. Now that they were traveling back to Little Horn, she shifted uncomfortably in her seat and rubbed a hand over her temple as she looked over the list of potential adoptive families they'd procured from one of Oakalla's ministers.

Frowning, he turned his attention back to the road. "You don't think we were too hard on the Walsh family, do you?"

She gave a tiny snort of disbelief. "My ears still haven't recovered from their children's incessant yelling, bickering and screaming. I can't fathom how Mr. and Mrs. Walsh can ignore it the way they do."

"They didn't ignore it completely."

"You mean the way Mrs. Walsh rapped the youngest on the back of the head."

David's eyes widened. "Did she? I heard him wail and guessed she'd done something but didn't see it happen."

"I might have said a few choice words to her while you were talking to her husband. I was about to give in to the temptation to rap *her* on the head when you said it was time to leave."

He barely held back a laugh. "Well, that explains the fire I saw in your eyes. I felt the same way when we left the McCormicks."

She sighed. "Oh, that was disappointing. They really seemed to want the babies at first."

"Oh, they wanted them, all right...as an investment."

"They were going to raise them as nothing more than farmhands."

He felt his jaw clench. "Until they found out we don't know what the triplets' mother was sick with. They figured she might have passed her 'weak constitution' on to her sons."

"And none of the other families were willing to take on all three of them." Caroline folded the list and tucked it into her skirt pocket. "That was a bust."

"It was a good effort. There are other towns nearby. We can try those another time."

She made a little humming sound that could have been agreement or disagreement. He glanced at her for clarification only to find that it was neither. Her languid lashes drifted toward her cheeks. "May I borrow your shoulder for a pillow?"

"By all means. We've had a long day." There was still a ways to go yet, but he didn't remind her of that.

She rested her head on his arm and dozed for a good thirty minutes. Glancing down at her flushed cheeks, he remembered the way she'd rubbed her temple as they'd left Oakalla. He stiffened in alarm. "Caroline?"

She didn't respond.

He moved his arm a little. "Caroline?"

"Hmm? Are we home yet?"

"Not yet. How long has your head been hurting?"

"I don't know. Awhile, I guess."

"Have you been drinking water like I told you?"

She groaned. "I don't know. You sound like my father. Did you practice your scales today? No, I did not."

"Drink some water."

She hushed him and snuggled slightly closer, which only emphasized the unnatural warmth of her skin.

"Caroline Murray—"

"Oh, all right!" She sat up enough to grab the canteen from beneath the seat. She slugged a few gulps down, then placed it in her lap. "Are you satisfied?"

"For now," he said as she settled back into her previous spot.

She pulled in a deep breath. "I'm sorry for being grumpy."

"It's all right." It was another one of the symptoms that had him concerned.

"It's just so hot."

"I know. Keep sipping that water. It will help you cool down." He left it at that, not wanting to alarm her. A few minutes later, he pulled over and stopped the wagon beside Rocky Creek. Caroline frowned at him. "Why are we stopping?"

"You need to cool off."

"I thought you said that's what the water is for. Honestly, I don't have the energy for this. I'm not feeling well. I'd rather we go straight home without any unnecessary stops."

He hopped down from the buggy and tied the horse to a nearby tree. "I know you aren't feeling well. That's why we're stopping. Now, I'm going to stay over here with my back turned. I want you to take off any excess layers and put them under the seat."

She stiffened. "Why in the world?"

"I'll never see them. Never know—"

"I'll do no such thing!"

He sighed, realizing he wouldn't gain her cooperation without giving her more information. He turned. "Caroline, I've seen the symptoms you're having before in cowboys who didn't take care of themselves in the heat. It can get serious real fast. That's why we're going to cool down now."

She was quiet for a moment. "Serious in what way?"

"Fainting, fits of seizure, vomiting, confusion…" Seeing the way her hazel eyes had widened, he stopped himself. "Need I go on?"

The energy from her indignation seemed to drain her. She shook her head. "Turn around."

"Tell me when you're ready." While he waited, he bowed his head and whispered a short prayer for her healing. They still had about an hour to go on their journey back to Little Horn. That was a long way to go in the heat for someone already feeling sick.

"Ready."

He hurried over to her side of the buggy. A cursory glance revealed no obvious change in her attire of a light blue top, navy shirtwaist and brown skirt. However, her boots rested on the floor beside her skirt, so she must have done something. He gave an approving nod. "Bring the canteen with you."

He extended a hand to help her down. She took it. Caroline stood a little too shakily for his liking, so he swept her into his arms. Gasping, she clung to his shoulders, then buried her face in the curve of his neck. He held her closer. "Dizzy?"

She nodded. "I don't want to be a bother."

"You could never be a bother."

Her breath hitched a little. Her lashes fluttered against his neck as though she was blinking back tears. He walked down the sloping white limestone to where the creek pooled into a pretty little swimming hole.

"Drink some more water." He set her down on the bank just shy of the bottle green water, then sat beside her to tug off his boots. Catching her watching him over the edge of the canteen, he turned away from her and said in a mock-peevish tone, "A little privacy, please."

She snorted, then started coughing and laughing all at once. She pushed him weakly on the back. "You almost drowned me."

He harrumphed as he made a show of rolling up his pants legs. "Just asking for some basic decency."

She covered her face with her hands and giggled. "You have to stop using that voice."

He grinned, then tapped the canteen expectantly. After waiting for her to compose herself enough to take a long drink, he helped her stand. He pulled his pants legs up a little more. He placed an arm around her waist to steady her. "Ready?"

"Keep your eyes on the creek, mister." She waited until he trained his gaze on the water before hiking up her skirts. "Ready."

They stepped into the creek...and plunged into pure nothingness. He forced himself not to catch his breath in surprise at both the depth and coldness of the water enveloping him. Realizing they weren't going to hit bottom, David propelled them upward. He released her as they broke the surface, gasping. David scanned Caroline's face for any sign of distress. "Are you all right? Can you swim?"

She nodded, drifting away a little as she treaded water. "I'm certainly awake now."

"I'm sure. This water is freezing. I'm so sorry. It didn't look anywhere near this deep."

She pressed her lips into a straight line even as laughter sparkled in her eyes.

He shook his head and rolled his eyes. "Oh, go ahead and laugh."

She did—so heartily that he had to hold on to her to keep her afloat. "I'm sorry. It's just..." She giggled. "When I think of all that effort we put into keeping our clothes dry."

He chuckled. "Rolling up my pants legs."

"Lifting up my skirt." Their eyes met, and they both burst out laughing again. She recovered first. Placing her hands over her cheeks, she grinned. "Oh, my cheeks hurt. I can't remember the last time I laughed this much."

Neither could he, and he didn't want to stop. He

snickered. "I wish I could have seen us from afar as we just plunked out of sight."

"Stop making me laugh."

"Sank like a stone."

"David!"

"All right. All right." He stared into the water. "Should I try to find the bottom?"

"No." Worry darkened her hazel eyes. "There's no telling how deep it is. If something happened to you down there…"

He tilted his head. "If something happened to me?"

A hint of a smile played at her lips. "It'd be an awful lot of trouble to drive myself back to Little Horn."

"Is that the only troubling thing about it?" He swam a little closer.

"Hmm." She glanced thoughtfully at the sky. "I suppose it would be a hard thing to explain to Maggie and Ida. How you disappeared while we were—" She blinked. Suddenly that vulnerability was back, along with something raw and intense. "I can't even joke about that, David."

He slid his arms around her and pulled her close as he treaded water for them both. "Why don't you float for a little while?"

"I can't. My skirt is too heavy."

"I'll help you. Want to try it?" After she gave her nod of approval, he turned her around. "Go ahead and float. I'll let your head rest on my shoulder while my hand supports your back. This is how I taught Maggie to float."

Caroline smiled as she relaxed in the water. "You did a good job. She swims like a fish."

He chuckled. "She sure took to it like one. She loves playing in the creek."

"She asks to go there nearly every day."

"I'll have to remember to take her down there myself. It's been a while since we've gone together."

"She would love that."

He loved this. Being with Caroline without the pressure of trying to push her away or protect himself was a lot like accidentally taking that leap into the creek. It was refreshing, exciting and unexpectedly immersive. It also left him vulnerable. He'd be lying if he said that didn't scare him. Maybe he should guard his heart a little more, not let her too close. The last thing he wanted to end up with was a broken heart.

# *Chapter Twelve*

Caroline was not in love. She could appreciate the sweet, attentive way in which David had been concerned about her health. She could hold on to the memory of floating in the limestone pool with his deep voice singing over her. She could melt just a little at the way he'd so carefully carried her back to the buggy even after she'd insisted she was feeling better. Surely she could do all of that without loving him for it.

Why, then, was love even a consideration? Why didn't her mind stop at appreciation or caring? Love wasn't even a possibility at this stage. She'd barely known the man for two weeks. He'd scarcely even been in the same room with her for most of the first.

It didn't make any more sense than why her errant hand kept sliding into the crook of his arm like it belonged there. She felt the muscles tighten as he guided the horse into a sharp turn. She peeked one eye open. Realizing they'd turned onto the lane that led to the

McKay ranch, she lifted her head from his shoulder and slid over to her own side of the buggy.

David grunted in displeasure. "Where are you going?"

She turned to give him a look, then couldn't decide what that look should be. Admonishment? Amusement? She felt so much more than that. Confused, vulnerable and unprepared for whatever this was. Yet not completely unwilling to find out. Feeling exposed, she dragged her gaze from his to the woods lining the road that led to the house. When he didn't slow down, she put a hand on his arm. "Wait."

"What's the matter?"

"We have to make ourselves presentable."

He lifted a brow as amusement curved his lips. "You mean put on our shoes?"

"Yes. Stop the buggy." As soon as they rolled to a stop, Caroline scrambled down from the buggy on her own, grabbing her boots. "I'll be right back."

She used the bottom of her skirt to wipe off the mud still clinging to her feet from the area around the swimming hole. With her socks on and shoelaces tied, she buttoned the high collar on her blouse. Feeling more presentable, she returned to the buggy. David hopped down from the buggy to assist her into it. He'd put his boots back on, but his sleeves were still rolled up and his collar unbuttoned. "Aren't you going to button up?"

He lifted an eyebrow. "It's blazing hot and we spent most of the day out in the sun. It would look odd if I hadn't done some adjusting."

"Your hair dried sort of mussed."

He obliged her by combing his fingers through it, which only made it worse. She had no intention of reaching up to fix it herself. Realizing her hair probably looked just as messy, she smoothed down the flyaways as best she could. "I wish I'd thought to bring a brush."

"Caroline, no one's going to think anything of our appearances—especially not my mother. She's the one who sent you on this trip, remember? She'd probably be pleased to know I'd done some wooing."

"Wooing?" Alarm tightened her voice. "Is that what you were doing?"

He rubbed his jaw. "If you couldn't tell, I must not have done it right."

"I didn't mean—it's just that you make it sound almost deliberate."

He frowned. "Well, it wasn't an accident. I mean I didn't plan on it happening on the road, but it would have happened eventually."

She hugged her arms over her waist. "David, I don't think this is a good idea. I'm not sure if I'm ready to even consider getting involved in another courtship so soon after what happened with Nico."

"So you want to ignore what's happening between us? I tried that, Caroline. It didn't work."

"It's only attraction."

"Do you really believe that?"

Did she? She bit her lip and glanced away.

His hands traveled over her arms, loosening them until he held her hands in his. "Look at me, sweetheart."

She reluctantly lifted her gaze to his steady, sincere green eyes.

"After what I went through with Laura, the fact that I'm even considering this… It shows how special I think it is. But the truth is I'm nervous about this, too. We can take our time. We don't have to make this something official. I just want your permission to get to know you better, spend time with you. For now, that can be our end goal. Not marriage." He gave her a funny little grin. "That sounds a little more scandalous than I intended. I promise I'll behave honorably."

She allowed herself a small smile. Why did he have to be so adorable and funny and sweet and understanding? This was never going to work. "You promise we can take our time?"

"As much time as you need. There's no rush."

Oh, but she wanted to rush. Deep down, she truly did. She wanted to rush straight into his arms, into his heart. That wasn't wise. That's why they'd take it slow. "All right."

His eyebrows rose. "All right?"

She nodded.

He let out a whoop that made her laugh. For a second she thought he might kiss her, but he simply squeezed her hands instead. "For now, I think it best we keep this between the two of us. I don't want Maggie to get disappointed if…"

If things didn't work out. If Caroline decided to go back to Austin in September. So many ifs. She nodded. "I understand, and I completely agree."

"Good. Now, are your clothes still damp like mine are?"

"Yes." Uncomfortably so, though there had been no point of mentioning it on the road.

"I know you'll want to check on Maggie and the triplets, but there is no use catching a chill on top of everything else. Promise me you'll go right upstairs and change into something dry."

"I promise."

"Let's head on home, then." He offered her a reassuring smile before he helped her into the buggy. They arrived at the ranch house only a minute or two later. She had no idea how tired she truly was until it was contrasted with Maggie's usual exuberance. Or perhaps it was the relief of finally being at her temporary home again. Her body must have decided it was permissible to relax, because she could barely keep her eyes open as she changed out of her still-damp clothes into something dry. A knock sounded on the door just as she was fastening the last button of her blouse. "Come in."

Ida stepped inside to survey her with concern. "David told me what happened. We both want you to take the rest of the night off. Understood?"

"Oh, but—"

"Good. You look asleep on your feet. I want you to go rest in my room. It's cooler there because it's farther from the kitchen. No arguments. Come along." Ida led the way to her room, which was as cool as promised and darkened by the heavy curtains over the windows. "I've put fresh sheets on the bed, though I think it's best you don't cover up. You need to stay cool. Make yourself comfortable. I mean that. I'll be the only one coming in and out, so don't be afraid to remove a few layers. I do hope you did so when you were on the road. Yes? Good. Do you need anything else?"

"No. Thank you, Ida."

"You're welcome, dear. Feel better." Ida gave her arm a quick squeeze, then left.

Caroline hardly remembered crawling beneath the sheets or closing her eyes. However, when she opened them again, soft light was easing through the seams of the curtain. Morning light. Eyes widening, Caroline sat up in bed. Had she really gone to sleep before supper and slept through the whole night in Ida's bed?

The clock on the nearby wall confirmed that she had. She threw aside the sheet, dressed in the clothes she'd intended to wear last evening and rushed down the hall to the nursery. The triplets' crib was empty. They must already be dressed and downstairs for breakfast. She pulled in a deep breath to slow herself down. She took a moment to finish her morning ablutions before heading downstairs. Ida was on her way up and they met in the middle. "Ida, I'm so sorry! I can't believe I slept that long."

Ida smiled. "No need to apologize. I figured you might end up sleeping for the night. That's why I suggested you take my room. I wanted you to be able to rest undisturbed while I saw to the triplets. Are you feeling better?"

"Much."

"Good. I was just on my way to awaken you so that you could eat breakfast. You must be starved after missing supper."

Caroline placed a hand over her stomach as it growled at the suggestion of food. "Excuse me."

Ida chuckled. "That's quite all right. Come to the table."

She followed Ida to the kitchen. Caroline couldn't help feeling a little hesitant as she entered the room. She instinctively searched for David. He was settling Jasper in a high chair and stilled when he caught sight of her. There was a hint of uncertainty in his smile even as his eyes filled with concern. "How do you feel?"

"Better." Something about him set her at ease, prompting her to answer his other, unasked question with a soft smile of her own.

Maggie breezed in from outside. "Duke's eating breakfast. Good morning, Miss Caroline."

"Morning, sweetheart."

Eli was the first of the triplets to catch sight of Caroline. His face brightened with a grin. He reached out to her from his high chair squealing, "La-la!"

She lifted him and cuddled him close. "Hello, my darling! Did you miss me? It feels like it's been ages since I saw you last."

"La-la!" He giggled and grabbed on to her ear, which she'd learned to leave free of earrings.

Ida turned from the stove to look at Caroline in confusion. "Is he calling you La-la?"

Caroline blinked. "Surely not. None of them have spoken any real words yet."

"Apparently," David began as he poured himself some coffee, "Jasper said his first word while you and I were gone yesterday."

Caroline gasped. "He did? What did he say?"

David winked at Maggie. "Do you want to tell it?"

"Yes." Maggie grinned from her seat next to Theo. "Grandma tried to feed him peas, so he turned his head and said, 'No!'"

She laughed. "Sounds like he knew exactly what he meant."

Ida shook her head. "There's no mistaking that for baby talk."

"What a smart boy you are, Jasper." With Eli still on her hip, she ruffled Jasper's hair. He shot her a playful grin, and she couldn't resist leaning over to kiss his forehead.

David set his coffee on the table, then called Eli's name to get the boy's attention. He waited until Eli turned toward him before tapping Caroline's arms. "Who's this? Who's this, Eli?"

He launched himself back to hug Caroline's neck. "La-la."

"Aw!" Caroline tightened her arms around Eli as her heart melted. "He gave me a name. Isn't that the sweetest thing?"

David watched them with a smile. "It sure is."

"Why La-la?" Maggie asked.

Caroline smiled. "I think I know. Eli in particular has been fascinated by words lately. The only way I've been able to get him to sleep is my substituting the lullaby lyrics for nonsense words like *la-la-la*. I guess that's where he picked it up."

Ida chuckled as she placed a plate of flapjacks on the table. "Well, that's adorable."

Maggie placed her chin in her hand and her elbow on the table as she stared at Theo. "It's your turn, Theo. Say something. Say Maggie. Maggie."

Theo stared right back at her, but he didn't say a word.

"Maggie. Mag-gie. I'll answer to Mag if that's easier. Mag."

The adults exchanged laughing glances as Maggie continued her coaching. Caroline put Eli back in his seat with a kiss on the head. Realizing Theo was the only baby who hadn't received any special attention, she quickly remedied that with a smacking kiss on his cheek, which made him chortle, much to Maggie's delight. Then Maggie looked so cute and had made so much progress when it came to getting along with the triplets that Caroline couldn't help kissing her cheek, too.

Maggie bashfully rubbed her hands over her eyes before tucking her fists beneath her chin. "What was that for?"

"Being such a good helper to your grandma and me."

Maggie pursed her lips to hide a smile. "I have been a pretty good helper, huh?"

"The best." Caroline winked, then went to help Ida chop up the triplets' food.

As soon as breakfast was over, David pushed away from the table. "Caroline, I usually do a performance review of our new employees two weeks after they start working for us. We may as well do it now. Would you come to my study? It should only take a few minutes."

"Oh. Of course." The McKays had treated her so much as a part of the family that she'd halfway forgotten she was David's employee. She couldn't deny that being reminded of it smarted a little, especially after what had happened between them yesterday. Pushing aside her silly pride, she preceded him into the study.

He closed the door behind them and leaned back against it. Conscious of his perusing gaze, she clasped her hands behind her back. It was always a nerve-racking experience to stand in front of one's boss while he offered criticism, constructive or otherwise. She'd hated having to do it at the music school in Austin. It was far too akin to facing her parents' criticism at the end of a practice or recital.

She went over the last two weeks of nanny duties in her mind, trying to prepare herself for anything with which he might find fault. No glaring mistakes came to mind. That didn't mean there weren't any.

David took a few steps away from the door. Caroline held her ground, though she couldn't help noticing how small the room seemed with David only an arm's length away. He rubbed the nape of his neck and offered a sheepish smile. "Honestly, I just wanted to have you all to myself for a minute."

Tension eased from her shoulders. She gave a relieved laugh, then instinctively stepped forward to wrap her arms around his shoulders. Belatedly realizing the brazenness of the action, she was about to pull away when his arm looped around her waist. His other hand pressed against the small of her back to ease her even closer. She relaxed in his arms, letting her cheek rest against the solid warmth of his chest. His deep voice rumbled in her ear. "I was afraid you might have changed your mind."

"I haven't." She smiled when he sighed in relief. "Do you really give performance reviews of your employees?"

"Yes, but I didn't mean to make you nervous about it. You've been doing a wonderful job. The triplets love you. Maggie listens to you. My mother dotes on you."

"What about my boss?"

"He thinks you're pretty special. You've made his life a whole lot easier of late. What about you? Any concerns I should know about?"

She was incredibly concerned about the way she felt so at home in his arms. However, that wasn't what he was asking about. He wanted to know if she had any work-related concerns. "None that I can think of."

"All right, then. I've spoken with my mother. We both want you to take it easy today."

She really was feeling better, but it was sweet that he was concerned. "I'll try."

"This evening, after everyone else turns in, we can go for a walk. How does that sound?"

"Wonderful." She paused. "We'd both better get to work."

"Yep."

Neither of them moved. She laughed, then let her hands slide to his chest, where they reluctantly pushed off. "Go."

He grinned and backed away. "Have a good day."

"You, too."

She lingered in his office for a moment. This was good. They would take it slow. Keep it secret until there was something worth telling, but that wouldn't be for a while yet. Of course, she would have to decide if she was taking that role in *The Pirates of Penzance* sooner rather than later.

Ida appeared in the doorway. "Everything all right, Caroline?"

"Perfect."

She wasn't sure how long it could stay that way, but she intended to enjoy it while it lasted.

A low rumble sounded in the distance. David reined in his horse and glanced at the sky. "Was that—"

"Thunder," Isaiah Upkins said with a smile as he rode past on his horse, pushing the lazy cattle forward. "Again."

Ephraim sent a speculative look at the clear blue sky, then set off after a rebellious calf while calling over his shoulder, "Let's just hope it actually rains this time."

"Please, Lord," David prayed, as the entire community continued to do after the special prayer meeting Brandon Stillwater had held at the church. In the week since David and Caroline had returned from Oakalla, it had threatened to rain twice. So far not a single drop had fallen. Still, the thunder was a good sign, and hopefully a harbinger of wetter weather on the way. He'd be grateful for even one good ground soaking before haying season began. The grass needed it, too. Bad. Thus, the reason they were already moving the cattle to a new pasture today.

With Joaquin taking point, the task was finished by midafternoon. The ranch hands moved on to their other duties while David headed back to the ranch house. He slowed on the porch steps as Maggie's singing drifted through the open parlor window.

"Whether she loves me or loves me not, sometimes it's hard to tell. Yet I am longing to share the lot of beautiful daisy bell."

Caroline sang in harmony for the chorus. Even his mother joined in, making his breath catch in his throat. He hadn't heard her sing or play the piano since his father had died. Unwilling to risk interrupting the moment, David stood by the front door singing along too softly for them to hear.

"I'm half-crazy all for the love of you."

And that was about all David could take of not being with his three favorite ladies during such a joyous moment. He quietly slipped inside, then stalled in the parlor's doorway. No one seemed to notice him at first. That gave him a second to work through the shock of seeing Maggie dancing around the parlor in the fanciest dress she owned.

Ida watched her granddaughter with pure delight in her eyes. Caroline could hardly sing for smiling. The triplets watched from their play area in fascination as the colorful skirt twirled and swung with Maggie's dance. Duke followed after her with his ears perked forward in confusion. David commiserated with the pup, who finally sat with the triplets to watch.

Of all the sights David may have expected to return home to, this was not one of them. He couldn't help grinning as his daughter twirled around the parlor as though it were a grand ballroom. Even more astounding, she looked perfectly content to have the skirt swirling about her—not at all the grimace her face usually bore when she was forced to wear one for church. She caught sight of him. A little gasp escaped her as she stopped in her tracks.

She looked so much like her ma with her hair swept back like that. He'd met Laura at a dance all those years ago. She'd been the prettiest girl in the room. For once David didn't push away the memory. Those early days with his wife had been good ones. He should remember them for Maggie's sake—even share them with her. One day, but not now. He didn't want to miss this moment with his precious little girl.

The music faltered a moment as he stepped into the room. He knew Caroline was sitting at the piano but didn't let himself look in her direction. He extended his hand to Maggie. She grinned. He twirled her under his arm, then deftly led her into the waltz steps he'd shown her at his brother Edmund's wedding.

As the music began to wind down, he swept her into his arms and turned in as graceful a spin as he could manage before setting her down again. Ida and Caroline clapped for them while he kissed her hand as though he were a grand duke and Maggie a lady of the court. "Thank you for the dance, Maggie. You sure look pretty in that dress."

Her blue eyes sparkled. Her cheeks, already flushed from the dance, turned pinker. She fiddled with the seams of the skirt and ducked her head. "Thank you, Pa."

He tweaked her nose. He was dying to know how this little scene had come about, why she'd chosen to wear a dress and if this had happened before. He didn't want to embarrass her by making too much of it. He did, however, intend to get a full account of it later from the other ladies in the room.

He stole a quick glance at Caroline. The affection in her eyes made his heart skip a beat. He'd gladly yield most of that affection to Maggie, but surely at least some of it was for him. Perhaps he'd even be so bold as to claim the full portion of the admiration he saw there, as well.

A week with her as something more than just his family's latest nanny had left him longing for even more. More time. More conversation. More long walks after the house had gone quiet.

She hadn't said a word about the prospect of leaving. He was hoping that if he ignored that possibility long enough, it would go away—not unlike the letter from the mail-order bride that he'd tucked into the recesses of his nightstand. He had no intention of marrying that woman. So why hadn't he written to tell her so? Perhaps she was a last resort should Caroline decide there were other offers more desirable than his.

"Pa, can you help us solve a mystery?"

He trained his eyes back on his daughter. He sat on the nearby settee and lifted her onto his knee. "What mystery is that, Magpie?"

"The case of the lost marbles."

For some reason, that made Ida and Caroline burst

out laughing. David exchanged a confused look with Maggie. "What's so funny?"

"I don't know."

Giving Ida and Caroline time to compose themselves, he asked Maggie. "You lost your marbles?"

"No. Grandma did."

He paused, glanced at his mother and grinned. There had to be a story behind this. "Ma, have you lost your marbles?"

"I surely hope not." Ida wiped away a tear of laughter. "Although I was starting to suspect I might have. Maggie must have overheard what I said to Caroline and misunderstood. Maggie dear, I didn't lose actual marbles. It's an expression that means…well, that someone has lost their wits."

Maggie frowned. "Wits?"

"Mind," David supplied. "I'm sure it isn't true. What's going on, Ma?"

"I thought Caroline had folded the triplets' diapers and clothes on laundry day twice now. I was grateful but wanted to let her know that it was unnecessary. Come to find out, she hasn't been folding the clothes at all. Maggie hasn't, either. I don't suppose you have?"

"I'm afraid I can't take credit for that."

"That's what Caroline said. I was afraid that somehow I'd folded the laundry, then forgotten all about it. That's when I mentioned the bit about losing my marbles."

David shook his head. "There has to be another explanation."

"By all means, offer one."

"Well, a couple of weeks ago, the ranch hands and I ran across a heifer and her calf with some scratches on them."

Caroline snapped her fingers. "I knew it had to be the cows."

That set Maggie giggling. Ida nodded seriously. "I should have thought of them first."

David rolled his eyes. "It wasn't the cattle. They were too busy breaking into the hay field to fold laundry. The scratches were from the barbed wire fence that was supposed to keep them out. Someone shooed them out of the field, then laid a tree branch across the opening to keep them out."

Ida frowned. "That doesn't sound like something your men would do."

"Exactly. They would have fixed the fence right away. Between that, the folded laundry and the bag of toys left in my wagon a while back, I'd say someone is looking out for us."

"And the triplets," Caroline added as she crossed the room to let them out of the cordoned-off area. Eli headed directly for Duke, much to the puppy's delight. Theo went to Maggie, who squirmed off David's lap to join the boy on the floor. Jasper took advantage of his brothers' absence to gather all the toys they'd left behind to his chest.

Maggie glanced up at him as Theo crawled into her lap. "Who's helping us?"

"I don't know." David shrugged. "I figured it must be one of the Colemans, since the hay field is near their border."

Caroline narrowed her gaze thoughtfully. "Or it could be Annie. She has a real soft spot for the triplets."

"That's a good guess. I suppose, technically, it could be anyone. We'll have to be on the lookout to see if we can figure out who it is."

Ida winked. "As long as we don't find out it's actually me."

"It isn't you," David and Caroline both assured her at the same time, with equal vehemence.

Ida eyed them suspiciously. "You two have been doing that more and more often."

"Doing what?" Maggie asked.

"Saying the same things at the same time."

That was probably because they were spending a lot of time together. He shot a quick glance to Caroline, who gave a casual shrug. "I've noticed that, too. Strange, isn't it? How about another song?"

Just like that she distracted Maggie. Ida appeared more reluctant to give up the line of questioning, but it was hard to conduct an interview over the sound of a piano, so she gave up. David could barely hold back a laugh of appreciation at Caroline's skillful maneuvering. Only a few hours more and he could have her all to himself. Let the wait begin.

# Chapter Thirteen

Maggie was asleep. His mother had retired to her room. The moment David had been waiting for all day had finally arrived. Caroline spun toward the soft sound of the front door closing behind him. He extended his hand at the same time she reached for his, and they set off down the porch steps into the moonlight. David savored the companionable silence between them until his curiosity could wait no longer. "How on earth did you get Maggie into a skirt?"

Laughter filled her eyes as she turned to look up at him. "That was entirely her decision. She wanted to be able to pretend she was a lady at a ball. It wouldn't have been the same without a flowing skirt."

Of its own accord, his gaze took in her dress from its puffy sleeves to the ruffled hem. The color, somewhere between blue and green, set off the richness of her hazel eyes. Only when her cheeks flushed did he realize he'd been surveying her like the heifers he helped judge at the county fair. "I think Maggie's found someone new to emulate."

"I think you're giving me too much credit."

"Never." He gave her hand a light squeeze. "What do you think? Any chance the change will stick?"

"Absolutely—when she's ready for that to happen and not a moment sooner." She shook her head. "She's got a mind of her own, your daughter."

"I've noticed."

"Speaking of noticing, I think your mother is onto us."

"She probably is. She isn't the type to miss much." He stole a sideways glance at her. "What do you think about telling them?"

She sighed. "I'm still afraid I'll end up disappointing Maggie somehow."

That could only mean she still wasn't completely certain they had a future together. Her doubt only increased his own. What would it take to convince her to stay?

Thunder rumbled in the distance. He groaned and glanced up at the sky through the branches overhead. "I wish it would make up its mind. Rain or don't rain. This endless taunting is unbearable."

Caroline faltered a step. She glanced up at him with wide eyes. His words suddenly took on new meaning. He swallowed hard. "I didn't mean… That was poorly timed."

They stepped out onto the ridge, where the view of the night sky was incredible, but their eyes never left each other's. She offered a soft smile to say she hadn't taken his statement in the wrong way. "I don't mean to be a tease, David. I just need more time. Everything has happened so quickly. A month ago..." She bit her lip, seemingly unwilling to mention Nico or Austin in what had become their spot. "Now I'm here with you. Everything within me wants to tumble headfirst into—"

He kept quiet, hoping she'd say *love*. That was where his thoughts had been headed of late. His feelings, too. He was certain of that. Instead she skipped it altogether. "I've done that before. At least, I thought I had. Now I'm all confused. And why haven't you kissed me?"

He blinked, gave his head a light shake, then felt his brow furrow. "What did you say?"

Her chin lifted incrementally. "You heard me."

Honestly, he'd thought his imagination had taken over in some strange protest against the rigid self-control he'd exercised since arriving home from Oakalla. Taking in the flush of her cheeks and the vulnerability in her expression, he realized it had taken quite a bit of courage for her to bring up the subject. He met her honesty with his own. "I've wanted to. There's no denying that. More than that, I wanted to prove to you and myself that this was more than just a flash-in-the-pan attraction."

She released his hand to hug her arms. "I knew it had to be something like that."

He caught her locked arms and eased her closer until she rested her forehead on his chest. "Well, don't leave me in suspense. Did it work?"

"Yes," she muttered, sounding none too pleased about it. "But I always knew there was more to our relationship than that. I just didn't want to admit it because then I'd have to take this seriously. Now what am I supposed to do?"

"That's up to you and God."

She was quiet for a moment, then finally admitted, "I do care about you, you know."

He made a low sound of agreement to let her know she'd been heard, but he couldn't force himself to return the sentiment. *Care* was such a small word. He cared about the weather. He cared about his livestock. He much more than cared about Caroline. He had a feeling she much more than cared about him, too. Like before, she was simply too afraid to admit it. Maybe he was, too.

However, during the first week of their unofficial courtship, he'd learned that her touch never lied, never equivocated and somehow wasn't subject to her doubts or insecurities. It was fascinating…outright confounding at first. Now that he understood it and her better, he was unerringly careful about not using that knowledge to his advantage.

Of course, if he was going to be honest with himself, he had to admit that holding back on the kisses was about more than merely proving a point. It was about keeping one last bastion of protection between her and his heart. He wasn't ready to give up that protection yet. Not with her so unsure of the future.

He wrapped his arms around her, despite her crossed arms, and rubbed a circle on her back to dispel her tension. Unlocking her arms and resting them against his chest, she relaxed into him. Her breathing steadied. *See?* This was perfect. This was safe. Except he still wanted to kiss her. Idiot that he was. Time to change the subject. "I've been thinking about trying to find the triplets a family again."

She pulled back just enough to look at him as if his words were the most important in her world. She'd been doing that a lot lately. It made him feel about ten feet tall. It also made him want to kiss her. Her lips tilted into a smile. "I think that's a great idea. Where were you thinking we should look next?"

"Joppa. It's accessible by train." He dragged his gaze from her mouth only to find her watching his.

Caught, she glanced away. "When do we leave?"

His arms tightened. "Actually, I think it's best if I go by myself."

"What? Why?"

"You got sick last time." *Not to mention all that time alone together.* He left that unsaid, since he was pretty sure she wouldn't appreciate the idea of him avoiding time with her. He didn't want to slip back into that habit, either. Maybe he should just kiss her now and get it over with. Then he'd stop thinking about it.

"That was easily preventable."

She was waiting for his response, but he couldn't think of one. Didn't care to, either. He lowered his head just as she turned her face away to stare at something in the distance. "David, what *is* that?"

"What?"

"That glow in the distance." She eased out of his embrace.

He stared down at his empty arms until his brain

caught up. *Glow. Distance.* Alarm stiffened his body. He turned to follow her gaze. Dread filled his voice. "Fire."

Her eyes widened. "Fire?"

He was already grasping her hand and urging her down the ridge toward the house at as close to a run as she could manage in her skirts. "It's on Hill land or maybe the Colemans'. They'll need help. You need to go back to the house. Awaken Maggie and my mother. Get them and the triplets ready to go."

"Go where?"

"To town. Take refuge in the church. We have no idea how fast or how far the fire will spread with conditions as dry as they are. Fires can move faster than a horse can trot. I don't want to take any chances. Have everyone stay calm, but hurry!"

She left his side to run into the house. He went to the bunkhouse to rouse his men. They were already awake and quickly scrambled to the barn while David called out orders. "Isaiah, I want you to rig up the wagon and take the women and children into town. Sound the alarm there if it hasn't already been raised. Ephraim, you're with me. We're heading to the fire. Joaquin, I want you to ride over to Matthew's spread and—" He stopped as Matthew drove into the barnyard with Emma clinging to the wagon seat beside him. "Never mind, men. Saddle up and head to the fire. I'll catch up as soon as I can."

Matthew set the brake and hopped down to meet him. "I saw the fire a few minutes ago. I sent a man into town to spread the word. The rest of my ranch hands are headed for the fire. I'm taking Emma into town. Figured I'd take the rest of the women and children, too."

David nodded. "Caroline is getting them ready now."

Emma called from the wagon. "Let me down. I'll help them."

Leaving Matthew to escort Emma inside, David saddled his horse, then met back up with his family at the porch steps. He drew a sleepy yet rather startled-looking Maggie into his arms and kissed her forehead before glancing up at his mother. "Y'all have everything you need in case you need to stay in town overnight?"

Ida nodded. "We're ready."

He lifted Maggie into the wagon, then his mother. Between the adults, they somehow managed to get the fussy triplets settled, too. Finally, it was Caroline's turn. She took a step back when he moved to help her. "David, the other women and I discussed this. I'm going with you."

"What?"

"No!" Matthew crossed his arms. "You're coming with me."

All three women offered their own argument as to why Caroline should attend. Apparently, Emma was going to help Ida look after the triplets in town. Ida insisted that they'd need every able-bodied person at the fire. Lula May was likely going to be there. So would Dorothy Hill. Caroline wanted to be there for Annie and in case the Coleman or Hill children needed looking after.

David sent a look to Matthew that must have clearly said, *She's your sister, so do something.* But Matthew did the wrong thing. "I don't think you'd be much help, Caroline."

Her mouth fell open. "Why? Because I'm from the city?"

"Frankly, yes."

"I'm not some delicate orchid who's going to wilt."

She had already done just that on the way back from Oakalla. However, he'd learned his lesson from Matthew's stumble and kept that point to himself. That didn't keep her from turning on him. "And don't say it's too dangerous. I'll stay well back from the flames."

He shook his head. "We don't have time to argue about this."

"Then don't argue." She stormed off toward the barn.

David sent Matthew a confused glance, lifting his palms in a silent question.

Matthew shrugged. "Don't ask me. I've never seen her like this. I've got to get the others to town. Keep her safe until I meet you at the fire, then I'll watch over her."

"Fine." He hurried to the barn to find her saddling her own horse. His men were already gone, so he didn't bother keeping his distance as he reached around her to take over the task. "This is foolhardy. You have no business being at the fire."

"I need to go, David."

The conviction in her voice made him glance down at her. Her hazel eyes were dewy with unshed tears. He caught her chin in his hand to study her more closely. It didn't help him understand her any better, so he released her and gave her a leg up. "Stay back from the flames, Caroline. I mean it."

He strode out of the barn without waiting for a reply. He mounted his horse and waited for her to join him before they followed the path his men had taken toward the border between the Coleman and Hill properties. After a few minutes' ride, David spotted silhouettes moving against the bright background of flames and smoke less than a quarter mile away. They headed in that direction as Tug Coleman rode up to meet them. A large man with a full brown beard and a commanding presence even on horseback, Tug didn't waste time on pleasantries. "Did y'all bring shovels?"

"Yes, sir," David said. "I've got a couple in a saddle bag. My ranch hands should already be here."

"They are. I've got them working on the fire line. I'd like you there, too. There isn't much else we can do about the flames until the fire wagon gets here." Tug shifted his blue gaze to Caroline and nodded his greeting. "Miss Murray, I've got two girls who are eleven and thirteen. They could use some looking after."

Caroline sent David a triumphant look. "I'd be happy to help."

David eased his horse a bit closer to hers. "She stays near me. I promised her brother that."

"I'll bring the girls by."

"And the youngest Hill boy, too, if his mother will allow it."

Tug's eyes narrowed at Caroline. To her credit she didn't back down from the request that would necessitate the two families interacting. Tug gave a quick nod. "I'll see what I can do."

Caroline helped dig the fire line at David's side without complaint until Tug brought his girls for her to watch. David split his focus between the bite of the shovel in the dirt and the soothing murmur of Caroline's voice behind him. The fire wagon finally arrived. Its water slowed the fire's progress somewhat, but wind kept whipping up the flames, sending them marching southwest toward his ranch and the general direction of town.

The air felt charged as clouds rolled overhead in the moonlit sky. He wasn't sure who started it first, but a murmur swept through the pastureland and rose in volume as more and more folks began crying out to the Lord, asking Him to let the rain fall. Lightning flashed. Thunder rumbled. One of the Coleman girls started crying. Still no rain. The fire crept closer, got hotter.

The fire wagon left to be refilled. Ash floated into the sky. Smoke stung his eyes. Tug rode down the line, telling folks to move back. The fire had already jumped the line in the north. Frustration filled David, but he didn't let up. Just because the fire had jumped the line elsewhere didn't mean they had to let it jump here. He was too close to joining his ditch to the one Matthew had started to give up now.

Caroline called his name. He motioned her and the children back and kept digging. The fire was close, but not near enough to make him stop. He dug harder and faster. He was only a foot or so away from completing the line when a rush of wind enveloped him.

He glanced up to see a wall of fire. Then it wasn't a wall. It was a living, breathing inferno, surrounding him and licking at his clothes.

Caroline screamed his name. Jolted from his shock, he turned and jumped through the flames toward her voice. He kept running once he was free of them. She yelled something about his shirt. He was already ripping it off. His panicked strength was too much for the few buttons he hadn't already undone. They went flying an instant before he tossed the flaming garment to the ground. He fell to the ground and rolled to smother out any other flames.

Caroline slid to her knees beside him. "It's out. It's out. Are you hurt? David—"

"Can you stand?" Matthew appeared next to her. "We need to look at your back."

David grabbed the hand Matthew extended to him and let the man help him to his feet. He saw Bo Stillwater stomping out the flames from his shirt a few yards away. The rancher joined Matthew and Caroline as they carefully lifted David's undershirt to examine the skin on his back. Some of Bo's wife's nursing skills must have rubbed off on the rancher for he said, "It's hard to tell in the dark, but the skin looks a little red. How does it feel?"

"It burns some. Nothing I haven't felt from accidentally touching my mother's hot teakettle. I don't think it's too serious."

David didn't notice the satchel strapped to Bo's back until the man removed it. "My father-in-law is out here somewhere with his doctor's bag. Louisa sent me with some supplies of her own. Aloe, bandages and the like. They should help."

Tug rode over to them. "What's happening here? Are you hurt, David?"

"Nothing too bad."

"Didn't you hear me say to move back?" When David couldn't find an answer to that, Tug frowned. "Miss Murray, if you'll take care of him, I'd like the other men to come with me. We need a new strategy. My girls can come, too. I'm sending them to town."

Caroline accepted the supplies from Bo as the men and children walked off. Her hands shook as she tried to open the jar of aloe. David took it from her and opened it before handing it back. He would have taken the time to comfort her, but a swath of skin on his back was really starting to burn. The cool gel relieved it some. Noticing she'd yet to speak after learning he was all right, he asked, "How long was I in the flames?"

"Only a second or two."

It had seemed like an eternity. It could have easily *turned* into eternity. If he hadn't heard Caroline's voice, who knew how long it would have taken him to recover from the shock of the flames. Worse yet, he'd been disoriented. He might not have known which way to go to get out of the fire. At the very least, he would have hesitated longer.

Life could be over in an instant. He'd seen it happen with his father and again with Laura. It had almost happened to him. And what would he have left behind? A daughter. No. Maggie wouldn't be anyone's daughter. She'd be an orphan like him, like the triplets, like the

Satler siblings. Of course, she'd have Ida to take care of her. But Ida was getting older. Running after an eight-year-old and raising a girl into a woman at a time when Ida should be slowing down wasn't fair to her.

David needed a wife. Not to take care of the triplets, though that would be helpful. He needed her for Maggie. That would give his daughter a better chance of having at least one parent around long enough to raise her. Thankfully, he was already courting, albeit secretly, a woman perfect for the task. It was time to stop playing it safe. He needed to put aside his fears and hesitancy. It was time to tell her how he felt and give her a real reason to stay.

## Chapter Fourteen

"I can't believe you almost got yourself killed." Caroline kept an eye on the approaching fire as she bathed David's burn using a cloth and some of the drinking water that the Coleman girls had left behind. She gave a little huff, remembering her panic at the sight of David disappearing behind a wall of flames. Her heart had frozen in her chest for those few seconds only to race back to life at the sight of him on fire. "And you called *me* foolhardy."

"I guess it's a good thing you came, after all, seeing as you saved my life."

She stilled, then dipped the bandage in water again. "I don't know about that."

"I do."

She'd like to say she'd had some sort of divine warning or directive that she would be needed here. Truthfully, she'd come simply because she'd *wanted* to be needed here. She'd wanted to feel as though she was a part of this close-knit community. She'd wanted to fight alongside them, especially Matthew and David, against the destruction of their homes and livelihood. It didn't make much sense for her to be this invested in the lives and fortunes of people she'd known for such a short amount of time, but something about this town and the ranches she was visiting made her feel like she had roots that extended beyond her disinterested parents. How could she not want to protect that?

A drop of water landed on her arm. It prompted her to blink away the tears in her eyes, though whether they were born from emotion, smoke or wind was anyone's guess. Another drop landed on her hair. Now, that couldn't have been a tear. She tilted her head back to stare up at the night sky. She hoped that what she felt was more than her imagination and more than a single errant raindrop. David must have felt something, because he stiffened, as well.

"Please, Lord," she whispered, then smiled as the sky let loose a steady drizzle.

She heard David murmur, "Come on. Rain harder. Rain harder."

A few exclamations of surprise and praise across the field was all the warning they had before the skies opened, and a drenching rain fell. David let out a shout of relief, pumped a hand in the air and would have taken off at a run to do who knows what if she hadn't dug in her heels. "Hold still. Let me finish."

Laughing as he fidgeted, she swiped a good portion of aloe on his burn, then let him go. He rushed toward the flames to watch them sizzling and dying away. He stomped a dying ember as though getting back at the fire for trying to maim him or kill him, whatever its intent might have been, before throwing his head back to let out another yell. Throughout the pasture, similar celebrations took place. She could hear them even though she couldn't see them in the darkness that grew with every flame the rain extinguished.

She watched David fall to his knees in a prayer of gratefulness and found herself doing the same. A funny thing happened while she was thanking God for His mercy concerning people whom, besides her brother and Emma, she hadn't even known a few weeks ago. She realized it had been a really long time since she'd humbled herself before her Father like this. Oh, she'd worshipped on the hillside with Maggie that moonlit night when she'd discovered David's talent with a guitar, but this was different.

The darkness, the rawness of nature, that delicate line between life and death all came crashing down on her at once. God had saved the day in His own way at His own time. He'd done the same for her at that altar in Austin. That salvation didn't mean that she wouldn't experience loss. The Hills and the Colemans had tonight, as well. It did mean that she could trust Him to see her through that loss, to make something good come from it even when she didn't see how. So what good would come of her botched wedding?

Obviously, being saved from whatever ill intent Nico might have had for her was a large part of it, but what about her future? Where was she supposed to go from here? She knew that she'd been putting off making decisions for too long. She needed to move forward in life. Unfortunately, she had no idea what that meant. "Please, show me what to do."

She spoke so quietly that the thrumming of the rain would have drowned out the words to anyone but the One it was meant for. No immediate answer presented itself. Frustration threatened to steal the joy of this moment, but she refused to let it.

Dampness seeped through her skirt to her legs. She was now kneeling in mud instead of dry dirt. Unable to stop a grin, she grabbed a handful of it, then smeared it between her palms with gusto. She stood and threw her arms open to the sky, letting the rain wash her hands clean of the mud. It was relentless and cold and absolutely energizing.

Somehow she felt David coming before she peeked an eye open to see his form moving toward her. Even so she let out a squeak of surprise as he wrapped his arm around her waist, lifted her off her feet and spun with her through the rain. She closed her eyes tight and clung to his shoulders as her laughter mingled with his. He set her down and they both swayed dizzily for a moment. While the world was still spinning, he kissed her.

At first it was little more than a natural progression of their previous exuberance. Then they both seemed to realize what was happening, what they were doing. They stepped apart. David searched her face. "Caroline..."

He hesitated, but she knew the words he didn't say. They filled the space between them with warmth. The rest of the world faded away behind a curtain of rain and smoke and a darkness that grew thicker with every dying flame. His touch erased even that as he wiped away the mud she hadn't realized was clinging to her cheek. His green eyes darkened with something much deeper than affection. "Caroline, I—"

She shushed him. She couldn't let him name it. Not yet. A kiss was by far the safest choice. Passion was an easy cover to hide behind. Yet when she eased closer and their lips met again, it wasn't passion that demanded expression. It was love. Pure, sweet, reverent love. That was what was in his kiss and in her response. How could that be? They'd known each other such a short time and...

They separated to take a breath, but his hands were already at her waist, pulling her closer. Cradling his jaw, she let him deepen the kiss. A voice yelled her name in the distance. It demanded her attention. "Caroline! Caroline, where are you?"

*Matthew.* She pushed away from David's chest and spun toward her brother's voice. Her mouth opened and closed without admitting a sound. David finally yelled, "Over here."

She turned away from them both to search the ground for the jar of aloe that Bo had given her. It was impossible to see anything in the dark. David's hand settled on her arm. "Don't get lost now."

She glanced up at his shadowy features as Matthew neared, holding a fiery branch as a torch. In its light, she spotted the jar and the sodden bandages. She scooped them up. The men were talking about the damage the fire had done. Apparently, the Hills and Colemans had both lost fencing and outbuildings, but nothing else. She found her voice to seek some much-needed reassurance. "The rain will put the fire out, won't it?"

Matthew led them in the direction the others had gone before the rain had started. "Maybe not entirely, but it should keep the fire from spreading and make it easier for the fire wagon to do its job."

She lifted her skirts from the mud, though that didn't do much to keep them from tangling around her legs. David caught hold of her arm to keep her from stumbling. He didn't immediately let go. She saw Matthew's gaze linger there, so she rushed on. "No one else was hurt? Besides David, I mean."

"Not that I know of." Matthew lifted an eyebrow.

Caroline had no intention of answering her brother's unspoken questions. She couldn't even answer her own.

David heaved out a sigh. "Uh-oh."

Matthew chimed in with his own groan.

Caroline frowned. "What is it?"

David shook his head. "The Hills and the Colemans are at it again. Listen. You can hear them yelling from here."

The sound of arguing grew louder and louder as they neared the gathering of ranchers, ranch hands and townsfolk who had come to help. A lamp on a nearby wagon illuminated the scene enough for Caroline to spot the two youngest Coleman girls. They were glaring at the two youngest Hill boys, but at least the girls were safe beside their father. For the first time since arriving at the fire, Caroline caught sight of Annie just in time to see her friend give a nod to Jamie.

He took a deep breath and yelled loud enough to

drown out their parents' fussing. "Annie and I are engaged!"

Shock rendered both families silent. None of the bystanders dared move or even breathe. He held out a hand to Annie, who immediately took it. United, they faced their families. "We love each other, and we're going to get married."

Dorothy Hill, Annie's mother, broke the silence with a sputter. "Over my dead and bleeding body!"

"Have you *lost* your mind?" Tug yelled at his son.

Annie lifted her chin. "We're going to be family. That means this fighting has to stop."

It didn't stop. It got physical. Annie's older brother Peter went after Jamie with his fists. Jamie must have anticipated it for he dodged and tripped his adversary. Peter dragged him into the mud on the way down. As they grappled, the children started throwing mud pies at one another with gleeful battle cries. Dorothy started shoving Tug, who ignored her to lecture Annie and Jamie. Annie was too busy yelling at Peter and trying to pull him away from Jamie to notice. Having had enough of being pushed, Tug stepped to the side as Dorothy tried to shove him, then used her momentum to pull her to his chest, where she was too close to do any damage. Caroline didn't have to hear his growling voice to read the warning on his lips. "Shove me one more time."

Dorothy froze. Caroline waited for Tug to release the widow, but he just stood there as Dorothy glanced up at him from beneath her lashes. Tug's countenance changed to something more vulnerable. Distracted as he was, he never saw the littlest Hill boy creep up behind him and kick his knee. Tug let out a howl of pain and released Dorothy.

"Oh my. Oh my. Oh my." Caroline nudged Matthew's side with her elbow. "Matthew, did you see that?"

"Ouch." Matthew rubbed his side. "Are you trying to start a feud with me now?"

"She likes him."

"Of course Annie likes him."

"No, I mean—" She gasped as a flying fist nearly landed on Annie's cheek. Caroline didn't realize she was stepping toward the fight until Matthew firmly pulled her to a stop.

"Don't you dare, Caroline Murray!"

"Well, someone has to—"

"Enough!" David roared from where he stood on the nearby wagon bed. Thunder clapped as though all of heaven agreed with him. The feuders froze, then slowly began to separate into their different camps. "This is not the time for fighting. The fire isn't out yet. We need to remain alert. We also need to remain grateful. We prayed for rain. God sent rain. The least we can do is get along with each other long enough to appreciate that."

He turned to face the feuders more fully. "And when you feel like fighting, I want you to remember something. Y'all could have lost everything tonight. More than some fence posts and a few outbuildings. Y'all could have lost people. Real, living, breathing people. People who are your blood, your neighbors, your family in Christ. People who are more important than the disagreements you have with them and, therefore, deserve your respect and kindness—especially at a time like this."

The fight seemed to drain from the two families, but David continued, "Now, y'all can ignore all of that and choose to fight anyway. If that's what you want, then do it on your own time. The rest of us have families waiting and praying for our safe return. And we'd like to get home to them." With that, he hopped down from the wagon.

"He's right," Matthew seconded.

Another man called out, "Yeah, we came here to help. Not watch you fight."

Lula May stepped into the light looking as mud-spattered as Caroline was. "Speaking of helping, I think most of the ranchers in the LSCL are here. I'd like to call an impromptu meeting now. I propose that some of the money raised by the county fair and already designated to go to families in need be used to help the Hill and the Coleman families."

Dorothy let out a sigh of relief. "That would be a big help, Lula May."

Preacher Brandon Stillwater stepped forward. "I know I'm not a rancher, but may I suggest one stipulation? The two families must work together to rebuild and try to make peace with each other."

Tug frowned. "Now just a minute."

Matthew grinned. "That is a great idea."

David's older brother Josiah stepped forward. "As the owner of the town's lumber mill, I'm willing to give the league a discount on any lumber purchased to re-build the Hill and Coleman properties."

Lula May crossed her arms as she looked at her brother-in-law with amusement. "Thank you, Josiah. I appreciate the enthusiasm from the non-ranching folks, but this vote is for league members only. All those in favor say aye."

A collective aye resounded over the rain.

"Opposed?"

Not even Dorothy and Tug spoke up, though they both looked like they'd taken a big swig of pickle juice.

"The ayes have it. Now, let's get back to work and finish putting this fire out."

Folks began to disperse. Caroline watched David walk over to speak with Dorothy and Tug. She would have gone over to talk with Annie, but Matthew kept a firm hold on her arm, not trusting that the hostilities were truly over. After a couple of minutes, David shook hands with both of them, then joined her and Matthew. "I should have said something about the feud a long time ago, but I was hoping it would resolve itself."

Matthew nodded. "Same here. This is a good first step."

Caroline had never seen anything quite like the fight she'd just witnessed, and she was impressed by the way David had stood up for peace. Commenting on any of that was impossible at the moment. It was all she could do to keep her teeth from chattering loudly enough for them to hear. How on earth could they appear so unaffected by the chilling rain?

Matthew was the first to notice her plight. That was

likely due to the fact that he was still holding on to her arm. "David, Caroline's freezing. Since tomorrow is her day off, why don't I take her back to my place? You still have some clothes there—don't you, Caroline?"

"Yes, but the triplets will need me when they get back to the McKays'."

"I dropped everyone off at the Stillwater ranch, since it was farther from the fire and I knew the triplets would be comfortable with Louisa. She offered to keep them there overnight so they wouldn't have to be disturbed again." To David, he said, "I can bring Miss Ida and Maggie back to your place, then drop Emma off at mine before coming back here."

David agreed to the plan, and Matthew whisked her away. She was grateful for a quick escape. Even more so when Matthew didn't take the opportunity to ask her about whatever he might have picked up on between her and David. It was a little odd to be all by herself in her brother's house, but she made good use of the time. By the time Emma arrived home, Caroline was finished bathing and had changed into a nightgown.

Her sister-in-law, who was also dressed for bed in a robe tied around her protruding belly, immediately lowered herself to sit on the bed. "I wanted to see if you needed anything, since you weren't expecting to stay the night."

"That's sweet of you." She smiled at Emma in the mirror, then finished combing out her hair. "It was a bit of a nuisance to cart everything back and forth on the weekends, so I left some things here. I should have everything I need. How are you faring after the long wagon trip?"

"I'm fine. Glad to be home again. Glad this place is still standing. The rain is absolutely pouring down. Isn't it wonderful? I hope it keeps up." Emma rested a hand on her stomach and gave Caroline a curious look. "Matthew tells me there seem to be some sparks between you and David."

Of course he did. Caroline blew out a huff of air. She should have known she wouldn't get off the hook that easily. "I can't say he's wrong."

Emma's thoughtful silence was a little unnerving. She began to braid her hair. "You didn't seem very much in favor of a romance between David and me the last time we spoke of it."

"It isn't that I wasn't in favor of it. I just wanted you to be cautious. I didn't want to see you get hurt again."

"I don't think David would hurt me." She hesitated a moment, then admitted, "Honestly, I'm a little afraid of hurting him."

Emma frowned. "What do you mean?"

Caroline tied off the loose braid with a ribbon. She turned to face Emma. "There have been a few moments when…well, the thought has occurred to me that I might be in love with him."

Emma gasped. "Truly?"

"Yes, and sometimes I think he might love me."

"Then why aren't you over the moon?"

"I'm too busy being scared stiff." She hugged her arms around herself. "After what happened with Nico,

I'm not sure I should trust what my feelings are telling me."

Sympathy filled Emma's voice. "What are they telling you?"

"That what I have with David is real and right and true. That he can be trusted. Even if all of that is true, what am I supposed to do about it? This isn't my life, Emma. This isn't who I am. I'm a music teacher who lives in Austin. I sing at high-society recitals. I love children, but I'm not responsible for them. I send them home at the end of the day."

Caroline shook her head. "*If* David wants a wife—I'm not entirely sure he does, by the way—I'll also become an instant mother. As much as I care for Maggie, the reality of being anyone's instant mother is intimidating."

Emma placed a hand over her rounded stomach. "Now, that I can understand, but you've been wonderful with Maggie and the triplets. Challenging as it might be, I'm sure you'd be a wonderful mother."

"I hope so." That didn't make it any less intimidating, but it probably wasn't a good idea to go over all of that with a woman who would give birth relatively soon. With a shrug, Caroline moved on to the next problem. "Then there is the whole aspect of actually getting married. The mere idea of standing at another altar... I don't know if I'm ready for that, either. I thought it would be fine if David and I took things slowly, but our feelings aren't progressing slowly. There's also the fact that I don't really have much time left here. I'm supposed to be back in Austin to start rehearsing for the musical in two and a half weeks. I'd have a leading part that could lead to another leading part and another. Time is running out. I have to decide."

Emma was quiet for a moment. "To be honest, Caroline, it sounds like you already have."

Realization widened her eyes. She tested the thought and found safety in it. With a nod, she determined her course. "I'm going back to Austin."

## Chapter Fifteen

"How can you even say that?" David stared at Caroline. They'd both stopped at the head of the mud-logged trail leading into the woods. He'd been on his way out the door to check the level of the creek when Caroline had hinted she'd like to tag along. He'd been quick to invite her, since they'd barely had a chance to talk since the night of the fire. He'd seen her at church on Sunday, but she'd slipped away with Matthew and Emma before he'd had a chance to say anything other than a quick hello. She'd gone straight to her room once she'd arrived back at the ranch instead of joining in with the music-making with the ranch hands as she had last week. This morning she'd barely said two words at breakfast. Now he knew why.

"How long have you been planning to leave?" It was a stupid question to ask, but it was all his stunned brain could come up with.

Her gaze darted from his to stare through the rain

falling around them into the woods. "David, you knew this was a possibility from the first."

Her tone was conciliatory. He didn't want to be consoled. A sudden thought filled him with hope. "You're coming back, though, after the operetta is over?"

She gave a hesitant nod, then dashed his hopes. "To visit Matthew and Emma. Occasionally."

In other words, not to visit him and not to stay. He turned away from her, clenched his jaw and tried to think. It was hard to do when the woman he'd planned on marrying was breaking off their...what exactly? He hadn't gotten around to proposing, so they weren't engaged. They weren't even so much as officially courting. Yet she had his heart in her hands, and she knew that. He'd told her that the night of the fire. Or he would have if she'd allowed him to speak it. Instead he'd told her in his kiss. He'd thought the message was unmistakable. Maybe it hadn't been. Maybe she'd misunderstood. Maybe he needed to be clearer.

He let his umbrella fall to the ground, then ducked beneath hers. She didn't step away from him. She stood there with those mesmerizing hazel eyes of hers and let him search her face. Didn't she know he'd see through that veneer of calm to the uncertainty and love beneath?

He closed his eyes, committing what he'd seen to memory. He forced himself to calm down. She was running scared. That much was obvious. He should be making it harder for her to leave instead of easier. Being angry wouldn't accomplish that. Perhaps love could. Unfortunately, taking time to fortify himself had allowed her to do the same. Her expression had turned guarded.

He'd broken those walls down before. He could do it again. He fell back on her truth teller—touch.

He traced her cheekbone with a gentle brush of his fingers, remembering how he'd wiped the tears from that cheek the first time they'd met. His fingers rounded to capture her chin like he had the night before last when she'd stubbornly insisted on traveling with him to the fire. He lowered his forehead until it hovered near hers. Then he kissed her with all his heart and soul. She kissed him back.

That was when he knew.

For her, this was a kiss goodbye.

Unwilling to accept it, he moved his hand to the small of her back. He pressed her closer, but the kiss was bittersweet and he couldn't bear it. He let her go.

Their quickened breaths resounded over the steady rain. She'd lowered her umbrella at some point and, while she still held it in her grasp, it seemed all but forgotten. She released it to cradle his jaw. Sorrow filled her eyes and her voice. "I'm sorry, David. I do love—" She swallowed hard, then continued. "I do love this life I've been living, but it isn't mine. I didn't choose it. It just sort of happened to me."

He couldn't stop himself from taking her hand from his jaw to brush a kiss against it. Foolish as it might be, he might never have a chance to do it again. "Nothing is stopping you from choosing it now."

"You should be stopping me. I'm not the woman you need, David. We both know that."

He nearly laughed at the ridiculousness of her statement. "You're everything I need, Caroline Murray."

"David, don't. You aren't going to change my mind." She tugged her hand from his and said the words he'd known would be inevitable. "I'm leaving. In two weeks, I'll be boarding a train to Austin. Consider this my final notice. I'm staying for the triplets and Ida and Maggie. I don't want to leave them in a lurch. However, I think it's best that I stay at Matthew's from now on. I'll arrive in time for breakfast in the morning and leave after I put the triplets to bed. They're sleeping through the night now, so they won't know the difference."

It would be hard enough being around her during the day. He nodded. "That's probably for the best."

"No more kissing or holding hands or flirting of any kind. Don't look at me like that. This isn't about how your charm may or may not affect me. It's because anything less would be inappropriate for an employer and his employee. More important, I don't want to confuse Maggie. She knows nothing of this. I don't want that to change."

"I understand." He took a deep breath and forced the tension in his jaw to ease. "Just let me be the one to tell Maggie that you're leaving."

With a nod, she lifted her umbrella back into place and calmly walked back toward the house. He watched her until she disappeared behind a veil of rain. This was not how things were supposed to turn out. Yet she had made her decision and he had no choice but to accept it. There would be no trying to win her back for all the reasons she'd so aptly outlined. Their breakup had happened so fast. It seemed almost surreal.

He left his umbrella where it had fallen and walked

down to the creek. The water level was as high as one might expect it to be after the almost nonstop rain they'd had since Saturday night. He wasn't sure why he'd bothered to check in the first place. Maybe just to assure himself there would be some relief from the drought.

With that done, he left his umbrella in the house and grabbed his slicker instead. He rode with the ranch hands for most of the day. He didn't want to go back into the house, but he couldn't put it off any longer. A man had to eat.

Ignoring the music in the parlor, David slipped unnoticed into his room and changed into dry clothes. Caroline's melodic singing seeped through the closed door. It was too muffled for him to understand the lyrics. Nevertheless, her voice drew him. He crossed the hall to find a living picture of everything he'd hoped his future would hold.

His mother sat at the piano with Theo on her lap. He joined in the accompaniment by pressing a key or two whenever he so pleased. Meanwhile, Maggie helped Eli balance on his feet while also managing to do a little jig that really should have gone with a faster-tempo song than what was being sung. If his grin was any indication, Eli didn't seem to mind a bit.

David's gaze finally settled where it had wanted to all along. Caroline had Jasper perched on her hip with one arm securing him there while the other held his hand as though he were a full-size dance partner. She swayed back and forth as she continued singing, "Poor wandering one! If such poor love as mine can help thee find true peace of mind, why, take it. It is thine!"

David crossed his arms over his chest, steeling himself as she continued her melodic encouragements. His ma seemed to be the only one aware that he was standing there, but of course she was too busy playing the piano to do much else. Caroline whirled in a circle. "Take any heart—take mine!"

Her gaze finally caught upon his. She swallowed the next note. She blinked as a blush rose to her cheeks. "I'm sorry, David. Did we disturb you?"

Did she disturb him? He clenched his teeth as he faced the fact that he was a world-class idiot. Here he was nursing a broken heart over a woman who was in the next room dancing for joy and practicing the song she'd sing in the operetta she'd chosen over him. A punch in the gut would have been less painful. To his shame, his eyes began to smart. Not since Laura had he made this much of a fool of himself over a woman so utterly uncaring of the havoc she'd wrought in him.

"David." His mother's sharp voice drew his attention. "Don't you have that Lone Star Cowboy League meeting in town tonight?"

He nodded. Taking the excuse for what it was, he turned on his heel and grabbed his hat on the way out the door. He'd forgotten all about the meeting. Couldn't care less about it, to be honest. It was an escape, though, and one he sorely needed.

David slipped into the back of the church right as Lula May called the meeting to order. He had a hard time concentrating on any of it until Casper Magnuson took the floor. The man cleared his voice a few times, but it still shook a little as he spoke. "I don't know how many of y'all have heard the news, but Saul Hauser got caught in a gully washer last night. He drowned."

David was stunned. He could hardly comprehend it. The weather had gone from a drought to a flood capable of drowning a man in a matter of days. It was stranger still to know Saul was dead. He'd seen the man at church yesterday. They had only been nodding acquaintances if that. Still, David's voice added to the murmur of sympathy and concern that swept through the crowd.

Casper swallowed hard. "Saul was a good man. He was my best friend. He was also a widower with three children."

A widower with children. Gone in a matter of moments. His children left to the mercy of those in the community. David's heart gave a little flip, then sank to his stomach. He stopped slouching in his seat and grasped on to the back of the pew in front of him.

Casper stared at the floor. "My wife and I have taken them in for now. With four teenagers of our own, we can't afford to keep them long-term. The reality of the situation has made me realize that...well..."

Casper glanced up and met David's gaze. "I was wrong to shoot down David McKay's idea of a children's home. We need one in this community. I know that financing it could be a challenge, but I think it ought to be reconsidered."

Shocked, David glanced around the room to find that everyone looked as surprised at the turn of events as David felt. Even so, David squared his shoulders and met the challenge head-on when Casper gave David a prodding nod. David stood. "Casper was right to worry about the financial aspects of the children's home project the first time. I admit that I got caught up in the idea. It ran away with me. My feet are firmly planted in reality now."

David squared his shoulders. "We don't need a lot of bells and whistles to make the idea work. Children in dire need don't care about those things. All they want is a roof over their head, food in their belly and someone to love them. The Lone Star Cowboy League can provide that. Perhaps not entirely on our own, but if we coordinate the effort and open it up to the community, I believe we can find a way."

"I'll help," Brandon Stillwater said from the back of the church. He'd joked before about how being the pastor gave him the prerogative to sit in on any meeting taking place inside the church. David was glad Brandon had chosen to do so this time for the preacher continued. "I'll lead the community involvement for the undertaking if David leads it for the LSCL. Between all of us, we'll find a way to make it happen."

David shot his friend a grin and gave him a grateful nod before glancing back at Casper. Even Casper, grieving as he was, seemed unable to hold back a smile. He turned to Lula May. "Shall we bring it to a vote?"

It passed unanimously.

Little Horn was getting a children's home. After promising to get together to discuss the details soon, Brandon left with Casper to help comfort the bereaved children. David stayed to talk with anyone and everyone who approached him, wanting to put off retuning home for as long as possible. He tensed when Matthew approached, then released a breath of relief when the man merely congratulated him on the children's home idea before moving on.

By the time David arrived back at the ranch, everyone had gone to sleep. He padded up the stairs to check on Maggie. She was only half asleep and reached out her hand toward him. He took it as he kneeled beside her bed. "I'm sorry I missed tucking you in."

She pointed to her forehead. He leaned over to give it a kiss. She sighed, then took her hand back to snuggle it under her pillow. "Why are you mad at Miss Caroline?"

He smiled. Leave it to his daughter to cut right to the chase. "That's grown-up business, sweetheart. Nothing you need to worry about."

She stared into his eyes through her sleep-laden lashes. Something she saw there must have prompted her suspicion. Her brow furrowed. Her mouth stretched into a frown as desperation filled her voice. "Please don't be mad at Miss Caroline. I love her. I want her to be my mommy."

"Maggie," he said as gently as possible. "Miss Caroline has to go back to Austin in a couple of weeks. We knew that all along."

"No."

"Yes." His tone brokered no argument, then softened again. "We enjoyed having her here. I want you to keep enjoying it until the very last minute before she leaves. Promise?"

"Yes, but—"

"Hush, baby." His fingers trembled slightly as they smoothed over her brow. "Go to sleep."

"I want a mommy. I want Miss Caroline. Please, Daddy." Her eyes filled with tears that spilled over. "I've waited and waited and prayed and prayed."

He swallowed hard against the lump in his throat. "I know, baby. I know. I'm sorry."

He wiped away the tears on her cheeks and hushed her again. Then because it worked for the triplets, he sang Maggie a quiet lullaby until she went to sleep. He waited a few more minutes before sneaking out of the room. He closed the door softly behind him. His hand covered his aching heart as he padded down the stairs to his room. He sat on his bed and stared unseeingly into the darkness.

"Lord, what do I do?" he whispered.

The echo of Maggie's words seemed to fill the darkness. *I want a mommy. I want Miss Caroline. Please, Daddy.*

He lit the lamp on his nightstand, then opened the first drawer. Moving his Bible aside, he picked up the letter beneath it. Elizabeth Dumont—willing to accept a business arrangement instead of a marriage. Ready to come as soon as he sent for her. It was almost too easy.

Maggie would have the mother she longed for. He'd have the assurance that he wouldn't leave his daughter an orphan should the worst ever happen. His mother would have the help she needed around the house. The triplets would have a caretaker until the children's home was built or they found a permanent family. As for Elizabeth, she would sleep in the nursery. He could smile, be polite and kind. He wouldn't have to trust her with his heart. He'd know better than to love her. He'd treat her as he would a sister. He could even go so far as to give her a kiss on the cheek at the wedding.

This was the solution. No more doubting or procrastinating. He'd made his decision.

The very next morning he sent Elizabeth a telegram apologizing for, though not explaining, the delay and asking her to come. An hour later, she responded that she would. She'd need a week to wrap up her affairs, then she'd travel to Little Horn. He wired her the money for the trip.

It was done.

Now he just had to share the news with Maggie and his mother and put his broken heart back together before she arrived.

Caroline arrived at the McKay ranch the next morning with no small amount of trepidation. Yesterday had been difficult to say the least. Her mind kept circling back to the moment she'd finally noticed David standing in the doorway of the parlor. It was obvious what his impression of her lighthearted act had been. That was all it had been, though. An act. She hadn't been Caroline in that moment. She'd been trying to portray Mabel—a carefree, innocent, if slightly dim, character from the operetta. Apparently, she'd assumed the part a little too well.

Surely David thought she was heartless, that she'd been playing with his affections this entire time. She might not be willing to trust her feelings or follow where her heart was leading her, but that didn't mean she was emotionless. Although, truth be told, she did feel rather numb and confused.

She'd never had the ability to hurt anyone. No one had cared enough to give her that much power over their emotions. It was a strange feeling and one she abhorred, to be the cause of someone else's heartbreak. Yesterday, it had taken all her strength not to rush after him and do everything she could to ease his pain even if it meant making promises she shouldn't keep.

With a tremulous sigh, she braced herself against whatever the day might bring and paused on the porch to remove her muddy boots. She entered the house feeling more like the visitor she'd first been than the almost family she'd like to think she'd become. She padded past David's closed bedroom door to step into the kitchen. Ida glanced up from the open oven with a friendly "Good morning."

"Good morning." She scanned the rest of the room.

"David has already left—probably for the day. Though why he needed to go to town in this weather is beyond me."

Caroline rubbed away the few drops of rain still clinging to her arms. "I never said I was looking for David."

"Looking to avoid him, more likely. That must have been quite a fight y'all had." Ida removed the pan of biscuits from the oven and set it on the stovetop. Glancing over her shoulder, she lifted an eyebrow. "Oh, don't look so surprised. I know y'all were courting."

"How did you know? Did he tell you?"

"He didn't need to tell me. I have eyes, don't I?" Ida turned to face Caroline, then leaned back against the counter. "So what happened?"

"I told him I was going home in two weeks." She took an apron from the drawer and tied it around her waist. "I shouldn't have gotten involved in the first place when my real life is in Austin."

"Your real life? Hmm. And what have you been living since you came to Little Horn?"

"A sabbatical of sorts. I suppose?" She opened the can of peaches.

"I see." Ida turned away and began cracking eggs into a mixing bowl. "So now it's over and you're going back to Austin."

"That sums it up." Caroline found a small jar and drained the peach syrup into it.

For a moment the only sound in the kitchen was the rasp of Ida whisking the eggs while Caroline chopped the fruit. Finally, Ida glanced up at her with a smile that was half amused, half compassionate. "Are you telling me my son really believed that load of nonsense?"

Caroline froze. "Nonsense? It isn't nonsense. It's the truth."

"The truth." Releasing a soft laugh, she set down the whisk to look at her. "Do you know that in the entire time you've lived in this house you haven't mentioned the name of one single friend waiting for you to return to Austin?"

"I…" Caroline set the knife aside and leaned her

hip against the counter. "What does that have to do with anything?"

Ida's voice softened. "Who was the maid of honor at your wedding?"

"I didn't have one." She rushed to explain. "Nico didn't have a best man, either, though. Neither of us felt it was necessary."

Ida nodded. "Is there anyone you're particularly looking forward to seeing when you get back to Austin?"

"My parents."

"Are you close to them?"

"No, I'm not close to my parents." The truth was she hardly saw them even though she lived in their house. That had always been the case, so she was used to it.

"And your former fiancé? Was he your first beau?"

"Yes." He was the first man who'd ever cared about her. Only, he hadn't cared, had he? She frowned. "Why are you asking me all of this?"

"I'm trying to find out if my suspicions about you are true."

"What suspicions are those?" She folded her arms while fighting away the tears trying to blur the edges of her vision. "That no one in my life cares about me?"

"Oh, dear, of course not." Ida reached out to touch Caroline's arm. "My suspicion was only that you are far too used to being alone."

What was the use of denying it anymore? She turned back to the peaches and began to chop them with too much force. "I suppose your suspicions are right, then. I am used to being alone—so much so that I hardly notice it anymore."

Would that still be true when she went back? Or would the time she'd spent here make the aloneness all the more acute? She shook away the thought. "Maybe that's why it was so easy for Nico to become my whole world. There was no one else in it."

"But that isn't true anymore. You have plenty of people in your life who love you. It's just that most of them happen to be right here in Little Horn." Ida frowned at Caroline's disbelieving laugh. "It's true. You have friends here with the potential to make even more. You have family here—your brother and his wife with a brand-spanking-new niece or nephew on the way who will be predisposed to love you, too. And you have the McKays.

"Caroline, each one of us loves you—especially my son." Ida shook her head in amazement. "I've never seen him as happy and content as he was when the two of you were together. I've also never seen him so utterly distracted by a woman. He couldn't keep his eyes off you."

She found herself searching Ida's sincere brown eyes. "Really?"

Ida smiled and gave a small nod. "Caroline, my dear, it would be a real shame to throw all of that away. Especially if it's only for the sake of returning to your former life because that's what is normal and expected of you by people more concerned with themselves than with your best interest. Who are you trying to make happy with that decision, by the way? It doesn't seem to be you because, despite what David might have seen yesterday, you've looked plumb miserable."

Caroline sighed. "I don't think I'm trying to please anyone. It's just that… I'm scared. I've never cared about anyone like this before. The closest I came was with Nico. I couldn't stand it if this blew up in my face like that did. It would be so much easier to walk away now before it has the chance."

"What does God have to say about that?"

"I'm not sure. I've prayed for direction, but…" She shrugged. "Sometimes God uses circumstances to provide direction, like me getting that role in the operetta."

"True. And sometimes circumstances distract us from what God is truly trying to lead us to do."

"How do we know the difference?"

"We stop listening up here." Ida gently tapped Caroline's forehead. "And listen down here."

Caroline lifted a brow as Ida poked her. "With our stomachs?"

Ida laughed. "No, with our spirit. There's a verse in the Bible that says it's the Holy Spirit that works within us to will and to do according to His good purposes. Submit your will to His. Follow His peace."

The sound of the front door opening and closing brought the conversation to a halt. David had returned. Her resistance melted a little more at the sight of him. His face was a study of weariness and defeat. His broad shoulders tensed when he caught sight of her before he seemed to consciously make them relax. He ran his fingers through his hair. "It's a maelstrom out there."

Ida shook her head. "There's no sign of it slowing down?"

"Not in the least." David finally met Caroline's gaze. "How did you get here?"

"Matthew brought me by the main road. He didn't trust the creek."

He gave a nod of approval. "It's probably ready to overflow its banks by now."

"Caroline, did you hear David's big news?"

She shook her head. She didn't bother to mention that this was the first time they'd really spoken since she'd ended their courtship. Instead she looked to him for clarification. "The LSCL decided to go ahead with the children's home after all."

"Oh, that's wonderful!" Knowing how much that must mean to him, she reached out to squeeze his arm.

He smiled and all the trouble between them seemed to melt away for one brief, shining moment. Then his gaze clouded. It faltered. He glanced down at the hand she'd placed on his arm. No touching. That had been their agreement. She wasn't sure what was worse—that she'd been the first who crossed the line or that she'd been the one to draw it in the first place.

She forced herself to release him and take a step back. "I should go check on the triplets."

Sounding slightly amused, Ida said, "Yes, and send Maggie down, too."

Caroline was nearly at the top of the stairs before she heard Ida say, "She's in love with you, you know."

David's voice was more like a growl. "I'm not having this discussion."

"Good. Don't talk. Just listen and think about it from her perspective…"

"Oh, Ida," Caroline whispered in exasperation. Shaking her head at Ida's meddling, she knocked on Maggie's door. "Wake up, sleepyhead."

When the girl didn't respond, Caroline opened the door. The covers of the bed had been thrown back. Her nightgown lay in a puddle on the bed. Dresser drawers were pulled halfway out of the chest as if the girl had donned her clothes in a hurry. The window was open, allowing the storm to spit its fury all over the room.

Alarm filled Caroline. "David!" she shouted. "Maggie's gone."

# Chapter Sixteen

David's running steps pounded up the stairs. Caroline turned in time to see him scan the room as he entered it. His eyes took in every detail, then settled on the open window. He caught hold of Caroline's arms, though whether that was to steady her or himself she couldn't tell. Murmuring his daughter's name, he strode past Caroline and peered into the storm before closing the widow. A hint of desperation filled his voice. "She never leaves by the window unless she's going someplace she shouldn't."

Ida stepped inside the room. "Where would that be this time?"

His gaze shifted to Maggie's bed. "I think she's headed to Matthew's ranch."

"Why my brother's place?"

"To see you."

Caroline shook her head. "Why would she go there if she knew I was coming back early this morning?"

"She was upset. Last night I told her you were leaving."

"Last night?" Ida's voice took on a frantic tone as she picked up Maggie's nightgown. "You think she's been gone since last night?"

"She didn't make it to Matthew's before I left, so maybe she hasn't been gone long."

David rubbed a hand over his temple. "Or she could have taken her usual shortcut along the creek."

The path that Matthew and David both felt the flooding had made too dangerous to traverse? Caroline bit her lip. "We don't know that for sure."

"You're right. We need to search the woods. I'll rally the men." He strode toward the door, then paused in the doorway. "Ma, will you stay here in case she comes back? Caroline—"

"I'm going with you."

A hint of a smile briefly curved his lips. "I know. Come on."

She hurried down the stairs at his heels and saddled up alongside his ranch hands. David even lent her a gun to signal with after she assured him Matthew had taught her how to use one before he'd moved away from Austin. David also made sure she was equipped with a rope and a rolled-up blanket. He gave her a boost into the saddle, then tucked her foot into the stirrup.

His hand lingered there. "Be careful, Caroline. Don't take any chances. The woods are flooded. Not just the creek. If you can't tell how deep the water is in a particular spot, go around it, not through it. Understand?"

He waited for her to nod before he turned away to mount his horse. They all rode out, each one of them peeling off from the group as David assigned them an area to search. He kept her on the same side of the creek he was on but urged her to check the woods while he traveled nearer the creek bed. The creek had already swollen to twice its normal size. She led her mount away from it and into the waterlogged woods.

As she picked her way around puddles and downed branches, her voice merged with the others shouting Maggie's name. She came to what appeared to be a shallow lake of floodwater that stretched twenty or thirty yards in front of her. She scoured the water in case Maggie had gotten stranded somewhere near its center, then heeded David's warning by going around it. The other voices faded away until she could hear only her own. "Maggie! Maggie, where are you?"

Through the rain, her gaze latched on to a flash of white against the muddy browns and greens of the flooded forest. A crumpled figure huddled at the base of a tree. "Maggie!"

Caroline urged her mount up the small rise toward the girl. After all but leaping from the horse, Caroline ran the last few feet, then dropped to her knees beside Maggie. The child was curled up in a little ball with her head resting on a bed of leaves. She appeared to be sleeping or unconscious. She placed a hand on the child's back and shook her slightly. "Maggie, wake up. Maggie?"

Maggie's lashes lifted. Her blue eyes focused on Caroline's face. She gasped in a breath and threw herself into Caroline's arms. Eyes filling with tears, Caroline held her tight. She swallowed against the ache of emotion in her throat. "Are you all right?"

Maggie nodded against the curve of her neck. "I was on my way to see you, but there's water everywhere. I slipped in the mud and hurt my ankle. After a while, I got tired of hopping, so I sat down to rest. Guess I fell asleep."

"Let me see your ankle." Caroline eased back enough to press a kiss to the girl's dirt-streaked forehead, then gently probed the ankle Maggie presented to her. It was swollen, but not broken as far as Caroline could tell. "Let's leave the boot on until we get back home, then we'll ask the doctor to check on it. Do you think you can walk to the horse with my help?"

"What horse?"

"That one." Caroline turned to point only to find there was no horse behind her or anywhere in view for that matter. She let out a disbelieving huff of a laugh. The horse must have kept right on going after Caroline had dismounted. And why not? She hadn't taken the time to tie off the mare. This was really no laughing matter.

Without the horse and the supplies it carried, she had no way to signal David and his men. She had no blanket to put around Maggie's shivering shoulders. She had no way to transport Maggie back to the house. Asking Maggie to walk on an injured ankle could easily injure it more. It would also make their progress incredibly slow.

She offered the girl a playful smile to cover her panic. "How would you like a piggyback ride?"

With Maggie safely stowed on her back, Caroline set off in the direction of the house. She made the long trek around the lake, making her way closer to the creek in the hopes that they might run into one of the men before they reached the house. There was no one in sight once they emerged near the creek.

Panting slightly from carrying Maggie, Caroline set her down. "Let's rest for a minute and try calling out for the men. Here—lean against this tree to keep the weight of your foot."

The creek seemed to rise two inches for every minute they lingered. Caroline couldn't risk staying any longer. Besides, she felt sufficiently recovered to make it the rest of the way home. "Hop on my back again, Maggie."

She'd barely made it a step before an odd rumble filled the air. *Thunder? No.* The sound wasn't coming from the sky. It was coming from the creek.

A brown layer of branches, dirt and debris turned the curve of the creek and marched across the top of the water. Maggie stiffened. "It's a gully washer! Run!"

Matthew had told her a rancher had died from one just the other day. According to her brother, they were nigh on impossible to outrun even without a child on one's back and Maggie would never be able to run fast enough with a bad ankle. Caroline turned on her heel and released Maggie's legs. Catching the girl's waist, Caroline positioned her beneath the lowest-hanging tree branch. "Climb the tree, Maggie. Climb!"

She boosted Maggie into the air. Maggie caught the branch and swung herself up into the tree. Sprained ankle seemingly forgotten, she scurried to the next highest branch. "Hurry, Miss Caroline!"

Caroline hopped up to catch the branch, then kicked against the tree trunk to haul herself into its branches. "Keep going! Find the strongest branch. Careful now."

Caroline split her attention between Maggie and the oozing brown muck that bumped against the bottom of the tree with an alarming amount of force. The branches, logs and rocks in its flow would have pulverized her. Maggie called, "Is this high enough?"

She glanced up to find the girl a few more feet overhead. Wishing they'd been close to a tree larger than the one they'd claimed, Caroline climbed to a branch near Maggie's. "This is fine for now."

The flow beneath them changed to a faster-moving mud, then brown water swept beneath them. It turned into a raging torrent, crashing and splashing ever harder against the base of their tree as it tore downriver. Maggie's terrified gaze found hers. "It's shaking the tree."

"Hold on tight."

Maggie nodded. The girl edged closer to the trunk. Her little knuckles turned white as she held on to her branch. Maggie was so busy staring down at the churning water beneath them that she didn't see the tree just upriver from them. It tilted, then fell into the creek with a loud splash. Dread filled Caroline. Her body began to shake. She moved from her branch to Maggie's. It was sturdy enough to hold them both with no trouble. The tree shuddered as the other one banged into it on its way past. Meanwhile, Caroline did her best to cocoon Maggie with her own body. She kissed Maggie's cheek. "I love you, Maggie."

Maggie glanced back at her in delight. "I love you, too, Miss Caroline."

She kept her voice as calm as possible. "I want you to hold tight to this tree until someone rescues you, all right? Hold tight. No matter what. Even if it falls."

"If it falls?" Maggie stiffened in alarm as the tree shuddered again, then began to tilt.

"Tight grip. Relax your body. Tuck your head."

Maggie did as instructed. Caroline prepared herself to break the girl's fall as best she could. The world turned sideways. Air rushed past them. Maggie's scream filled her ear. All Caroline could think was that Ida was right. This was real—this life, her feelings for David, all of it. She loved him. She had for some time. She simply hadn't wanted to accept it. Now it was too late.

They hit the creek. Pain lanced her body. The world was nothing but water. And she was drowning in it. *No.* She couldn't. Not yet. Not until Maggie was safe.

Her grasp tightened on the branch above her. She hauled herself upward. A watery scream wrenched from her lungs at the overwhelming pain that throbbed in her other arm at the movement. It was cut short as she broke the surface of the water and coughed out muddy water. "Maggie!"

The girl was clinging to the tree trunk beside her. Blood smeared across her bottom lip. She spoke not a word. Her terrified gaze clung to Caroline's, seeking reassurance. Their locked eyes jarred apart as the trunk crashed into something. Maggie screamed. And as they careened down the river at breakneck speed, Caroline prayed for rescue.

* * *

David and his men had searched the creek all the way to Matthew's property without finding any sign of Maggie. Now it seemed that Caroline was missing, as well. Clenching the reins in his fist, David watched the debris flow of the gully washer roll downstream from the safety of a nearby hill. Isaiah had sounded the alarm early enough for them to get out of its way and had continued on by horse to warn the folks at the Murray ranch.

Meanwhile, David couldn't stop worrying about Caroline and Maggie. The words came out through gritted teeth before he could stop them. "Where are they?"

"Maybe they're together," Ephraim suggested.

"Then why didn't Caroline signal?"

Ephraim didn't have an answer to that, but Joaquin took up where he left off. "We've searched by the creek and Maggie wasn't there, so she shouldn't be in harm's way. Neither should Caroline if she was searching the woods where you sent her."

David appreciated the comfort his men were trying to offer, but there was no shaking the uneasy feeling in his gut. "Something isn't right. We need to keep looking for them. Just stay clear of the creek."

As they headed toward the woods, screams sounded over the rumble of the water. His heart leaped into his throat. "Maggie!"

He turned his horse and galloped toward the sound. He was running toward the creek with a rope in hand when his daughter rounded a curve in the creek. His little girl was caught in the rushing floodwaters with the woman he loved clinging to the branch beside her. Everything around him slowed down, compressing until the world consisted of only them and the danger they were in. "Caroline! Maggie! Catch the rope!"

Maggie didn't hear him, but Caroline did. Her eyes met his with a mixture of hope, relief and panic. She said something to Maggie to make the girl cling to her. David tossed the lariat with a cattleman's precision. Caroline released the branch to grab it. Her face blanched at the movement even as she instructed Maggie to hold on to the rope, too.

David hesitated, not wanting to pull too hard on the rope and accidentally wrench it out of Caroline's hand. Thankfully, with him anchoring the rope, the river moved them closer to the banks in its effort to carry them downstream. It also did everything it could to pull him into its clutches, as well. Joaquin stepped in front of David to add his strength to the effort. David cautioned him, "Don't pull it. Just hold it."

"We'll hold it still," Joaquin said as Ephraim took his place on the rope, as well. "Go get them, *jefe*."

David didn't need to be told twice. He left the rope in their hands and rushed to the river. The current was swift, but his determination to reach Caroline and Maggie was stronger. He met them in waist-deep water.

"Daddy!" Maggie lunged for him.

He grabbed her before she could be carried downstream. He shifted her to one side and caught up with Caroline, who had drifted closer to the shore. "Are y'all hurt?"

Caroline gave a single nod. "My arm. Maggie's ankle. Is that all, sweetheart?"

Maggie nodded. David helped Caroline stand. With her good arm around his shoulder and his around her waist, he walked them out of the water. "How bad is Maggie's ankle?"

"Probably sprained." She bit out the winded words, betraying her own pain.

"Your arm?"

She swallowed hard. "Maybe broken."

Joaquin was already coiling up the rope. "Should I get the doctor?"

"Yes. Bring him to the house." Feeling the way they both trembled in his arms. "Ephraim, the blankets?"

Ephraim was already grabbing them from his and David's saddles. Joaquin passed his to Ephraim, then rode off toward the town. Caroline wobbled a little. "I need to sit down a moment."

David sank to the ground with her and watched her in concern as he hugged Maggie closer. The girl seemed completely spent. He wrapped her in the blankets Ephraim gave him, while the man placed the other one around Caroline's back. Ephraim nodded toward Caroline's arm. "Do you want me to bring the wagon?"

"I can ride." Caroline pulled the blanket closer around her. "My arm will hurt no matter what, but the sooner we're away from the creek, the better."

David nodded. Caroline was right. They needed to get to safety, and Maggie needed to get warmed up as soon as possible. "Ephraim, if you'll take Maggie, I'll help Caroline. Don't wait for us. Go by the road and bring Maggie to her grandmother."

"Yes, sir. Let's go, Magpie."

Maggie easily went to the ranch hand she'd known most of her life, and the two were soon riding off on Ephraim's horse. David followed them with Caroline. He set a much slower pace, not wanting to cause Caroline any more discomfort than necessary. With that same intention, he led her to his room rather than to the nursery. She stopped short as they entered the room. "David, I can't stay here."

"This will be the easiest place for the doctor to set your arm, and it will afford you the most privacy."

She gave a slow nod but continued to stand in the door awkwardly. "I'm drenched and muddy. I don't want to dirty anything."

"It's probably best for you to wait to change clothes until after the doctor sets your arm. I don't mind the dirt, though. Everything can be washed." He pulled back the hunter-green-and-dark-blue quilt on his bed to reveal the blue sheets underneath, then swept his arm toward it.

She merely perched on the edge. "I'm too nervous to lie down. I've never broken my arm before. No. Don't look at it. It's unnatural looking, ugly."

"You broke your arm trying to help my daughter, didn't you?"

"I— Yes," she said as she pulled the blanket more securely in front of it to block it from view.

"Then it isn't ugly. It's a testament to your bravery, dedication and caring."

"I'm sorry I got us caught in the flood. I found Maggie, but the horse ran off with our supplies. I went to the creek because the woods were flooded. I hoped to find you or one of the ranch hands."

He kneeled down in front of her. "No one expected that gully washer, Caroline. It isn't your fault. You have nothing to blame yourself for."

"I exercised poor judgment."

"No. You made the best decision you could at the time with the facts you had. Things didn't turn out the way you hoped. That doesn't mean the decision itself was bad. That doesn't mean you're to blame for the unexpected outcome. There are a lot of things I wish I could do over in life, but we can't be omnipotent. We don't know the end from the beginning. We can't change the past. We just have to learn from our mistakes and move on." He paused, then shook his head and offered a self-deprecating smile. "I don't know why I'm saying all this."

"I do." She carefully scooted a bit closer. "You're saying it because I need to hear it. I've been blaming myself for what happened with Nico. So much so that I've tried to do everything I can not to repeat that mistake—even if that meant pushing you away."

Cautious hope sprang in his chest, but he ignored it to stay focused on getting through to her. "Please tell me you will finally accept that you weren't at fault for that. Nico was a con artist. You weren't his first victim, but you were his last. Didn't Matthew tell you that?"

She shook her head. "I think he started to, but I told him I didn't want to hear about anything having to do with Nico."

"Well, it's true, and Nico will be paying for his crimes against you and everyone else he took advantage of."

"I don't want to be a victim anymore," she said thoughtfully, softly. Then her eyes took on a new light. "Do you know what I was thinking about when the tree we were in toppled into the water?"

"You were in a tree that toppled over?" Alarm filled his voice as he glanced at where the blanket covered her arm. "No wonder you broke your arm. You must have been terrified."

"I thought I was going to die. I *could* have died. All I could think about in that moment was how wrong I'd been about you, about everything. I wanted a chance to tell you how sorry I am for hurting you, for making you feel as though you weren't enough or that what we had wasn't real. The truth is I've never felt this way about anyone before. It scared me, but I don't want to be afraid anymore. I want this. I want you. David—"

A knock on the half-open door announced Ida's arrival only an instant before she stepped inside with a steaming mug of tea. David stood and released Caroline's good hand, though he had no idea when he'd reached for it. Ida hesitated as she glanced back and forth between them. "I'm sorry. I didn't mean to interrupt. I wanted to check on Caroline, but I see she's being taken good care of."

David turned away and rubbed the back of his neck. Still reeling from Caroline's words, he was grateful for the moment to gather himself. She seemed sincere. He wanted to trust that she was. Still, he wasn't sure his heart could take it if she changed her mind again.

His mother chatted on. "Here you go, Caroline. Some cinnamon tea to warm you on the inside, since we can't do much for the outside yet."

"It's delicious. Thank you, Ida."

"You're welcome. I'm so sorry you broke your arm, but I'm glad you're all right otherwise. Now, I have to get back to Maggie." Ida's wave fluttered in his periphery vision. "Y'all go back to whatever you two were doing."

With that, Ida left as quickly as she'd appeared. Her footsteps retreated upstairs until they no longer filled the silence between him and Caroline. He turned to her again with his defenses rising. In contrast, her eyes were a study in vulnerability. Her hair was a mess of mud-streaked brown waves spilling from their normal style to rest about the shoulders of her tattered dress. Her face was leeched of its usual color and tense from pain. Yet she watched him as though he was the only thing that mattered. Finally, she spoke with calm assurance. "I love you, David."

"Will you marry me?" The words came out before he realized she'd slipped past his defenses. They were an automatic response to her confession because he wanted proof. He wanted to know with certainty that she wouldn't recant her words. Still, the proposal took him by surprise as much as it did her. He recovered first.

Taking the mug of tea from her hand, he set it on the nightstand. He went down on one knee before her. He caught hold of her uninjured arm and trailed his hand down until it caught hers. He kissed it. Capturing her gaze, he urged, "Marry me."

Uncertainty flickered in her eyes. Only then did he realize how much he was asking her to give up—the operetta, her home, living near her parents. He was asking her to take on a lot, too—a daughter, a live-in mother-in-law, ranch life, small-town living. It might be too much. If so, he'd rather know it now. Would she stay with him? Was she ready to be his now and forever?

Her lips tilted into a beautiful smile. "Yes, I'll marry you."

Relief and joy overcame his caution. He rose just enough to kiss her. His arms began to close around her, but he remembered her injury in time to stop himself from hurting her. Instead he planted his hands on the bed on either side of her, framing her in. He kissed her again, then pulled back just enough to ask, "When?"

"Hmm?"

He couldn't help smiling because she sounded a little dazed. He gently bumped his nose against hers. "When will you marry me?"

"Oh, I don't know." Her free hand tangled in the back of his hair. "Is tomorrow too soon?"

"Not for me, but you'll need some time to recover from today." Still, he had no intention of waiting for long. "How about Saturday?"

She stilled, then pulled back a little more. Probably to see if he was serious. "Saturday? Four days from now Saturday?"

"I'll take care of everything. You would only need to rest and decide what to wear."

She blinked thoughtfully. "I suppose my parents could make it here by then if they wanted."

"Then it's settled?"

"Saturday," she repeated almost as though she wasn't sure how she'd gotten herself into this. "Why so soon?"

"You almost died today. I almost died last week. I don't want to waste any more time."

She seemed to melt a little at that. Finally, she nodded. "I don't, either. Saturday it is."

He moved in for another kiss. A pounding on the front door brought him up short. "That must be the doctor."

Her eyes widened with a hint of panic. "You'll stay with me while he's here?"

"If you want me to."

"I do." She caught his shirt and tugged him forward to kiss him briefly. "I love you."

The knock sounded again along with footsteps on the stairs as his mother called out that she was coming. Unwilling to be caught in an embrace just yet, David moved away and met Ida in the hall.

Then the doctor took charge of everything. Caroline maintained a brave face while the doctor set her arm, though she couldn't stop the tears. Matthew arrived while the doctor was finishing up on the cast. David went upstairs with the doctor to check on Maggie. The girl had fallen asleep and barely awakened enough to see that her ankle was being wrapped before snuggling back into her covers.

While Ida took care of the triplets, David walked the doctor out to the porch and paid him for his trouble. David stepped back inside just as Matthew closed the bedroom door softly behind him. "The pain medicine put her to sleep. I didn't know if you wanted me to move her to the nursery or take her home."

"She's fine where she is. We'll see how she feels after she's had some sleep and go from there."

Matthew nodded. "She told me congratulations are in order."

"Thank you," he said, though he knew full well Matthew hadn't offered his. "I'm sorry I didn't wait to speak with you or your father. It all happened pretty quickly once I found out she'd almost died today. I don't want to waste any time."

Finally, Matthew grinned. "You aren't. Want me to send a telegram to my folks?"

*Telegram.* Realization flashed through David even as he nodded. "That would be great."

"I'll be back to check on Caroline after dinner."

"Sounds good," David said despite the fact he could barely hear over the roar of panic in his ears. He closed the door behind Matthew and just stood there a minute. "I have two fiancés."

How in the world had this happened? Well, he knew how it had happened. He'd sent for a mail-order bride, then he'd proposed to Caroline. Elizabeth Dumont hadn't even crossed his mind. He hadn't been thinking. He'd been feeling. It was what he'd always done when it came to women. He'd hoped he'd grown out of it. Apparently not.

There was only one solution. He'd wire the mail-order bride and tell her not to come. It had been only two days since he'd sent the telegram. She'd needed a week to prepare for the trip, so she wouldn't be on her way yet.

No one ever need know. That was a good thing because he couldn't imagine trying to explain this to Caroline. After what she'd been through with Nico, it could easily make her bolt. The last thing he wanted was to give her a reason to change her mind…and break his heart.

# Chapter Seventeen

Her parents weren't able to arrive until the night before the wedding. Their train had been delayed, so it was too late for them to have supper with the McKays as planned. Instead Emma fixed them a quick dinner, then retreated to her bedroom to work on the wedding dress Caroline's mother, Priscilla, had brought with her. Although Caroline hadn't seen her parents in a month, she almost wished she could slip away, too.

Priscilla's blond hair glinted in the lamplight as her green eyes watched Caroline in concern. "My poor girl. It's so unfortunate that you broke your arm. You couldn't possibly take on the role of Mabel in *The Pirates of Penzance* now."

Caroline shrugged her left shoulder—the one not attached to the broken arm. "No. I suppose I couldn't, but I'm getting married. That's hardly a disappointment."

A beat of silence filled the parlor. Priscilla bit her lip. Caroline's father shifted uncomfortably on the settee beside his wife. Matthew, who sat in a chair across from Caroline, narrowed his eyes at his parents. Caroline met her mother's gaze in defiance. "Well, it might be disappointing to you, but it isn't to me."

"I never said it was disappointing," Priscilla protested. "It's only that…he's a rancher!

Matthew straightened in his chair. "What's wrong with being a rancher?"

"Why, nothing, of course. It's only that Caroline isn't like you. She loves music." Priscilla turned toward her. "Are you really willing to give that up?"

"I wouldn't be giving it up. The McKays have a piano that I've been using. I'm sure David would support me giving lessons on it if that's what I wished. You should hear him play the guitar. He's amazing. It's one of the first things that drew me to him. That and his voice. It's untrained but beautiful."

Lawrence rubbed a hand over his chin. "I suppose that's something."

"Yes, and Maggie has a sweet alto. I've already started voice lessons with her."

That perked her father's interest. "Have you?"

"Ida plays the piano. All of his ranch hands play instruments, as well. Living at the ranch, I'm surrounded by music." As opposed to living at her parents' home in Austin, where she'd often been surrounded by a silent house.

"Well, Priscilla, that doesn't sound so bad now, does it?"

"I suppose I do feel a little better about it."

Her father looked to Matthew. "You approve of this man?"

Matthew looked a bit surprised to have his father seeking his opinion. His shoulder squared. "Yes, I do."

Lawrence nodded, then gave a resigned sigh. "I just hope he doesn't have any skeletons in his closet waiting to jump out at us like the last one."

"Lawrence, what a thing to say."

"I'm sorry, but the speed of all this is making me jumpy."

"I'm uneasy about it, too." Priscilla's voice shifted to a persuading croon. "Why not wait awhile, Caroline? If only until you're out of the cast."

She smiled. "It's easier this way. I'll need a lot of help during the next six weeks. Emma's in the family way, so it wouldn't be right to burden her with my care. You and Father are busy with your work. There would be no one to look after me."

"We could hire a nurse," Priscilla offered.

"Thank you, but I don't need a nurse. David and his mother will take care of me. Besides, David and I are in agreement. Life's too short to waste it waiting around simply for the purpose of waiting around."

Lawrence frowned. "But you have barely known this man a month. We've never even met him."

"You met her last fiancé," Matthew couldn't seem to help interjecting. "It didn't exactly help any."

Her mother glared. Her father's voice turned colder. "That man fooled us all."

"He might not have if you'd been paying closer attention to your daughter."

The argument escalated from there, but Caroline took it as a cue to step outside for a breath of fresh air and some peace. She was just in time to see David riding up on his horse. She waved at him, then walked out onto the grass to meet him as he dismounted. Mindful of her arm, he met her with a gentle embrace. His voice was both teasing and a little grumpy. "I've been away from you for a whole day. It was awful. I hated it. I'm never doing it again."

She smiled into his shoulder. "I promise you won't have to after tomorrow."

"That is why I thoroughly approve of the shortness of this engagement." His lips pressed a glancing kiss against the curve of her neck.

Her breath caught in her throat. She pressed a hand against his chest. "My parents are here."

"They made it?" He glanced at the house behind them. "I'm glad. I know you wanted them here."

She sighed. "I'm not so sure about that anymore."

"Why?"

She traced the edges of his concerned frown. "They're questioning my every decision. It's only making me surer of my choices. Not less."

He relaxed at that. "Good."

"How is Maggie's ankle?"

"The swelling has gone down. I thought the sprain would slow her up some, but somehow she's even faster on those tiny crutches of hers."

Caroline laughed. "We'll be a sight in the morning. The flower girl on crutches and the bride with a broken arm. How are the triplets?"

"They're as giggly as ever. Annie worked out well as a temporary helper today."

She bit her lip at the word *temporary*. "David, I don't think I'm going to be much good for the triplets for a while yet. Y'all were struggling with it before I came. I don't know how we'll manage it now."

He sighed. "We may not need to manage it at all."

"What do you mean?"

"The sheriff came by today. He thinks he may have a lead on some relatives of the triplets."

She gasped. "Really?"

"Nothing has been confirmed yet. He just wanted to let me know so that we wouldn't get attached."

"Oh, it's too late for that."

"I know." He shook his head. "I'd be lying if I said I haven't been secretly hoping to adopt them, but a relative would trump my claim a thousand times over."

She squeezed his arm. "I'm sorry, David."

"So am I. We'll have to see how this all plays out."

"Speaking of playing." She tapped the guitar strap slanted across his chest. "The natives are restless and could use some subduing. Come meet my parents."

David laughed as he followed her inside. Within minutes of meeting her parents, he'd charmed them both. His guitar playing even coaxed Emma from the bedroom, where she'd been hiding out by working on Caroline's wedding gown. With the family in a far more peaceful mood, he persuaded Caroline to sing a duet with him. Normally she hated singing in front of her parents, but she forgot all about them as her voice blended with his and she looked into his eyes.

Love stared back at her. She knew it was love even though he'd yet to say those three precious words. Why was he withholding them from her? Did he even realize he was doing so? Sure, she appreciated how he showed his love through his care and concern for her, but she wanted to hear it at least once before she walked down the aisle toward him. Her wish wasn't granted for he said goodbye to her in front of the others with nothing more than a kiss on the cheek and a promise that he was looking forward to tomorrow.

There was little time to wallow in disappointment for Emma insisted that Caroline try on the wedding dress one last time to make sure the sleeves had turned out all right. Since the fashionable puff sleeves narrowed at the forearm, it would have been impossible for Caroline to wear it with a cast on one arm. Emma had cut off the narrow part and refashioned the puff to make it appear as though the sleeves had always been short.

Caroline turned this way and that in the mirror to admire the dress. "I think it looks perfect. Thank you, Emma."

"You're welcome." Emma leaned her hip on the dresser as she surveyed her work. "I'm so glad it worked out."

"Do you think it's odd for me to wear the same dress I wore at the other wedding?"

Emma sent her a disbelieving look. "You had four days to come up with something to wear."

"So...no?"

"No, I don't think it's odd, since you already had a perfectly good wedding dress hanging in your closet. The dress is perfect and isn't to blame for the problems at your last wedding."

She grinned. "That was a case of having the right dress and the wrong man."

"Exactly. Now you have the right dress and the right man." Emma hugged her. "It's so nice to see you so happy."

"It's nice to be this happy." It was also a little scary, she admitted to herself as Emma helped her into a nightgown. Caroline almost felt as though she was waiting for something to go wrong. It was like singing an aria with one troublesome note. She couldn't help anticipating it.

If only David had said the words. It would have given her something to hold on to, something to battle the nervousness fluttering through her stomach. But he hadn't. That along with the pain in her arm and the discomfort of the cast kept her awake long into the night.

Caroline awakened with a start when her mother knocked on the door. "Good morning, bride."

It was meant to be sweet. Caroline knew that, but Priscilla had said that exact same thing a month ago. It only drove home the point that she'd done this before. It had ended in disaster then. What if it happened again? Caroline pushed aside that thought along with the mess her hair had become and smiled. "Good morning."

"Emma is cooking breakfast. I thought I'd help you with your hair and your dress…" Her mother chatted on as the smell of breakfast drifted in through the open door. It only made Caroline's stomach roil.

"I couldn't eat a thing," Caroline said when her mother took a breath. "I'd rather start getting ready.

Why don't you eat while I take care of my morning ablutions?"

"All right, dear, if you insist, but you really should try to eat something before the ceremony. I can't believe it's only two hours from now. That's hardly enough time. But then, I suppose country folks do start their day unforgivably early."

Caroline had a precious few minutes alone to steady her nerves before Priscilla and Emma bustled in to help her get ready. Before she knew it, she was standing on the church steps wondering how on earth she'd been coaxed into getting married only a month after the disaster of her previous wedding. And she was in the same dress. It shouldn't have mattered, but suddenly it did. Emma had assured her the dress was fine. The doubts besieging her were her parents' concerns, not hers.

She glanced at her father, who waited beside her. His tension was almost palpable. Lawrence caught her watching. "If this man hurts you, so *help* me. So help *him*."

She appreciated the fierce protectiveness of his statement, but it was hardly encouraging. Her heart began pounding in her chest. Was David this nervous?

"Miss Caroline!"

She turned on the steps to find Maggie hurrying toward her on crutches with Ida and Edmund McKay not far behind. Caroline accepted the girl's hug and everything within her calmed down as a rush of love flowed through her. Tears gathered in her eyes, though she did her best to blink them away. She caught the girl's chin in her hand and tilted her face upward. Before Caroline could say anything, Maggie's eyes widened. "You look beautiful."

"Thank you. So do you." The girl wore a fancy blue dress that brought out that same color in her eyes.

"Daddy says you're going to become my mommy today."

Caroline laughed. "He's right. I am. I can't wait."

Maggie grinned in relief. "Me neither. I've prayed and prayed and prayed. I might have doubted a little bit, but deep down I knew God would give me what I asked for."

Oh, for faith such as that. Caroline wished she had that same measure of trust that this would all work out for her. Before she could find a response, Ida finished introducing herself and Edmund to Lawrence, then gave Caroline a quick hug and kiss on the cheek. "You are beautiful, my dear. I just brought Maggie by because she insisted she'd die if she didn't see you."

"I'm glad you did." Caroline turned her smile to Edmund as he gave her a quick hug. David hadn't wanted to pick between his brothers, so he hadn't chosen a best man. Instead he'd asked them both to serve as groomsmen. "Hello, Edmund. How's David doing? Is he nervous?"

"He seems pretty calm to me."

"That's good." Wasn't it? Probably. Still, part of her had hoped he was suffering as much as she was. After all, getting married only four days after the engagement had been his idea, not hers.

Maggie tapped Caroline's leg to get her attention.

"Uncle Edmund is going to carry me down the aisle so that I can throw the flowers."

"What a smart idea."

"Maggie, Edmund, you'd better take your places. Caroline and Lawrence, someone will knock on the door from the inside to let you know when to enter." Ida gestured to two other children who'd appeared seemingly out of nowhere at the bottom of the stairs. One boy and a girl slightly older than him smiled shyly at her. Ida introduced them as Gil and Jo Satler. They were the orphans whom David hoped to help with the creation of the children's home. "They generously offered to hold the doors open during the ceremony. Now, I'd better take my seat. They'll be starting as soon as I do."

Finding herself alone with her father and the Satler siblings, Caroline chose to engage the children in conversation. Gil seemed the only one willing to talk. However, she hardly knew what she was saying. All she could focus on was the church door. Finally, the knock came. The Satlers opened the doors. Caroline stepped inside the church on her father's arm. The guests all oohed and aahed at the sight of her. She did her best to smile at them through the veil.

Emma and Annie waited at the front in mismatched dresses with bouquets of flowers that had sprung up after the rain had cleared out. On the other side of Pastor Brandon, Edmund and Josiah stood beside the man waiting for her at the altar. Her heart skipped a beat at the sight of her groom. He was devastatingly handsome in his formal suit.

And he was all hers. Only hers. A smile blossomed on her lips, and she couldn't have stopped it if she'd tried. Their eyes locked. The intensity of his gaze spoke of so many things. Promise, certainty, joy and love. Love. Oh, why hadn't he said the word?

He would be required to before the ceremony was over. Of course, he didn't have to mean it or necessarily feel it. People got married every day for many reasons—not all of them were love. But why else would David marry her?

Maggie poked her head into the aisle. Caroline couldn't look away from the pure rapture on her soon-to-be daughter's face. What had Maggie said earlier? *Daddy says you're going to become my mommy today.* But that was a plain fact. It didn't mean that was why David wanted to marry her. It didn't mean he had ulterior motives.

Her father removed her veil and kissed her cheek before placing her left hand in David's. His hands were warm. His hold secure. She lifted her gaze to meet his and found herself drowning in his eyes. Oh, what did it matter if he said the words or if he meant them?

She loved him. She wanted him. Nothing else was important. Still, that niggling sensation in her gut told her that wasn't true. She tried to ignore it, but a new refrain marched through her mind. *Something isn't right. Something isn't right.* Over and over. It drowned out the preacher's words, yet it seemed to amplify everything else. The pounding of her own heart. The sound of Lula May's fan stirring on the second row. A whisper from someone near the middle of the church. The soft clunk of the door opening and closing to admit a latecomer.

David squeezed her hand. She met his gaze again, unsure when hers had drifted away. She forced herself to focus on what Pastor Brandon was saying. Something about the sanctity of marriage. Then it was time for the vows. "David McKay—"

A little gasp sounded from the back of the church.

Pastor Brandon continued as though he hadn't heard it. Caroline might have as well, if her eyes weren't already focused on the lone woman standing at the back of the church. A shaft of sunlight illuminated the woman's shifting expression. Confusion. Hurt. Disappointment.

Their eyes met. The woman's widened with something akin to panic. Dread filled Caroline's empty stomach. *Something isn't right.*

Caroline was nervous. It was impossible not to notice that. She shook like a leaf. He wished she'd look at him. Instead, other than that first transcendent smile she'd bestowed on him, she'd focused on anything and everything but him and their marriage vows. This was not a good start. With everyone watching, there wasn't much he could do about it.

He'd tried squeezing her hand. That had only helped for a moment. David glanced at Brandon. The preacher was watching Caroline, too, and looking slightly worried, though his voice remained as confident as ever. "David McKay, do you take this woman to—"

"Who are you?" Caroline demanded.

She was peering through narrowed eyes at the back

of the church. A woman stood there. While everyone else twisted around to see whom Caroline was addressing, David looked back at Caroline. Her mouth was drawn into a line. Her body was as tense as a too-tight guitar string. He didn't know whether to be exasperated, confused or concerned. What did it matter who the stranger was? They were in the middle of their wedding ceremony. He was about to speak his vows.

Before he could say any or all of that, the woman in question spoke. "I'm sorry. I didn't mean to interrupt."

Lawrence stood. "Answer the question."

David barely stopped himself from rolling his eyes. He understood why the Murrays would be jumpy after what had happened with Nico. But he wasn't like Nico. He certainly didn't have a wife just waiting to…

*Oh.*

*Oh, no.*

David turned to survey the woman. How had Elizabeth Dumont described herself? Auburn hair. Brown eyes. This woman had both. Still, it couldn't be. He'd sent her a telegram breaking off their engagement. Yet it was her. She said as much with her next breath.

He closed his eyes as Caroline asked a question that might as well have been his death knell. "How do you know David?"

"I'm engaged to him."

# Chapter Eighteen

Gasps rent the silence that followed his former fiancée's statement. Elizabeth's panicked eyes widened even more. "Or I was. I mean, obviously there has been some kind of mistake."

Caroline wrenched her hand from the grip he hadn't realized he'd tightened. "Yes, there has."

"Caroline, I can explain." He reached for her again, trying to sound calm despite the panic racing through him.

"Don't." She flinched away from his touch, which stung more than any slap could. Without another word, she lifted her skirt in her good arm and rushed out the side door.

David stood in stunned silence. He was the only quiet one in the church. The loudest was Caroline's father. Matthew held Lawrence back as the man threatened to tear David limb from limb. Maggie's voice pierced through the fog. "Pa!"

He snapped to attention. "What?"

Her hands jerked outward until they landed palms up in a silent question. "Go get her!"

"Right." He turned on his heel and ran out the side door. Caroline was nowhere to be seen, so he headed for the front of the church. Again, nothing.

Then he saw Jamie Coleman standing near the street holding what looked to be a box of supplies for the reception that might not happen if David didn't find Caroline. Jamie caught sight of David and the befuddled look on his face cleared. "She borrowed Annie's mare and headed east. Take my stallion."

"Thank you!" David hopped into the saddle and set off after Caroline. He spotted her as soon as he left the town behind. She glanced back at him. He called out, "Caroline, wait!"

She urged the mare faster.

With a groan, he gave chase. The stallion's hooves pounded on the packed dirt at a steady gallop. Knowing she wouldn't hear him or heed him, he murmured half in warning, half in prayer, "Slow down. Slow down. You have a broken arm. Please, slow down."

A disconcerting feeling of déjà vu clouded his mind as they flew down the road. He'd done this before. He'd chased after a woman he loved on horseback. The last time he'd arrived too late to stop her, too late to save her or even hold her in his arms as she'd breathed her last. Since then, he'd done everything he could to protect himself from once again experiencing the heartbreak that Laura's unfaithfulness had inflicted up to that final moment.

Nothing had worked. He was still chasing after

heartbreak. Only this time it was of his own causing. He was the one who'd inflicted the pain because he'd been too afraid and too prideful to tell the truth. No. It went deeper than that. He'd needed to feel in control. He'd assumed his judgment was best and had acted according.

Obviously, it wasn't best. It was flawed. It needed guidance. And so he prayed. He prayed for forgiveness. He prayed for guidance. He prayed that God would give him another chance with Caroline or make it clear that he needed to let her go. By that time the stallion had caught up with her. David reached for the mare's reins, but Caroline veered away to avoid his grasp. David followed her and spoke calmingly, "Whoa. Whoa. Slow down."

She urged her horse faster. "Go away!"

"No." He stuck with her. This time when he reached for the reins, he managed to catch them. He forced her horse to slow to a walk. "I don't care how angry you are at me. I'm not going to let you break your neck by galloping on an unfamiliar horse while you're nursing a broken arm."

"Let go of my reins." Her chin jerked upward. "I'm perfectly capable of riding one-handed."

"That doesn't mean you should."

She refused to look at him. "Go back to your fiancée. I have nothing to say to you."

"Maybe right now you don't, but even if you hightail it back to Austin on the first train that comes through, you're going to want answers from me eventually."

He watched her jaw clench. "You might as well hear them now."

She stole a quick glance at him. He saw a hint of curiosity in her eyes, so when she tried to jerk the reins from his grasp, he tested her by letting them go. She turned her horse as though intending to head back to town. He followed, realizing only too late it was a mere feign. The mare surged back in its original direction, but the stallion was faster. He cut her off. "It might not be as bad as you think."

She gave a laugh of disbelief that had an odd little hitch to it.

Their horses danced in and out of the shafts of sunlight as they circled each other like two fighters waiting to see who would try to land the first blow. The woods became little more than a blur of rich greens. She ducked her head, but it was too late.

He'd seen the truth. She wasn't just angry. She was devastated. He'd done that to her. "Caroline, I'm so sorry that I hurt you."

Her lashes fluttered as she tried to blink away her tears, but they were still there when she looked up at him. Despair stared back at him. And, surprisingly enough, a tortured sort of longing. He reined in his horse immediately. He took the chance of dismounting, then strode toward her with all the confidence he could muster to lift her down from the saddle. She stared at him through guarded eyes while her free arm cradled the broken one. He took her hand and laid it over his heart. "It's still yours, Caroline."

Her fingers curled into a fist. Fire sparked in her eyes before she closed them. "I don't want it."

"I don't believe you."

She stepped closer, her eyes narrowing. "You are awfully confident for a man with two fiancées. No. Make that one."

He held on to her arm when she would have pulled away. "She isn't my fiancée. Not anymore."

"But she was. Until just how recently?"

"Elizabeth Dumont is a mail-order bride."

Surprise filled her eyes. "Mail-order what? Why?"

"I contacted her out of desperation before you agreed to be the triplets' nanny." He relaxed his hold on her arm slightly. "Hiring you allowed me to consider less drastic measures than marriage. The children's home, finding the triplets a permanent family to stay with—all of that eventually fell through. Meanwhile, Maggie had fallen in love with you. She desperately wanted a mother."

Her brow furrowed at that, but he rushed on. "It seemed selfish of me not to provide one for her, especially after the night of the fire."

She bit her lip and glanced away, but he could see that she was listening, considering, weighing his words for truth.

"When you told me there was no hope for us, I was devastated. I didn't want to put myself in a position like that again."

"But Maggie still needed a mother."

He nodded. "That's all Elizabeth was intended to be. We'd talked on having a marriage in name only.

Nothing more. It seemed like the perfect solution at the time. I sent Elizabeth a telegram asking her to come. I rescinded that invitation the day you agreed to marry me. I don't know why she's here."

She pulled in a trembling breath. "Why am I only hearing about this now?"

"I didn't tell you because…" He searched his brain, then released her completely. "I'm sorry. I can't think of a good enough reason. I should have told you from the first. I was afraid. I didn't want to lose you. I didn't want to think I was like your former fiancé—for all the good that did. I ended up looking just like him, and I'm losing you anyway."

Caroline eyed him warily. "You could be making this entire explanation up."

"Have you ever known me to be a liar?"

"No, but I wouldn't if you were good at it."

"I have proof. Elizabeth and I each wrote one letter to each other. You're welcome to read them. They prove everything I'm saying, including the fact that there was no deeper attachment between the two of us."

"And your attachment to me?" Her voice rang with a challenge. "Is it any deeper?"

He frowned. "You know it is."

"Why did you ask me to marry you?" Another challenge.

"Why did I…?" He rubbed the nape of his neck. "Because I didn't want you to leave."

Her voice was harder, more demanding. "Why?"

"Because I love you." Once those words were out, it was impossible to stop the deluge that followed. "I can't imagine going through the rest of my life without you. I barely made it through yesterday without wanting to tear my hair out."

She smiled. It was a hesitant one, but a smile nonetheless. It spurred him on. "You've driven me crazy from the start. Didn't you know that?"

She shook her head.

"From the first moment we met, I haven't been able to get you out of my head. Every thought is full of you. I tried to stay away, but I couldn't. I tried to give you up, but I can't. You're everything to me. I only wish that I'd met you sooner. That I could know you more deeply. That you—"

"David, why didn't you tell me?" Joy and wariness battled for dominance in her voice.

"I didn't want to give my heart away until I knew for sure that you would stay. That you were mine." He shrugged. "I was also being an idiot."

She laughed just a little at that, which made him grin. "Caroline, the truth is you already had my heart. I've known it ever since you called me a horrible father."

She groaned. "That can't be the moment you fell in love with me."

"I think it might be. And you? When did you fall in love with me?"

She replied hesitantly, but at least she didn't deny loving him. "The first time we sang together, though I refused to accept it at the time."

"Music."

"Passion," she mused softly, then bit her lip as though she'd spoken out of turn.

"I still want to marry you. I understand why you might not want that anymore. I understand if you'd rather not trust me again. I messed up. I'm sorry for that. I was making decisions out of fear when I should have allowed myself to be guided by love." He took her hand in his again. "I promise that from here on out I'll always be truthful with you. I promise I'll stop holding back, but I'd like to do more than that. I'd like to prove it."

He took a deep breath, then said exactly what he felt God was leading him to say. "I'm going back to the church. I'll wait there until you make your decision one way or the other."

Conviction told him he'd done the right thing and a peace followed that confirmed it. Whether or not that meant Caroline would show up at the church ready to marry him again wasn't clear. However, he'd be ready if it did. Either way, he was determined to trust God with the future. Of course, that didn't mean he wouldn't give the Lord as much time as He needed to work on Caroline's heart. Or that he wouldn't be praying all the way to town.

He set out to church, keeping the horse to a leisurely walk. He might have glanced back toward the patch of road where he left Caroline a time or two or three. "Come on, Caroline. It's your turn. Come after me."

As David rode away, his words stayed with her. *I was making decisions out of fear when I should have allowed myself to be guided by love.*

*Fear.* Was that what she'd been struggling with? Fear of making another mistake. Fear of never having that perfect love story like her parents and Matthew had. Were those love stories perfect, though? Maybe for them, but not necessarily for her. Who wanted a fairy tale anyway? That wasn't real. David was. No, he wasn't perfect. It was unfair to expect him to be, especially since she wasn't and never would be. Perhaps it was their imperfections that helped make them perfect for each other.

She had to allow for the fact that mistakes were going to be made by both of them. Maybe that was permissible—even necessary for learning and growing in this life. The problem came when a person clung to them like a comfortable old coat in the summertime. That was exactly what she'd been doing. It was also exactly what David had been trying to tell her not to do.

Where did that leave her? Loving David. That was a given. But could she trust him? To be honest, it wasn't David she had a problem trusting so much as herself and her decisions. Yet she'd surrender her will to God's. She'd sincerely asked for His guidance. Surely that meant He was leading her heart now and it was all right to follow it to...

"Where Lord? David or Austin?"

Before she finished speaking, she knew. Deep inside beyond the places fear was able to reach, she'd always known. She smiled at the sky that peeked through the trees above her. "Thank You."

She carefully remounted, then spurred Annie's mare into a canter. The trees opened up a little more, allowing her to catch sight of David ahead of her on the road.

He hadn't gone far. Peace enveloped her as the distance between them shrank beneath her mare's gliding gait.

David glanced back, pulling his horse up short. Caroline ducked her head to hide her expression as she circled him. Bringing her horse alongside his, she came to a stop, facing him. She finally lifted her lashes to meet his hopeful gaze. She offered him her reins. He took them with no little amount of confusion. Hand free, she caught hold of the lapel of his open suit coat and tugged. She leaned forward to meet him halfway, then pressed a soft kiss to his lips. "I love you, too. Let's get married."

He released her reins before she could take them. Her mouth fell open. "David!"

He'd already wrapped his own reins around the saddle horn. His hands settled onto her waist. She automatically removed her boots from the stirrups as he lifted her from her horse onto the saddle in front of him. She sputtered out a protest. "You're going to break our—"

Then he kissed her and she couldn't think of a single thing to complain about. She was too busy melting into his arms. That went on for a while, though exactly how long she couldn't say. Finally, he pulled back with a satisfied grin. "Now, let's go get married."

As they neared the church, Caroline could see that most of her guests were milling in groups outside the church. One figure stood alone and apart from the others. Elizabeth Dumont. David saw her, too. Caroline watched his brow furrow with worry. This would be awkward at best and difficult at worst. A wave of compassion overcame her for both of them.

"David." Caroline waited for him to look at her before continuing. "We'll figure this out, but for the record, she can't have you."

Tension broken, he laughed, then leaned over to kiss her cheek. They surrendered their horses to their rightful owners before David took her hand. She walked over to meet Elizabeth with him. Her husband-to-be reached out to briefly clasp the woman's hand. "Miss Dumont, I'm so sorry. There seems to have been some sort of mix-up. I sent you a telegram letting you know that I planned to marry someone else. I thought for sure that you'd receive it in time to cancel your traveling plans, since you said you would need a week to be ready to leave Boston."

"I was able to leave much more quickly than I anticipated. Your telegram must have just missed me." Elizabeth's remorseful brown gaze shifted to Caroline. "I'm the one who's sorry. I didn't mean to ruin your day."

"It isn't ruined," Caroline said, then removed her hand from David's to extend it to Elizabeth. "I'm Caroline Murray."

"Elizabeth Dumont." Elizabeth shook her hand. "You are soon-to-be Mrs. Caroline McKay, I hope. I would never want to come between a love match. Please tell me you are going to continue with the wedding."

Caroline nodded. "We are. And what about you? What will you do now?"

Elizabeth clutched her reticule tightly. "I'm not sure yet. Going back to Boston isn't really an option at this point. This town has a boardinghouse, doesn't it? I'll stay there while I think of something. Perhaps someone might need a teacher or a—"

"Nanny?" Caroline's gaze flew to David. He caught on immediately. Reluctance filled his eyes, followed by resignation.

"Why, yes. That would be perfect. I adore children. Do you know of someone in need of a nanny?"

"We are," David said quietly. "Caroline broke her arm, as you can see. We need someone to take care of the triplets until their distant relatives arrive to claim them."

"Oh, but you two are about to get married. You wouldn't want me hanging around your house. Perhaps I could keep them with me in the boardinghouse."

David gave a slow nod. "I suppose that could be arranged. We can talk about it more after the ceremony."

"That would be wonderful." Elizabeth smiled at them without so much as a hint of hard feelings. "I truly hope you two will be very happy."

"Thank you," Caroline said as David led her toward the church. Once they were out of Elizabeth's hearing range, Caroline rose to whisper in David's ear. "I actually like her. She seems so sweet. She might not have been a bad choice for you."

He stopped in his tracks, looking highly affronted. "Excuse me? There is only one woman for me. How dare you suggest otherwise."

She giggled. "Just testing you."

He growled.

"I do think she's sweet, but I've already staked my claim on you. She'll have to find herself another man."

A throat cleared. She turned to find Pastor Brandon standing beside them. He glanced at their joined hands with interest. "Shall we continue with the ceremony, then?"

Caroline sent David a wink. "Yes, please."

David grinned. Matthew slapped him on the back. Emma stood beside him with concern in her eyes that changed to relief when Caroline smiled. She caught a glimpse of Elizabeth explaining things to an uneasy Lawrence and Priscilla while Pastor Brandon herded the wedding party toward the front. The rest of the guests hurried in as they took their places at the altar again.

Caroline hardly noticed them. Her eyes were locked on David. Every bit of her attention was focused on him. She watched in fascination at the play of emotions on his handsome face, the deep love in his vibrant green eyes, the joyful curve of his smile. His vows rang out strong and clear—undisputable. She pledged herself to him in the same manner with not so much as a tear in her eye. She felt only joy, certainty and love.

Then their union was sealed, unbreakable. He released her from the kiss, but she lingered to look up at him in wonder. As the guests celebrated, she stepped closer again and whispered for his ears only. "You're mine. Forevermore. How did I get so blessed?"

He searched her eyes as a sheen covered his. "Caroline."

That was all he said. All he needed to say. Everything he felt for her was in that one word.

A light tug at her skirt brought her attention down to a grinning Maggie. "We're a family now?"

David lifted his daughter, settling Maggie in the

curve of his arm before the other reached around Caroline's waist. "We sure are, Magpie."

Caroline and Maggie reached for each other at the same time to complete the hug. Over Maggie's shoulders, their family and guests lingered. All of them, even her father, smiled at them.

She ducked her head into the curve of David's neck. She couldn't help smiling, too. The future stretched out before her, and it was so much better, so much more beautiful, than she'd ever imagined. This was real. Better yet, this was hers.

\* \* \* \* \*

*Don't miss a single installment of*
LONE STAR COWBOY LEAGUE:
MULTIPLE BLESSINGS

*THE RANCHER'S SURPRISE TRIPLETS*
*by Linda Ford*

*THE NANNY'S TEMPORARY TRIPLETS*
*by Noelle Marchand*

*THE BRIDE'S MATCHMAKING TRIPLETS*
*by Regina Scott*

*Find more great reads at www.LoveInspired.com*

Dear Reader,

Writing has always been something hugely personal to me. It's also always been something rather private to the point where most of my friends and even family had no idea I was interested in writing until surprise, surprise! I had a book being published. Back then, I learned a very valuable lesson about not hiding your light under a bushel.

Five years later, I was honored to be asked by my editor to take part in this series. I am so glad that I said yes. Writing this book has taught me so much about what it means to share, to let what I create become a collaboration and to appreciate the ideas others bring to the table.

For this intensely personal and private writer, it was very much a chance to get back to the basics of the lesson I learned when I was just starting out. Writing, by its nature, is something meant to be shared. The story that begins in my imagination takes on a life of its own in yours. I think that is downright incredible.

I am so blessed that I was able to share that process with my editor, Elizabeth Mazer, and the two other authors in the Lone Star Cowboy League: Multiple Blessings series, Linda Ford and Regina Scott. Please be sure to read the other books in the series to see how the search for the triplets' family begins and ends. I'm sure you will enjoy the other installments as much as I hope you've enjoyed this one.

To find out more about me and the other books I've

written, be sure to go to NoelleMarchand.com. You can also search for me on social media sites such as Facebook, Goodreads, Twitter and Pinterest. I'd love to hear from you.

Blessings!

*Noelle Marchand*